74 MILES AWAY

OTHER BOOKS BY J.D. CARPENTER

POETRY

Nightfall, Ferryland Head
Swimming at Twelve Mile
Lakeview
Compassionate Travel

FICTION

The Devil in Me
Bright's Kill

74 MILES AWAY

A Campbell Young Mystery

J.D. CARPENTER

A Castle Street Mystery

THE DUNDURN GROUP
TORONTO

Editor: Barry Jowett
Copy-editor: Andrea Waters
Design: Jennifer Scott
Printer: Webcom

National Library of Canada Cataloguing in Publication

Carpenter, J. D.
    74 miles away : a Campbell Young mystery / J.D. Carpenter.

ISBN-10: 1-55002-649-6
ISBN-13: 978-1-55002-649-8

    I. Title. II. Title: Seventy-four miles away.

PS8555.A7616S44 2007   C813'.54   C2006-904593-3

1   2   3   4   5   10   09   08   07   06

Conseil des Arts du Canada   Canada Council for the Arts   Canada   ONTARIO ARTS COUNCIL CONSEIL DES ARTS DE L'ONTARIO

We acknowledge the support of the Canada Council for the Arts and the Ontario Arts Council for our publishing program. We also acknowledge the financial support of the Government of Canada through the Book Publishing Industry Development Program and The Association for the Export of Canadian Books, and the Government of Ontario through the Ontario Book Publishers Tax Credit program and the Ontario Media Development Corporation.

Printed and bound in Canada   www.dundurn.com

Dundurn Press
3 Church Street, Suite 500
Toronto, Ontario, Canada
M5E 1M2

Gazelle Book Services Limited
White Cross Mills
High Town, Lancaster, England
LA1 4XS

Dundurn Press
2250 Military Road
Tonawanda, NY
U.S.A. 14150

For my brother, Peter Conway Carpenter,
with thanks for his support and companionship

17 As he loved cursing, so let it come unto him: as he delighted not in blessing, so let it be far from him.

18 As he clothed himself with cursing like as with his garment, so let it come into his bowels like water, and like oil into his bones.

— Psalm 109

PART
ONE

PART
ONE

Thursday, November 8, 2001

The body found on the floor of Room 711 of the Sutton Place Hotel in Toronto was that of a mixed race male — African and Caucasian — twenty-five to thirty years of age. What was striking about the condition of the corpse to pathologist Elliot Cronish as he knelt on one knee beside the body, which was on its back at the foot of one of two queen-sized beds in the room, was not so much the rictus on the dead man's face, suggesting a painful and far from instant death, nor was it the open staring eyes, the aesthetic of the dead man's copper skin against the eggshell white of the broadloom — something Cronish, who considered himself to have a painterly eye, couldn't help but note — nor the careful arrangement of the naked body: ankles crossed, arms folded across the chest. While all of these ingredients added spice to the mix, it was the neatness of the suite, indicating the absence of struggle, and the eleven glass soda bottles —

seven Kist and four Wishing Well, forming a perfect oval around the corpse — that brought the recipe together. Some of the bottles contained fluid, greyish in colour; others contained what appeared to be dirt. They were old: the glass they were made of was chipped and cloudy. As well, there was an instrument case open on the floor, two feet beyond the top of the dead man's head. In it — as if casually tossed — lay eleven coins of foreign currency. Cronish's inclination was to pick up one of the coins to examine it, but because he respected crime scene integrity, he resisted the temptation.

He searched carefully but found no wounds on the front of the body. With his latex-gloved hands, he probed behind the ears and moved his fingers across the scalp like a group of volunteers combing a field for a missing child. Nothing in the mouth or under the jaw. He checked armpits, navel, and nether parts and came up empty. When he was given the okay by the senior Homicide man, Detective Sergeant Gerald "Big" Urmson, to roll the body, what he discovered shocked him: the back, buttocks, thighs, and calves were blue in colour, a dark, iridescent, almost midnight blue, and they were covered in lesions. As he held the body in position on its side, the skin of the shoulder broke free beneath his hand and slid like pizza topping. In various areas, Cronish noted, the epidermis was falling off as if drawn by nothing more than its own weight. He searched carefully — in the hair at the nape of the neck and in the crack of the buttocks — but found no entrance or exit wounds, in fact no punctures of any kind.

When the evidence team had finished dusting and tweezing and collecting, the photographer had taken his photographs, and the body bag boys were zipping up, Cronish asked Big Urmson what he had so far.

"A ton of evidence," Big Urmson said, drawing the back of his wrist across his heavy blond eyebrows, "but it's hard to know what any of it means. What's with all these bottles, anyways?"

Cronish said, "Looks like voodoo to me."

"Voodoo? Are you serious?"

Cronish shrugged. "That's what it looks like."

"What do you think's in the bottles?"

"Graveyard dirt, probably. I don't know about the liquid. Virgins' tears?"

Big Urmson regarded him uncertainly. "I'll send them off to the lab. We'll know soon enough."

Cronish nodded his head at the body. "Who was he?"

"Some kind of big deal musician from down in the Caribbean. What about cause of death?"

"Nothing obvious, I'm afraid," Cronish said over his half-glasses. "No external wounds. But the strange colouration on the back of the body intrigues me."

"Lividity?"

Cronish shook his head. "I've seen lividity in thousands of bodies, and it's never looked like this. It's the wrong shade of blue, for starters, and the spread of it is too uniform. Add to that the blistering. No, it's something else. As soon as I get back to the shop, I'll do an exam."

"Let me know."

Cronish headed for the elevators with a spring in his step. There were days when he absolutely loved his work, and this was one of them. There was nothing he welcomed more than a challenge, a puzzle. When he was relaxing at home, he did every acrostic he could lay his hands on. He did the *New York Times* crossword. He played chess on-line. He did five-thousand-piece jigsaw puzzles. At work — lucky man that he was — his happiest hours were spent with murder victims, determining when and how they died. On rare occasions, if the killer had moved the body after death, Cronish helped determine where the murder had taken place. Sometimes, if there was no ID on the body, he helped determine who the victim was, usually through dental records or DNA. And sometimes — not often — he was able to offer an opinion as to why the murder had occurred. This murder had potential. Aside from the unusual condition of the cadaver, there was the paraphernalia: the bottles of dirt and water, the coins in the instrument case. Cronish's considerable skills as a medical technician just might be tested. *Ah*, he thought as he stood inside the elevator, his eyes idly watching the little light above the door move from six to five to four, *battle joined*.

On weekday mornings, while other people were going to work, Priam Harvey smoked cigarettes and listened to his jazz station in the kitchen of his bachelor apartment. He never tuned in the AM news stations: he couldn't bear to hear what the Israelis and the Palestinians were doing to each other, or the Muslims and the Hindus, or the Tutsis and the Hutus, or the Serbs and the Croats, or the Protestants and the Catholics; it depressed him to hear about posties taking Uzis to work, or pit bull attacks on children, or mothers out partying while their babies dehydrated in their cribs. He didn't even want to know what the weather would be like. Except for his jazz, Harvey preferred to be solitary in the mornings, unwilling — at least until noon — to face society in any of its manifestations.

The FM station he listened to, CJOT, was a low-budget community network. The disc jockeys did their best, but they were unpaid amateurs who frequently fumbled the ball; they would cue up the wrong tune or forget to turn off their microphones and talk all the way through the next cut — sometimes to someone in the booth with them, sometimes on the phone. One man was let go because he talked to a friend about cunnilingus throughout Miles Davis' six-minute-and-twenty-two-second rendition of "Seven Steps to Heaven." Harvey was amused that the man, who had a pompous, self-important black man's baritone — a baritone noticeably absent during the cunnilingus conversation — and an annoying habit of repeating certain phrases ("… and the drums, of course, belong to the great Art Taylor") wasn't made aware of his gaffe until he hung up and someone called to tell him what had happened. Harvey had laughed aloud in his little kitchen. *That's what you get*, he thought, *for running a station on the cheap; no one in the next booth to wave you down.* Harvey didn't suffer fools gladly, and the man was a fool, no better than the caffeine-crazed AM deejays Harvey particularly detested.

For some people, jazz in the morning is as unpleasant as cigarette smoke, but Harvey could listen to jazz anytime, all the time, even as he was hacking his way into the kitchen for his first cigarette of the morning and his start-me-up Scotch, his threadbare dressing gown hanging open over his pale, unhealthy flesh, his yellow-grey hair in confusion; and so it was on this morning when he heard CJOT's Thursday morning announcer — a syrup-voiced young woman with a preference for West Coast bebop — inform her audience that the phenomenal young tenor saxophone player, Talmadge Cooper, had been found dead in a Toronto hotel room.

Campbell Young had decided to take the day off. Since retiring from the Metropolitan Toronto Police Department's Homicide Division a year earlier, he had established and operated, in desultory fashion, A-1

Investigative Consultants. Given that his full-time staff consisted of himself, he was, in fact, the only consultant, but A-1 Investigative Consultant, he thought, sounded stupid. Young's part-time secretary, Stella — a wiry, Greek-extracted, unmarried mother of a four-year-old boy — worked on an entirely unpredictable schedule of her own design. Whenever Young offered input on the topic of her schedule, he was politely ignored. He might say, "Stella, I want you here a bit early tomorrow, say around ten," to which she would reply, "You don't need me till noon, Boss. I'll be here at noon." In the year since she had started working for him, Stella had demonstrated that she was always at work when he needed her, and when he didn't, she wasn't. The third member of the crew, a still-unnamed puppy Young had acquired to replace his lamented British bulldog, Reg, was on the premises whenever Young was, but all she did was lie on the floor and suck the necks of empty beer bottles.

Young was still asleep when the phone rang, shattering the images of a dream he was in the midst of — a dream in which he was trying to negotiate his pickup truck down a set of rapids. As he rolled over to the bedside table he came close to crushing the puppy, which squeaked and fell in a tumble on the floor.

Young said "What?" into the phone.

"Priam Harvey here."

Young squinted at his clock radio. "Mr. Harvey, are you aware that it's eight-thirty in the morning?"

"I phoned your office and there was no answer, so I figured you'd still be home."

"I'm never in the office before ten. I'm retired, I make my own hours."

"Sorry, I —"

"What's so important?"

"I need to talk to you. A musician's been murdered."

"A musician?"

"Yes. I knew him."

Young hoisted himself into a sitting position. "Knew him how?"

"Well, his mother and I were quite friendly once upon a time. Almost thirty years ago. In the Bahamas. I worked in a casino down there for a few years."

"I thought you always worked at the racetrack."

"I had a couple of lean years when ... well, let's just say my presence wasn't welcome at *Sport of Kings* magazine."

"You got fired?"

"Yes, I was seriously into the juice back then, but after my stint in the Bahamas, they hired me back. I was still into the juice, but they hired me back anyway."

"So what's this got to do with the musician?"

Harvey took a breath. "I was floor manager at the Princess. It was tedious work, and noisy, and the hours were crazy, but in some ways it was a good life. Wine, women, all that. But eventually it got to be too much, even for me, so I came home." Harvey paused again. "But not before I'd had a relationship with one of the croupiers. And, a month or so after I got back, the croupier, whose name was Eula, contacted me. She'd had a baby."

There was a pause. "And you were the father."

"That's right."

"And the boy grew up to be the musician in question?"

"Yes."

The puppy was whimpering at Young's feet. He leaned down with one hand and scooped her up and placed her in his lap. "I'm sorry," he said.

"I started sending her money, and I went down to Freeport the following winter. I went down regularly, every year or every other year, for about ten years. Just for a week or two. If I didn't go, I sent him gifts. Eventually I stopped going. I kept in touch for a while longer. Phone calls, mostly, or Christmas cards and birthday cards. I went one more time when he was about fifteen. I'd gotten to know him in a kind of absentee father fashion. I liked him. When his mother told me he had musical talent, I started sending him jazz CDs. I sent him all the Blue Note Sonny Rollins CDs. I gave him his first saxophone and paid for his lessons. A few years ago when the Juilliard School offered him an audition, I paid the airfare."

"The Julie Art School?"

"Joo-lee-ard. It's the best music school in the States." He stopped for a moment. "My son that I hardly knew is dead."

Young looked across the room, then said, "How do you know he's been murdered?"

"It said so on the radio."

"When did it happen?"

"He checked in yesterday —"

"Checked in where?"

"The Sutton Place."

"He was here in Toronto?"

"Yes. I called Urmson at Homicide before I called you. He'd already been to the crime scene. He says the time of death was late last night or early this morning. A house dick found his body around three a.m. People in the next room phoned the front desk complaining of suspicious noises, but by the time the dick got there it was over."

"What was he doing in Toronto?"

"He was scheduled to play tomorrow night at the Sapphire. Don't you remember? You were going to go with me."

"This the kid you told me about last week?"

"Yes."

"I'd forgotten all about it." Young paused. "I don't remember you telling me he was your *son*. That sort of detail I'd remember."

Harvey hesitated. "I didn't tell you. My relationship with his mother — and with him, for that matter — had already pretty much ended by the time you and I got to know each other. Besides, I was embarrassed about it. I was a shit-poor father."

"Urmson know it's your kid?"

"No."

"What else did he say?"

"At first he wouldn't say much, but you know Urmson. It doesn't take much to get him talking. He said the crime scene was unusual."

"Unusual how?"

"He said the body was on the floor, naked, and it had unusual colouration — dark blue — on the back. And blistering. And it was surrounded by bottles."

"What kind of bottles?"

"Old glass pop bottles. He said the bottles were standing on the carpet in a formation around the body. Some of them had liquid in them and some of them had sand or dirt."

"Some kind of cult thing or some freaky sex thing?"

"I don't think so. It sounds like obeah."

"O-who?"

"Obeah. It's a type of voodoo practised in the Bahamas. I remember Eula telling me that people would hire these witch doctors — they're called obeah workers — to 'fix' people they didn't like."

"Fix them?"

"Put a curse on them, cause them pain or misfortune, even kill them. Usually by making their stomachs swell up till they explode."

"But the young man was murdered, right?"

"That's the assumption, but there are no obvious signs of trauma. Your friend the pathologist — what's his name?"

"Cronish, but he's no friend of mine."

"Well, anyway, he hasn't done the autopsy yet. So, what I did was I phoned Eula."

"In the Bahamas?"

"Yes, in Freeport."

"She already know?"

"Yes, the police had already talked to her. So I just, well, you know, offered my condolences. We talked for a little while. We hadn't spoken for about the same length of time that Tal and I hadn't — five or six years. Then she said, 'The police told me he was dead, but they didn't say why or how. He was murdered, wasn't he?' I said it was a possibility, his death was certainly suspicious, but no cause of death had been established."

"Why would she think he'd been murdered?"

"I don't know, but then she asked me to hire someone to find out what happened. I told her the police were already investigating, but she said that wasn't good enough. She asked me to hire the best private eye I could find and tell him money was no object."

"That's why you're calling me?"

"I was hoping you would help, yes."

The puppy was chewing on Young's thumb, so he lowered her to the floor and began to feel around with his feet for his slippers. "I'm sorry, Mr. Harvey, but I'm leaving for Florida on Monday."

"What are you doing in Florida?"

"I'm catching the first two weeks of the Gulfstream meet."

There was silence on the other end of the line.

"Look," Young said defensively, "after twenty-four years of walking the beat and patrolling high school dances and football games and breaking up domestics and working fraud for four of those years and larceny for two and being in Homicide for twelve and generally finding out how disgusting people really are, I've earned the right to do what I want — in this case, sit in the grandstand at Gulfstream and wear flip-flops and tropical shirts and play the ponies till I'm busted, if that's what I feel like doing."

Harvey said nothing.

"Don't pull this silent act on me, please, Mr. Harvey, 'cause it's not going to work. I've done my time." He found one slipper, and as he worked his left foot into it, he watched the puppy head out of the bedroom with the other slipper in her mouth.

Harvey said, "It's okay, don't worry about it. You're right, you've done your time. It's just that Eula's heartbroken over the boy's death, and, quite frankly, so am I. He was my son, a fact that I was able to ignore for much of his life, but now that he's dead ... well ..."

Young shook his head low and heavy like a buffalo. "What I *will* do," he said, "what I *will* do is I'll see what I can find out before I leave."

There was a pause before Harvey said, "Thank you, Campbell. That means a lot to me."

Arthur Trick was at home in his apartment when Young phoned him. When he picked up, Young said, "It's me."

Trick said, "What's that slurping sound?"

"That's the puppy. She's washing my face."

"You're disgusting. You need to find a woman, someone to look after you."

"No woman will have me. Listen, the reason I called is I need your help on something. I was just talking to Priam Harvey. Seems there was a murder last night —"

"The one at the Sutton Place?"

"That's right. Jazz musician."

"You on it?"

"No. He asked me, but I've already got my plane ticket."

"Oh yeah, you're off to visit Goofy."

"I feel kind of bad leaving him in the lurch —"

"Hey, you don't have to explain to me."

"— so I thought maybe you could help."

"Oh, you did, did you?"

"Turns out Mr. Harvey knew the dead guy's mother a long time ago. He has kind of a personal interest in the case."

"What kind of personal interest?"

"Well, I'm sure he doesn't want it made public, so just keep it under your hat. The dead guy was his son."

There was a pause. "Wow, that's terrible. I didn't think Mr. Harvey had any family."

"Neither did I."

"Isn't Homicide on the case?"

"That's what *I* said, but he said the mother wants a private eye, and that's her right. Besides, if it's the Sutton Place, that's Homicide's turf, so you'd be fine with whoever's on it."

"I'm not a private eye."

"Fake it."

"I hate to remind you of this, Camp, but I'm not as mobile as you."

"I might consider cutting the trip short. Just get it started for me."

"All right, fine. What do you want me to do?"

"I want you to get on the Internet and find out everything you can about a Bahamian brand of voodoo called obeah."

Trick manipulated the keypad with his left hand and effected a ninety-degree swivel in his wheelchair so that he was facing his computer. "O-b-e-a-h, right? I'm typing it in."

Friday, November 9

Big Urmson was staring out the large window behind his cubicle at Homicide — snow clouds were gathering, and the traffic on College Street was glacial — when the lab report on the crime scene evidence came in.

The seven glass Kist bottles contained salt water mixed with an undetermined type of ash. The mineral content of the brown dirt in the four Wishing Well bottles was common to the metropolitan Toronto area. The bottles bore no fingerprints. As to their origin, they were so old they had no doubt circulated, like money, through many hands over many years before coming to rest on the floor of the dead man's hotel room.

As his eyes scanned farther down the lab report, Big Urmson felt perspiration gather at his temples. The eleven coins found in the instrument case — it had been determined that it was a tenor saxophone case — had been divided into two groups. The first group included two coins: a copper penny bearing the head of Queen Elizabeth II and the Latin inscription "*Expulsis Piratis Restituta Commercia*" on one side and a starfish on the other; and a nickel bearing the same portrait of the Queen and the same inscription on one side and a pineapple on the other. The second group included nine coins: three copper pennies with a starfish on one side; three nickels with a pineapple on one side; a dime with a crenellated edge and two bonefish on one side; a fifteen-cent piece, square with rounded corners and a hibiscus on one side; and a quarter with a sailing ship on one side. The other side of all nine coins bore a coat of arms featuring a swordfish and a flamingo on either side of a shield that showed one of Columbus's ships, a sunrise, ferns emerging from a bowl, and a conch shell; the inscription below the coat of arms read, in English, "Forward Upward Onward Together." Appearing in raised letters on the nine coins were the words "Commonwealth of the Bahamas." A note informed Big Urmson that the first two coins were in circulation in the Bahamas prior to 1973 and that the second group was currently in circulation.

Big Urmson scratched his chin. The case was becoming very confusing very fast. *Who should I call first?* he wondered, and scratched his chin again. Then he pursed his lips, reached for the phone, and dialed Campbell Young's number.

"What?"

"Sarge?" Big Urmson said. "Oh good, I caught you at home."

"Who's this?"

"It's Urmson."

"Well, say so, for fucksake. It drives me crazy when people phone and don't say who they are."

"Sorry."

"Why do people do that? Is it some sort of test, like if I can't identify their voice I'm not really their friend?"

"I don't know, I never thought —"

"What do you want?"

"Well, the thing is —"

"This about the musician?"

"Yes, how did you know?"

"Mr. Harvey already talked to me. Yesterday. I'm leaving for Florida on Monday, so I'm not much good to you, but Trick's doing some research. Talk to him."

"Sarge, I really need your help on this one."

"Urmson, for fucksake, you can't keep calling me up and asking me what to do. You're a big boy now. You wanted to make detective sergeant and you did, and now you have to go it on your own."

"I know, Sarge, but —"

"But nothing. Besides which, I'm not your Sarge anymore. I'm retired, remember, which means I get to do whatever I want, which includes not talking to you every time you get a new case."

"I know, but the evidence is pretty strange, and I —"

"Talk to Trick."

After hanging up the phone, Young looked at the clock. Eleven-fifteen. At noon he would make himself a sandwich and watch an episode of *City Confidential*, and then maybe *American Justice* at one, if he felt like it. He liked *City Confidential*, he liked Paul Winfield's narration, but he thought too much time was spent on the travelogue aspect of the show. It was true that you got a good look at some interesting places, but really it just stretched a half-hour story to an hour. But he liked them both, and he liked *Investigative Reports* and *Cold Case Files*, as well. He watched *Cops*, too, but didn't admit it to anyone.

Forty-five minutes until lunch. He sat down in the La-Z-Boy. The puppy bounded into the room with one of Young's sweat socks in her mouth. She lay down on Reg's old rug and began to tear the sock apart. A wave of ennui swept over Young. *Maybe the puppy's a bad idea*, he thought. *Five years since Reg died, but maybe it's still too soon. Or maybe I don't really want another dog.* His daughter, Debi, and his grandson, Jamal, had been at him about it so much lately that he'd finally given in and visited the Humane Society dog pound. Jamal had gone with him and picked the puppy out. *Fine for them, they don't have to train it and feed it and clean up after it.*

He thought about turning on the TV. Instead he picked up the CD remote from the little round table beside him and hit "play." At first, he didn't remember what he'd been listening to last — he would have guessed the Stones or Bob Seger or John Lee Hooker — so he was surprised when the music that came out of the speakers was jazz.

He had owned the Miles Davis CD *Kind of Blue* for a week and had listened to bits and pieces of it. But this time he listened to it all the way through. As he listened, he read the liner notes and tried to understand pianist Bill Evans's comparison of a particular form of Japanese watercolour painting to the improvisation required of jazz musicians. "Erasures or changes are impossible," Evans wrote. Young studied the titles of the tunes: "So What," "Freddie Freeloader," "Blue in Green," "All Blues," "Flamenco Sketches." He had never seen an album with only five titles on it, and the titles intrigued him; they were like the names of comic strips and racehorses and paintings.

When the CD ended, Young phoned Priam Harvey's apartment. There was no answer, so he phoned McCully's Tavern. The bartender answered, and Young said, "Dexter, is Mr. Harvey there by any chance?"

"He's right here. That you, Sarge?"

"What kind of shape's he in?"

"He's good, he's talking some poor sap's ear off right now."

"Put him on, please."

The previous Friday night, Young had accepted Priam Harvey's invitation to catch a set of jazz at the Sapphire.

"Normally, I'd do everything in my power to avoid jazz," Young had said as they walked south on Victoria Street towards the nightclub. "My idea of good music starts and ends with the Silver Bullet Band."

"Just give this a listen," Harvey said. "It's the All-Mingus Band." Harvey was resplendent in his white plantation suit and Panama hat.

"Never heard of it," Young said.

"Charles Mingus was a jazz composer. He died in 1979, but his music lives on, as they say, and that's what this band plays. We missed the first set, but that's okay, the night's still young."

After Young got past the shock of the ten-dollar cover charge, and after he and Harvey were seated at a tiny table and their drinks brought to them, he began to relax. In a gesture towards moderation, he hadn't had any Jack Daniel's in almost two weeks, and he chewed on the first sip for a good thirty seconds before swallowing it. As the old familiar warmth spread down through his chest to his stomach, he sighed contentedly. He chased the Jack with a long swallow of beer, then lit a cigarette.

"Enjoying yourself?" Harvey asked.

"So far, so good."

Harvey nodded towards the stage. "They're about to start."

Without introduction, the pianist began to play. Except for his hands, he sat completely still at the keyboard with an unhappy expression on his face.

Young said, "What's wrong with that guy?"

"Shh," Harvey said.

One by one, the other musicians joined in. The drummer, a fat man with a pasty complexion and slicked-back hair, was wearing a lime green polo shirt and let-out trousers that came right up under his nipples. Young figured he was about sixty, but from the wrists out he had the speed and dexterity of a teenager. The sax player was small and hunched, and he played with a stiff, contorted style, as if he were in agony and ecstasy at the same time. The trumpeter was a tall man who leaned back when he played, and his sound was big and bold. The bassist was the leader of the group, and between numbers he did all the talking — announcing the titles of the tunes, telling anecdotes about members of the band; too much talking, Young thought — but when he was folded over the shoulders of his bass, plucking like a madman, he was something to see. When he slowly straightened himself up at the end of a long solo, Young could see the pain in the man's face.

"I know a bad back when I see one," Young said.

"Shh," said Harvey.

When the second set ended, Harvey said, "You in any hurry to leave?"

"Hell no," Young replied. "I'm good for another hour. I'm enjoying this. I'm getting some culture is what I'm doing."

From time to time throughout the evening, Harvey had been scribbling notes on a serviette. Young leaned over and said, "What's that you're writing?"

"I'm making a list," Harvey said. "These are the titles of the tunes they've played: 'Goodbye, Porkpie Hat,'

'Peggy's Blue Skylight,' 'Three or Four Shades of Blue,' 'My Jelly Roll Soul,' 'Better Git Hit in Your Soul,' and 'No Private Income Blues.' Six tunes in all."

"Only six?" Young said. "Seemed like more."

"Yes, but you have to keep in mind that each one was about fifteen minutes long."

Young let his gaze drift across the crowd. Many of the other tables were occupied by bearded, bespectacled men nodding their heads intently in conversation.

"Pretty geeky crowd you run with," he said.

"Shh," said Harvey, looking up at the stage, "the musicians are back."

After the last number of the final set, the leader laid down his bass with the same care a mother takes as she lowers her baby into its crib. The drummer placed his sticks on his snare, the sax player stood his sax in its stand, the trumpeter drained his trumpet, and the pianist wiped his keys. The faithful kept up a steady applause, several of them shouting "More!" and "Encore!" until the leader raised his hands and said, "Okay, one more. But before we begin, I'd like to acknowledge the presence in our midst of one of Canada's finest homegrown saxophonists, Mr. Buddy Drown. Won't you please take a bow, Mr. D?"

From the shadows at the back of the room there emerged a short, powerfully built bald man in a shiny blue sports coat. He nodded to the scattering of people still seated at the little round tables, who all twisted in their chairs to see him and clapped even louder. As Drown began to slip back into the shadows, the bassist said, "Mr. D, you wouldn't happen to have your axe with you, would you?"

While the other musicians resumed their places, Buddy Drown walked the length of the room carrying his instrument case.

Harvey leaned over to Young. "Buddy Drown used to be the pre-eminent tenor player in the country. I haven't heard much about him lately, but still, this is pretty special. We're in for a treat."

On stage, Drown took a few moments to prepare: he shook off his sports jacket, unbuttoned his cuffs, and rolled his sleeves halfway up his muscular forearms; he lifted his saxophone, which was old and tarnished, out of its case and fitted a fresh reed into the mouthpiece; he blew a few quiet riffs, his back to the spectators, then faced them and said, "Thank you, ladies and gentlemen. It's always a pleasure to sit in, especially with as fine a band as this one." He half-turned to the bassist. "What are we playing, Scotty?"

The tune they played, an extended version of Charles Mingus's "Wednesday Night Prayer Meeting," began slowly, stirringly, like a storm brewing. Soon Drown was front and centre, his sax tipped high as if he were drinking the elixir of life, and for almost five minutes he soloed — he honked and squawked and screeched and bellowed and cajoled — and when he was finished Young and Harvey and the rest of the audience stood and hollered, the other sax player got down on his knees and made gestures of obeisance, the bassist and pianist and drummer, grinning and shaking their heads like imbeciles, played on, and the trumpeter, nervously fingering his valves, awaited the leader's nod.

When the number was finished and the applause had died and the musicians were once again laying down their instruments, a woman with a salon tan appeared at the side of the little stage, stepped up to one of the microphones, and said, "Don't forget, folks, next Friday night the brilliant young sax man Talmadge Cooper, whose debut CD, *Goombay Bop*, is taking New York by storm, will be here direct from Freeport, Grand Bahama, en route to the Big Apple. Come early and stay late. Good night and safe home."

Out on the street, Young and Harvey walked west to Yonge Street, then turned north. Young lit a cigarette. "They cooked up there," he said.

"Indeed they did," Harvey said. "And, listen, since I've made a convert out of you, I should tell you about this kid who's going to be here next week. It will be an evening not to be missed, and I will definitely be here, and I hope you will, too. The kid's a prodigy, a genius, the real McCoy. He's the next Coltrane."

Young, exhaling, said, "Who's Coltrane?"

"Who's Coltrane?! Just the best tenor man ever!" Harvey looked up into Young's face with an earnestness Young had never seen before. "He took this ungainly instrument that was only ever used in German marching bands and turned it into the sexiest, most soulful instrument in music. The guys who came before him — Lester Young, Coleman Hawkins, Ben Webster — they were the real pioneers, but when Trane played tenor, it was pure poetry. And he was better than anybody who's come after him, too. Even the new cats like Joshua Redman and Branford Marsalis. He's even better than David Murray, whom I love. And this kid we're going to see next Friday plays in the same hard, driving style."

"All right, I'll come."

"Wonderful. Now let me buy you a nightcap."

"I can't," Young said. "I've got the new puppy at home, besides which I'm done in."

"Ten minutes, Campbell. Surely, you won't —"

"Next time, I promise." He glanced in the window of the music store they were standing in front of. "Do they sell jazz in there?"

"Absolutely."

"Sign says they're open till midnight. I'm going to buy me some jazz. What should I start with?"

Harvey considered. "You could start with Mingus, but what I'd really recommend is Miles Davis. Tell the clerk you want *Kind of Blue*. It's like a primer for jazz novitiates. You'll love it. And what's more, Coltrane's on it!"

Young nodded. "Good," he said. "See you next Friday." He disappeared inside the store. Harvey watched him go, then buttoned the collar of his overcoat against the wind, turned around, and began to walk back down Yonge Street towards the Sapphire Tavern.

Inside, Harvey joined a small lineup of people who were waiting their turn to talk to Buddy Drown. He heard one man say, "Way to blow, Buddy!" and a teenager with long hair and a weak moustache say, "Mr. Buddy, you are the coolest, man!"

Drown nodded and smiled. The lineup shortened until only Harvey and a young redheaded woman were left. Drown autographed a menu for the woman, who said, "I started listening to jazz at my father's knee, Mr. D. He'll be thrilled when I show him this."

After she left — Harvey still standing there, waiting to compliment Drown on his solo in "Wednesday Night Prayer Meeting" — Drown turned to the band and said, "Not half as thrilled as *you'll* be when I show you *this*," and patted his groin. The musicians laughed.

Harvey cleared his throat and said, "Mr. Drown, I just wanted to tell you how much I enjoyed —"

"Sorry, old man," Drown interrupted, "autograph time is over."

"I don't want an autograph, I just —"

"Back tomorrow night?" the leader asked.

"As long as I'm welcome," Drown said.

"You're always welcome, you know that."

Drown turned his back to Harvey. From his pants pocket he removed a plastic baggy and handed it to the leader. "Small token of my esteem."

The leader said, "Much obliged."

"Street name is Kingston Red. It's sixty a quarter, if you want more of it."

The leader tucked the baggy into a pocket of his suit coat. "Who's this young cat Marion was talking about?"

Drown shrugged. "There's a lot of talk. *Downbeat* did one of their polls, and he's supposed to be the second coming of Christ." He chuckled and shook his head as he laid his saxophone on the velvet lining of his instrument case. "There's a new one every year. Pampered, classically trained, never gone hungry a day in their lives. It's a different world, Scotty. These young musicians — hell, I don't even like to call them musicians, it's a title they haven't earned — they're like so many of these athletes you see on TV: the downhill skiers and the equestrians, they're all from rich families. They're all children of privilege." He unrolled his sleeves and buttoned his cuffs. He pulled on his electric blue sports coat, and smiled. "Well, you know what I say? I say fuck it."

The leader smiled. "You'd better hurry, Buddy. That redhead's not going to wait around forever."

Drown closed the latches on his instrument case and picked it up. "Baby, I got twenty in my pocket says the bitch is down there right now, waiting for the man."

Young heard Dexter say, "Mr. Harvey, Sarge is on the line."

A full minute passed before Harvey came to the phone.

"Good afternoon, Campbell. What a pleasant surprise."

"It's barely lunchtime, Mr. Harvey. Isn't it a little early for McCully's?"

"Well, I was in the neighbourhood, and I needed some nourishment. Sorry I took so long getting to the phone. Gentleman here was trying to convince me of his point of view, and I was trying to convince him of mine."

"I listened to that Miles Davis CD. It's pretty good."

"I told you you'd like it."

"Your son's CD, is it sort of the same?"

Harvey was quiet for a few seconds. "Yes, it is. It's what's called cool jazz."

"Where can I get a copy?"

"There's just a couple of stores in Toronto that carry it. I'll lend you mine if you promise to return it."

"I promise. I'll get Trick to burn me a copy. When can I get it?"

"It's at home. I'll drop it by here."

"When?"

"Tomorrow, I guess. Or tonight. If I'm not here, Dexter can keep it under the bar for you. Have you found out anything?"

"Not yet, but I wanted to ask you a question about jazz."

"Go ahead."

"When we were at the Sapphire last week, each musician had a chance to do a solo on just about every tune, right?"

"Right."

"How come the solos are so long? 'Night Moves' is only five minutes and twenty-five seconds, and I figure it tells you everything you need to know about life."

"It's about creativity," Harvey said. "Each musician has a chance to be creative for as long as he wants with the rest of the band supporting him. He'll go anywhere his instrument and his talent and his imagination take him. And, Campbell, one of the amazing things about jazz is that no two solos are the same. That sax player in the All-Mingus Band? His solo in 'Better Git Hit in Your Soul' was at least three minutes long. That's a long time, eyes closed, no music on the stand. It's like going three minutes with Muhammad Ali. That band will play the same tune every night they're here, but the sax man's solo will be different every time."

"On purpose?"

"No, it's more that he'll let his mood and the atmosphere in the club and the tightness or looseness of the band influence his playing. Remember Buddy Drown's solo in 'Wednesday Night Prayer Meeting'?"

"I remember."

"Stunning stuff. Rough and sexy and emotional. Musicians aren't very good at expressing their emotions in words, but they sure can play them." He paused. "Isn't it strange to think that just a week ago we made plans to see Tal play? I wish we'd been able to."

"Me too, Mr. Harvey."

"I wish we'd been able to hear him express himself. He had a great rhythm section lined up, all of them veterans of the New York scene. Mulgrew Miller on piano, Ray Drummond on bass, Victor Lewis on drums. They're as good as they come, and the fact they were travelling up here to Toronto to play with Tal tells you what they thought of him."

"Are they in Toronto now?"

"No, they probably never got here. Marion at the Sapphire would have phoned their agents and told them what happened. Saved them the trip."

"I thought Tal would have had his own group."

"In the Bahamas he did. That's who he cut his first album with, but when he got a chance in the States and Canada, he wanted to play with the big boys."

"Wouldn't that piss off his homeys?"

"Maybe, but he was right to do it. He was the one with the gift, the rare talent, and he needed the right musicians to play with him — the ones who *could* play with him, who not only have the technical skills but also the ideas, the creativity."

Young said, "I'd be pretty steamed if I was his original drummer or something and he left me behind."

Harvey shrugged. "Jazz, like anything else, is a business, and if you're going to be successful you have to make the tough decisions. You can't keep people around who aren't earning their way." He paused to light a cigarette. "Was there anything else you wanted to ask me?"

"No, that's it."

"All these questions, are they part of your investigation, or because you're a budding jazz fan?"

"Both. I'll be in touch."

Young turned on *City Confidential*. It was half over, but he quickly picked up the story: a young man in Fresno, California, had hired a hit man to murder his parents and sister so that he could inherit $7 million. When it ended Young began to watch an episode of *American Justice* dealing with a Florida prostitute who had a penchant for killing customers. Ten minutes into it, Young turned off the TV and turned on the stereo. He pressed "play," and the haunting opening chords of "So What" followed him into the kitchen.

Saturday, November 10

Young had finally bought the vehicle of his dreams —
a GMC half-ton, dark red and fully loaded. It had been
four years old when he got it the previous spring, but it
was in mint condition, and he looked after it as if it were
new. The day he'd picked it up he'd taken Trick for a ride
and proudly listed its features: cruise control, air, 315
V8, ABS brakes, stereo, cassette, rust-proofing. Trick
said, "You sound like you're describing a woman:
blonde, blue-eyed, nice rack, legs up to here."

At 9:00 a.m. Young started up his truck and drove to
the A&P to do his weekly grocery shopping. He explored
every aisle, starting at the frozen food side of the store
and working his way across to the produce side. Into his
cart he piled a five-pound three-cheese lasagne, a tub of
orange sherbet, six frozen Michelina egg noodle and
Swedish meatball dinners, four cartons of orange juice
(no pulp), a pound of butter, a carton of milk, a rubber

chew toy for the puppy, six cans of baked beans, two cans of tomato rice soup, a box of Grape-Nuts, a tray of Nanaimo bars, two bags of Bridge Mixture, a bag of lemon cream cookies, a triple pack of Hawkins Cheezies, dishwasher detergent, a six-pack of paper towels, a case of twenty-four rolls of toilet paper, an inch-thick New York strip loin steak, three dollars' worth of thinly sliced hot mortadella, ten slices each of smoked provolone and creamy havarti, loaves of light rye, caraway rye, pumpernickel, and twelve-grain, a jar of kosher dills, a jar of sauerkraut, a bag of Reddi-Snack peanuts, two bananas, and a grapefruit.

After driving home, putting away his groceries, and eating lunch in front of the television, Young got back in the truck and drove out to Etobicoke in Toronto's west end to visit his aunt Gladys. Gladys was his mother's sister, and, until a year earlier, Young had thought she was dead. The last time he had seen her he had been a boy, and all he could remember was that she had sometimes babysat him, that she was tall and angular, and that she had gotten down on all fours in her long dress to help him set up his lead soldiers. Then she'd disappeared from his life. Young remembered once asking his mother about her and being told that Gladys had moved back home to Uxbridge to look after their ailing father, Young's grandfather, whom he never met.

When Young was seventeen, his father died, drunk, at the Legion, his face in his dinner. Four years later, Young was a starting defensive tackle for his police college football team when cancer killed his mother. Over the next two decades, he graduated, married badly, worked too hard, drank too much, watched his daughter grow up and away from him, got divorced, and lost track of what few relatives he had. He had not seen his aunt Gladys for almost forty years when, the previous

December, he'd answered the phone and a pleasant-sounding woman introduced herself as Aileen Struthers, director of Crestwood Nursing Home. She told Young that Gladys, who had been living at Crestwood for eight years, had asked for him. All she knew, however, was his name, and because there were over seventy listings in the phone book for C. Young, it had taken three days before Ms. Struthers dialed the right number. One afternoon shortly before Christmas, Young visited his aunt for the first time, and he had done so every Saturday since.

Crestwood was nothing to look at. Housed in a dilapidated mansion, it appeared from the outside to be a refuge of last resort. The hallways were crowded with old people sitting in wheelchairs or walking aimlessly. Many of the residents suffered from Alzheimer's, and, over time, Young learned to recognize them because of their restlessness and air of distraction. Several of the women spent hours each day standing in the hallways, bent at the waist, picking up phantom pieces of lint from the linoleum. One old man on Gladys's floor paced incessantly, drool swinging from his lower lip, a folded newspaper in one hand, a teddy bear in the other. A collection of used handbags — acquired at yard sales and flea markets by Aileen Struthers — hung from the wall railings for the Alzheimer's ladies to pick up and carry. Each handbag contained a paperback novel and some Kleenex and costume jewellery. As well, all manner of ladies' hats — from little felt berets to floppy sunhats — hung from pegs on the walls. Convinced that they were on their way to work or shopping, the Alzheimer's ladies would pick up whichever hat and purse appealed to them and head off down the hall with a soon-vague sense of destination. After Young had become a regular visitor at Crestwood, these ladies would sometimes stop him as he walked towards his aunt's room. One woman thought Young was her son; another thought he was her piano student. A woman named Mabel, who always held a purse protectively in front of her chest, constantly complained there was a man in her room, and Young would escort her down the hall, stick his head in the door, and reassure her no men were in sight. A balding woman with a red-veined nose was always whimpering, and Young would walk her along the hall, patting her hand. Her story, according to Aileen, was that her husband had failed to come home from work one day during the fifties, and she was still looking for him.

Gladys, unlike most of the other residents, was as sharp as a tack. Her body had betrayed her — her skeleton had twisted in on itself and she was in chronic pain — but she didn't miss a beat, and she had summoned Young because he was the only blood relative she had left. As Young soon found out, Gladys kept mostly to herself; she rarely attended singalongs or went on bus excursions. Most of the time she was parked in front of the television with her roommate, a tiny, heavily wrinkled Jamaican woman named Petergay.

As Young tugged loose the Velcro end of the bright yellow banner stretched across the doorway to keep the Alzheimer's patients from wandering into Gladys and Petergay's room and wandering off with the TV remote or one of Gladys's Dick Francis novels, he could tell something was up. The women, seated side by side on a threadbare loveseat, were in a state of high agitation.

"Hello, ladies," he said, closing the door behind him.

Their heads swivelled towards him, and Gladys said, "Oh, Nephew, it's you."

Young pulled two cans of Labatt Blue out of one of his jacket pockets and a third out of another. "What's all the excitement?"

"What is this world coming to," Gladys said, "when people are being murdered in our finer hotels?"

Young looked at the television and saw a news anchor with, superimposed in the upper-right-hand corner of the screen, an image of a smiling young man holding a saxophone, and below it, his name: Talmadge Cooper.

The women returned their attention to the television. Petergay, who was fine-boned and mahogany-coloured, said, "He were just a boy. Twenty-five year old, and somebody gots to kill him. For what? I say. That man say he a musician. That why they kills him? 'Cause he make beautiful music?"

Young stepped across the small room to his aunt's bedside table, opened the top drawer, and, from the clutter of candy, jewellery, playing cards, greeting cards, and tubes of ointment, lifted two clear plastic cups. He snapped open one can of beer, filled the cups about halfway, and handed them to the women. Without taking their eyes off the television, they accepted the cups and sipped from them.

Young said, "I know his father."

The heads swivelled again. Petergay said, "You know the dead boy father?"

"Yeah, he's a journalist ... among other things."

"White man?"

"Yeah, the mother was black."

Petergay said, "Mmm-hmm, mix-race child. I thought so when I seed the picture."

The women's eyes returned to the television.

"He wants me to help with the investigation."

Gladys said, "Well, I hope you said yes."

Young shook his head. "I can't."

"Why not?" Petergay said. "'Cause he black?"

"No, of course not."

"Then why?" said Gladys, looking up at Young. "Why can't you help?"

"Because I'm going away, that's why. Day after tomorrow."

Petergay said, "Where you going?"

"Florida for a couple of weeks." He turned to his aunt. "I told you last time I was here I was going to Florida."

"I don't think you did, dear. I would remember something like that."

Petergay said, "What so important 'bout Florida?"

"I'm sure it has something to do with horse racing," said Gladys.

"Horse racing!" Petergay shook a finger in Young's direction. "Wages of sin!"

Gladys said, "Really, Nephew, how can you leave when your friend needs you?"

Young said, "It may interest you to know that he's involved with horse racing, too. He's a journalist for *Sport of Kings* magazine. Well, sometimes he is. Anyway, the point is he writes about horse racing."

The women returned their gaze to the TV screen. Gladys said, "I don't understand how you can go on vacation —"

"— when your friend need you," Petergay said.

Young placed the unopened second and third cans of beer on the coffee table in front of the women. "I've got to go, Aunty," he said. "I'll see you when I get back."

"But you just got here," Gladys said. "Won't you at least have a refreshment with us before you go?"

"I have a lot to do before I leave."

Gladys nodded towards the two cans. "Well, open those before you go. You know we can't manage those tabby things."

Young leaned across her and snapped open the cans.

She fixed him with her gaze. "I wish you'd stay and help your friend."

"I know —"

"I pray for that," said Petergay. "Me and Glad, we both *prays* for that."

"Well, I'd like to help, but —"

"That news man say it look like a voodoo murder. That what you hear?"

"There was some evidence, yes."

"You might better talk to my grandchile. He know all about voodoo."

"Your grandchild?"

"Yes, my daughter boy."

Young took his notepad and pen out of his shirt pocket. "I probably won't get to it till I get back from Florida, but I'll definitely look him up. What's his name?"

The features of Petergay's face twisted together in thought. "I don't recall. I think it begin with a C."

"Do you have his phone number written down somewhere?"

"He don't have no phone."

"What about his address?"

"That he do have, and that I do know. Millhaven Penitentiary. But I don't know what cell he in."

Five years earlier Trick had been reluctant to become computer-literate. For him, doing research on the Internet was a poor excuse for police work, but over time he had come to regard it as an improvement — like upgrading your hydro from one hundred to two hundred amps — and it made him feel useful and once again interested in life. In the past six months alone, the Homicide Division of the Metro Toronto Police Department had asked him to provide them with information on the construction of baseballs, the effects of gasoline fumes on the human brain, and the various edge types used by an English knife manufacturer; now Campbell Young had asked him to dig up what he could about obeah.

Trick printed out a dozen pages of information and placed them in a file folder. Before he turned his computer off, he checked his e-mail. He had only one new message: "As per your Request, an Appointment has been scheduled with one of our Finest Representatives, *Miss Leventhorpe*, who will call at your Residence on Monday, 3:00 to 4:00 in the Afternoon. Please Confirm by checking the Box below and by selecting a Mode of Payment."

Trick scrolled down, read some additional information, then clicked "Confirm" and "Visa."

Young phoned Priam Harvey from the lobby of the nursing home. This time he tried McCully's first.

"Campbell, what a pleasant surprise, *encore*," Harvey said after Dexter had passed him the receiver. "When are you coming over for the CD?"

"That part about money being no object. Do you think it's on the level?"

"You mean Eula? Sure it is. She's married to an architect. He's building one of the new hotels the Chinese are putting up. She's got *tons* of money."

"I don't like to interfere with my brothers in blue, but as a personal favour to you — and because there's a good chance I might actually get paid — you can tell her I accept."

"That's wonderful news! But what about Florida?"

"It'll still be there."

"Oh, thank you, you don't know how much I appreciate this. And if I can help out at all ..."

"I'll let you know."

"You may need me, Campbell. Tal was a jazz musician, and for someone who can't hold a tune or play an instrument, I know just about everything there is to know about jazz."

"I'll be in touch."

"One of the great regrets of my life."

"What?"

"That I never learned how to play an instrument. That I never learned how to make music. You know what I tell people?"

"What?"

"I tell them I'd give my right arm to play the tenor saxophone."

That evening, Young put on his windbreaker, opened the door to the little balcony off his kitchen, let the puppy out, filled a plastic sherbet tub with black oil sunflower seeds from a fifty-pound sack he kept in a garbage can and scooped an old chipped coffee mug into a bag of niger seeds he kept in the same garbage can, and carefully descended the steps to his backyard. He unlatched the roof of a large bird feeder that stood on a pole below a mountain ash tree in a corner of the yard and dumped the sunflower seeds into it. He poured the niger seeds into a finch feeder that hung by a short length of picture-hanging wire from one of the tree's lower branches. A previous tenant in the building had left the feeders behind, and for several years Young had been stocking them. He kept a bird guide and his racetrack binoculars on the sill of his kitchen window. In the winter he had blue jays and cardinals and nuthatches and chickadees and goldfinches. In the spring, the blackbirds, grosbeaks, and sparrows would arrive — first the tree sparrows, then the song sparrows, then the whitecrowned sparrows. He made notes on a piece of paper he kept in the bird guide. His first sighting of a robin the previous spring was March 25, the same day the cedar waxwings made a one-day appearance.

Young returned to the balcony and was watching the puppy sniff around the yard when the telephone rang. He went inside and picked up the receiver.

"All packed?" Trick said.

"I'm not going."

"You're not going? Why?"

"I decided to take the case."

"Really. Why the change of heart?"

"I don't know. What's up?"

"I just called to tell you I got the dope on obeah."

"I'll come over and take a look at it."

Young whistled the puppy back up the stairs and into the apartment, retrieved his keys and wallet from the change dish he kept by the front door, walked out to his truck, and drove over to Trick's high-rise. Trick buzzed him in, and Young took the elevator to the seventeenth floor. The door of Trick's apartment was open, and Young stepped in. Trick was in the living room in his wheelchair watching television. When he heard Young he clicked off the TV and turned his wheelchair to face him. He had the file folder in his lap. He was wearing his black and purple Raptors jacket.

"Going somewhere?" Young asked.

"Yeah, you and me are going to McCully's for a beer."

"What's the occasion?"

"The occasion is I haven't been outside in five days. Also, you owe me for this." He held up the folder.

"Okay," Young said, "get your purse and let's go."

Trick had two wheelchairs: a cumbersome, battery-operated, state-of-the-art limousine of a wheelchair worth almost as much as a limousine, and a simple, fold-up, manual wheelchair that weighed almost nothing. Although Trick preferred the former, because it allowed him some control over his movements and because he enjoyed showing off the bells and whistles and impressing people with his independence, on those occasions when he was going to be in a crowd, he used the latter, so long as he had a friend along to chauffeur. The friend was always either Young or an enormous Haitian taxi driver named Boum-Boum.

McCully's was busy — all the tables were occupied — but when Jessy the barmaid saw Young and Trick at the entrance, she ordered three young men wearing college jackets to vacate their table and join the mob at the bar, which they did willingly enough once they saw a black man in a wheelchair being pushed towards them by a six-foot-eight, two-hundred-ninety-pound white man with kinky red hair and a nose like a potato. A minute later Young had two bottles of Labatt Blue in front of him and Trick had a bottle of Tuborg and a glass.

As they sat talking, Young's eyes never rested; he scanned the room, not for anything in particular, but just in case something should show up. Old habits die hard, and Young was an old homicide detective who knew better than to let down his guard. Trick was an old homicide detective too, his career cut short because nine years earlier he hadn't been surveying his surroundings when a man named Lawrence Woolley approached his cruiser and shot him through the neck.

"So," Young said, "what have you got on obeah?"

Trick nodded at the file folder on the table in front of them. "It's harmless," he began by saying. "People use it to ward off evil, like people who believe in vampires wear garlic around their necks. In Spain, people wear strings of garlic during those bullfight fiestas."

"Why?" said Young. "Not to get gored?"

"No, because they're basically drunk for six or seven days and they don't want anything bad to happen to them."

"And obeah's like that?"

"Well, not exactly, but the point is it's more passive than aggressive, if you know what I mean."

"I don't have a clue."

"They don't use it to kill people is what I'm saying. They use it to protect their property, to scare children away from their mango tree, or whatever. Wives use it to scare their husbands' mistresses away."

Young said, "You want a pickled egg?"

Trick shook his head. "I thought you wanted to hear about obeah."

"I do. I'll be right back." Young stood up and made his way through the crowd to the bar.

Priam Harvey was sitting in his usual spot at the corner of the bar. As Young waited for Dexter to fish an egg out of the jar for him, he said, "What's up, Mr. Harvey?"

Harvey turned his head in Young's direction, and Young knew right away that Harvey was drunk: his head was unsteady, his eyes were unfocused and pink, and the front of his rumpled white plantation suit was stained with gravy. Young said, "You'll be happy to know that Trick's helping me with the case. He's already done some research —"

"I'm a jazz fan," Harvey interrupted. He lifted his chin. "But not just any jazz. I'm partial to quintets. Drums, bass, piano, tenor sax, and trumpet. Or maybe alto sax in place of trumpet. Maybe baritone. If it's alto, I want Cannonball Adderley. Gerry Mulligan if it's baritone. Freddie Hubbard on trumpet. Mingus on bass. Monk on piano. Philly Joe Jones on drums. And tenor? Well, Coltrane, obviously. Or Ben Webster. If it's Webster, then I want Ray Brown on bass, Kenny Drew on piano."

Harvey's nose had a drip dangling from the end of it, and there were white flecks in the corners of his mouth.

"And I'll tell you something else. I am so much an aficionado of jazz that I will not turn off a CD in the middle of a tune, not even if I have to go somewhere, not even if I'm late for an appointment. I consider it rude. People don't walk out in the middle of a concert and they shouldn't do it at home. It's all about respect for the musicians."

Dexter placed the egg on a paper napkin in front of Young. Young said, "Give me a shot of JD, as well, please, Dexter." When Dexter placed the shot in front of him, Young picked it up and knocked it back. He waited for the burn.

"See this trail mix?" Harvey said, and he indicated the small bowl in front of him on the bar. "I like the cashews best. To me they're like saxophones. They even look like saxophones … curved and sexy. Other tenor players I admire are Johnny Griffin, Lockjaw Davis, David Murray, Sonny Rollins, Dexter Gordon and Lester Young." He paused to belch. "And Coleman Hawkins."

Young said, "What about your son? You thought he was pretty good, didn't you? He was in their league, wasn't he?"

Harvey selected a cashew and popped it into his mouth. "The almonds I like less well. They're like trombones. And just as there's no place for trombones in a quintet, there's no place for almonds in trail mix. Maybe if they're roasted, but not raw like these ones." He picked out several almonds and dropped them in an ashtray. "Clarinets are the worst. Dixieland shit. That's not jazz. Clarinets are like these things." He held up a tiny cheese log. "Maybe they're acceptable in nuts and bolts or Bits 'n' Bites, but they've got no place in trail mix. They're salty, while the rest of the ingredients — the raisins and sunflower seeds and bits of peel and the unsalted nuts — they're all sweet. What these things are is discordant." He dropped the cheese log in the ashtray with the almonds and the smoking cigarette butts.

"I've got to get back," Young said. "I'll be in touch."

Slowly, Harvey rotated his head to the right. One of the college students was leaning on the bar trying to get Dexter's attention. "I'm a jazz fan," Harvey said to him.

Back at their table, Young said to Trick, "Mr. Harvey's sitting at the bar."

"Is he drunk?" Trick asked.

"Of course he's drunk." Young took a long draught of beer. "When isn't he drunk? I told him you were helping with the case, but it didn't seem to register. I don't think he even remembered I phoned him today and told him I'd take the case."

"I like Mr. Harvey, but he's got no willpower."

"Well, I know, but his son's dead, after all. Maybe we should cut him some slack."

Trick shrugged the one shoulder that worked. "He's been drinking like a fish for years. His son just died two days ago."

Sunday, November 11

"Excuse me, Miss Young?"

Debi looked up from her salad. "Yes?"

"I'm sorry to disturb you, but I saw you here and thought I should seize the day, as it were." He extended his hand. "My name is Berry, Edgar Berry. I've recently bought a race horse from a friend and I was hoping I might interest you in training it for me. I've asked around, and your name comes highly recommended."

Young, sitting opposite his daughter in the clubhouse dining room at Caledonia Downs, glanced at Trick, seated to his right, and gave him a veiled look, as if to say, *It's Sunday, we're here for a little personal time, why can't the bastards leave us alone?* but Trick's head was bowed over his *Racing Form*, his fork and its cargo of mashed potatoes suspended in the air.

Debi said, "Nice to meet you, Mr. Berry. If you'd give me a number where I can reach you, I'll give you a call."

Berry, who was short and rotund, took out a billfold and extracted a business card. "Truth be told, I didn't exactly buy the horse. I accepted it in trade."

"Trade for what?" Debi asked.

"For my services." He handed her the card. "My friend and I are both very shady characters. He's a gambler, I'm a lawyer." He laughed and nodded at Young, who nodded back unsmilingly, and at Trick, who remained oblivious to the man's presence.

Debi smiled politely. "Tell me about the horse."

"It's a two-year-old colt. Unraced. The sire is Carson City, so it should have some speed."

"Carson Citys don't come cheap. Your friend must owe you plenty."

Berry nodded. "Let's just say I've always wanted to get into the racing game and never had the opportunity till now. The colt is worth considerably more than my services, but it was all he had to barter with. He paid eighty thousand for it at a yearling sale."

"What about the dam's side?"

"The dam's by Risen Star. Won a couple of minor stakes in Louisiana, and it's already produced two winners."

"Where's the colt now?"

"Still on my friend's soon-to-be-repossessed farm. I should tell you, Miss Young, it's barely broken and hasn't even been worked yet."

Debi shook her head. "That's just plain irresponsible, a colt with that kind of potential. I'll phone you sometime in the next week, Mr. Berry, and I'll certainly take a look at him, but that's all I can promise for now. It's too late to do anything with him this year, but maybe we can get him ready for next spring."

Young stood up, said, "Excuse me, but there's some roast beef over there with my name on it," and headed for the buffet.

As Berry watched him go, he made a comical face. "My God, look at the size of him," he laughed. "If he ever fell over, he'd be halfway home."

Debi said, "That's my dad."

Berry turned to her. "No offence intended. I'll look forward to your call." He smiled and walked away.

Young returned a minute later. "Must be nice," he said.

"What?" Debi said.

"Everybody wants you."

In the five years since Debi had become a full-time trainer, she had risen from being an unknown with four or five washed-up claimers to number six in the trainer standings at Caledonia Downs with twelve quality horses in her barn, four grooms in her employ, and fourteen wins in fifty-nine starts at the current meet.

"It's nice all right," Debi said. She looked down at her plate. "Now, where was I? Ah yes, the next order of business was the cabbage rolls." A cellphone chimed. "God*damn* it!" she said. She picked up her purse from the floor beside her chair and rummaged inside it.

"Trick," Young said, "want to come to the Bahamas with me?"

The forkful of potato still hung in midair. Trick's eyes remained on the *Form*. "No, thank you."

"Why not?"

"My wheels would get stuck in the sand."

Young frowned. "I'm serious."

"I am, too." Trick looked up. "I'd just be a burden. People would stare at me or take pity on me or pat me on the head like a boy in short pants. Drunks would feel sorry for me, and I'd end up picking a fight. But thanks for asking." He laid the forkful of potato down on his plate and resumed his scrutiny of the *Form*.

Debi folded up her cellphone and replaced it in her purse. "I gotta go. That filly I've got in the ninth has heat in her leg. We may have to scratch her."

"You want me to pack you up some of that buffet to take with you?" Young said.

"No thanks, I've had enough."

"Will you be back later?"

"No, I'm going to be busy at the barn for the rest of the day. What was that you were saying about the Bahamas?"

"I'm going to the Bahamas on a case."

"You're not flying, are you?"

"No, I was thinking I might paddle."

Debi stood up and pulled the strap of her purse over her shoulder. She was her father's daughter, tall and big-boned and fleshy, and she was wearing a chocolate muumuu over tan boots. Her hair was short and brunette, with blonde highlights. "I thought you hated flying. I thought the seats were too small and you always felt hemmed in."

"Thanks for reminding me."

"It scares me when you fly."

"Why should it scare *you*? You're safe on the ground. I'm the one should be scared."

There was a Jazz Lunch that afternoon at Nathan's Ribs on Mount Pleasant Avenue. The leader of the house band — the banjo player — was delighted to see Buddy Drown in the audience, and thrilled when he agreed to sit in. The clientele at Nathan's Ribs was upscale — their idea of jazz was Dixieland and Diana Krall — but Drown was flexible, and his solo on "Tin

Roof Blues," based on Pete Fountain's clarinet mas-
terpiece, left them shouting for more.

During the break, a man with an unlit cigar in the
corner of his mouth approached Drown at the bar. "I
wish I could do what you do," he said. "All I'm good
for is straightening the teeth of spoiled brats. Buy you
a drink?"

"Certainly," said Drown. "Courvoisier."

"Listen," said the man, "my wife and I were just
talking — that's her waving over there — and I know
it might sound unusual, but we were wondering if
you would do us the honour of playing at our son's
bar mitzvah."

Drown shrugged. "Depends when and where and
what my agent has lined up for me."

"So you might do it?" the man said.

"I might."

The man gave a thumbs-up to his wife, who
shrieked and turned to the woman beside her. "It's not
until next May," the man said, "but we were thinking
it's never too early to plan ahead, and when we heard
you play today we said to each other, 'We love his
music, and Dustin' — that's our son — 'loves Kenny G.
It's a match made in heaven!'"

"I appreciate it, thanks."

"We were thinking in the garden would be best, and
you could bring your own rhythm section."

"I'd want more than union rates," Drown said.

"Of course, of course!" The man squeezed Drown's
arm. "Name your price. I'm serious, Mr. Drown, name
your price." He reached inside his jacket. "I'm going to
give you my card, I'll write down the date, and you give
me a call or have your agent give me a call when he
knows if you're available — and both Esther and I sure
as *hell* hope you are — and tell me your price."

Drown nodded. "Having money must afford you many pleasures."

The man seemed not to have heard him. He was watching his wife, who was gesticulating. "Oh, I almost forgot. Esther wanted me to ask you if you do any Herb Alpert."

As he was eating his supper — two nuked Michelina dinners — in front of the TV, Young's telephone rang.

"What?" he said, his mouth full.

"Priam Harvey here. Wondered if I could entice you into a beer."

Young identified the background noise as McCully's. "You caught me in the middle of my supper."

"Come when you're done."

"All right, I'll be there in half an hour."

Young found Harvey on his usual stool at the corner of the bar.

"When Tal was sixteen or seventeen," Harvey said as Young settled in beside him and raised two fingers to Dexter, "I sent him a Thelonious Monk CD. It's the one with Gerry Mulligan on baritone sax, Wilbur Ware on bass, and Shadow Wilson on drums. The CD's unusual because of the alternate tracks on it — tracks that weren't included on the original LP, which was released in 1957, but were included on the more commodious compact disc thirty years later." Harvey paused to light a cigarette. "For the serious jazz fan, listening to two versions of the same tune is fascinating stuff because at first they may sound pretty much identical, but after you've listened to them four or five times, you start to hear subtle differences. For instance, on the first take of 'Straight, No Chaser,' Monk's piano is subdued and ordinary, whereas about two and a half minutes into the second take he gets all bluesy and gospelly. It's wonderful. But you have to listen carefully, because all these nuances are happening behind Mulligan's saxophone. And Monk's piano work on the first take of 'I Mean You' is, again, ordinary, uninspired, whereas five minutes into the second take he does this tiny little boogie-woogie riff — it can't be more than five seconds long — but it adds spice to the whole thing."

Dexter brought Young his two Labatt Blue and said, "Mr. Harvey?"

"Oh yes," Harvey said.

Dexter took a fresh glass from the little freezer behind the bar and placed it under the Creemore tap.

"So anyway, I basically introduced Tal to jazz, and I told him stuff like I've just told you, and he really dug it, and he saw how jazz could be mysterious and fun and complicated, like math problems, which he was also very good at, as was I, and which we'd also worked on together years earlier, when I was still a presence in his life." He tapped the ash off his cigarette. "Anyway, I'm telling you all this because I want you to have some of the background — and I haven't even told you how amazed his teachers at the high school in Freeport were, and how he just took off in high school, which I was no longer present to witness, and how he won a partial scholarship to Juilliard, and how the community he grew up in at Pinder's Point held a fundraiser to cover the rest of the tuition. This was before his momma married the rich man. Anyway, I told you all this so you'd see what a special kid he was, and why it's so important to me not only that you take the case but that you physically go down to Freeport and see for yourself what this kid's background was like and how well he was thought of down there."

Dexter placed Harvey's pint in front of him.

"Thank you, my good man," Harvey said to Dexter. He turned back to Young. "What do you say?"

"I told you yesterday, I'm in."

Harvey drew his head back. "You did?"

"Yes, I'm in."

"You know, it's funny, I remember you telling me you'd do it, but I assumed I'd just dreamed it. Yesterday's a bit of a blur."

Young said, "There's something fishy about this obeah business, which to my mind may be the key to the whole case, and where better to research it than where it comes from, is the way I figure it. So I'm not only in, I'm going to the Bahamas."

"You're serious?"

"I'm serious, all right — on one condition."

"What?"

"You come with me."

Harvey's eyes widened. "I don't think so."

"You told me you knew everything about jazz, and if I needed any help you were my man."

"I meant up here. To tell you the truth, I don't want to see Eula again. Especially right now. She was fiery enough when things were going well, but my guess is she blames me for Tal's death."

"Why? You had nothing to do with it."

Harvey examined the coal on his cigarette. "I got him interested in jazz. If he hadn't been a jazz musician, he wouldn't have been in Toronto, and if he hadn't been in Toronto, he wouldn't have been killed."

"You don't know that. No offence, but maybe it was drug-related, or maybe there was a contract on him for some reason we don't know about. Maybe he'd have been killed wherever he was."

"He wasn't that kind of boy, Campbell. And even if he was, that's not the way Eula will see it."

"Well, whatever, I still need your help. You know your way around down there, you know who to talk to, and you claim to know everything about jazz."

Harvey studied his beer. "I don't have any money. I can't afford to go."

Young said, "You're my consultant. I'm hiring you. I don't expect you to pay. Besides, it's a business expense, I can write it off. All you need is pocket money."

"I don't have any pocket money."

"Find some. Look at it this way, Mr. Harvey: if you want me to go, you have to go, too."

Harvey butted out his cigarette. "I know the whole reason for going down there is investigation and research — sad research — but I suppose we could have a bit of fun while we're at it. We could go on a booze cruise, I could show you the International Bazaar and Count Basie Square. We could go to the casino. And we'd eat well. Lobster and grouper and calamari. Conch salad and conch fritters. Cracked conch. Conch's good for your prick, gives it muscle."

"Maybe I'll get a chance to flex it."

Harvey looked around the bar. "I could use a change of scenery. Get me out of this hole for a while. When are we leaving?"

"Tomorrow."

"Tomorrow! That's awfully soon. Will you be able to get tickets?"

Young patted his shirt pocket. "Find yourself some pocket money."

The phone was ringing. Young was dreaming about cracked conch. He'd never eaten conch in his life, cracked or otherwise. He knew it was some kind of shellfish, but he didn't really know what it looked like.

In the dream a chef came to his table — who was he sitting with, was he alone? — and began smashing a pile of big pink shells with a sledgehammer. Shell fragments flew everywhere, into Young's mouth, into his eyes.

He roused himself from the clutter of his La-Z-Boy. "What?" he said into the phone.

"Daddy, I'm worried about you flying."

Young rubbed his face. On TV, the Titans were playing the Colts. "What?"

"I'm worried about you flying. What airline are you flying with?"

"I don't know."

"Well, check your ticket."

The tickets were still in his shirt pocket. He looked at them. "American Airlines."

Debi said, "Oh my God, do you realize that two of the planes in 9-11 were American Airlines, and that was only two months ago. Jamal's twelve years old, he's too young to lose his grandfather. When are you coming back?"

"Saturday. The girl said Monday to Saturday was the cheapest."

"I'm so worried. Ant'wawn's worried too. He doesn't think you should go either."

"Who?"

"Ant'wawn."

"Who the hell's Ant'wawn?"

"You know perfectly well who Ant'wawn is. I introduced you to him at the Horsemen's Ball."

"Was he the one wearing pink bellbottoms and a tea cozy?"

"Daddy, I wish you'd —"

"I didn't realize him and you were hooked up."

"We've been together since October."

"By 'together' I take it you mean he's moved in."

"He moved in two weeks ago, yes, but he's promised to help with the rent —"

"What is he, an exercise boy, a hot walker?"

"He's a groom. He works for Westwinds."

"Who's his boss?"

"Will you stop with all the questions! Sometimes you treat me like I'm one of your suspects."

"Debi, you go through these black boys like a hot knife through butter, why is that? You collect them like stray dogs."

"Daddy, please —"

"You're doing so well for yourself, sweetie, you're one of the best trainers on the grounds, and yet you insist —"

"Please don't start on me."

"Well, you woke me up —"

"Woke you *up*? It's not even ten o'clock yet."

"I don't care what time it is. I'm retired now. I sleep when I want, and when I get woken up I get cranky. Besides, I liked Eldridge."

"I liked him, too! We were together five years, goddamn it! But the important thing is what you just said: you're retired, so you don't have to go down to the Bahamas if you don't want to."

"Ah, but I *do* want to. And excuse me, but that's not the important thing. The important thing is what's Jamal think of the new guy? Does he like him? He hasn't mentioned him to *me*."

"He likes him okay, I guess."

"You don't sound too convinced."

"Daddy, I called about the Bahamas, not about my private life. Me and Ant'wawn —"

"Okay, let me see if I got this straight. Antsinhispants who I met maybe once and who moved in with you all of two weeks ago's already got a say in whether or not I get on a goddamn airplane."

"Daddy, please —"

"Maybe I should have a say in how he dresses himself."

"Daddy, *I* don't want you to go."

"Well, I'm going!" Young shouted. He took a breath and in a calmer voice he said, "I love you, sweetie, but you have to stop worrying. Nothing's going to happen. Now good night."

After he hung up, Young let the puppy out and made himself a snack of Hawkins Cheezies, lemon cream cookies, and milk. He ate, let the puppy back in, sat back down in the La-Z-Boy, and promptly fell asleep again. He dreamed he was at the controls of a bush plane flying over a northern lake whose shallow rocky bottom was clearly visible. The plane began to lose altitude, but Young couldn't figure out how to make it climb. There was someone seated behind him in the cabin, talking calmly to him, but the water and the rocks were rushing up at him, and he couldn't risk turning around to see who it was. He hauled back on the joystick for all he was worth; then, just as the plane was about to hit the lake, he let go of the joystick. He wasn't panicking, he wasn't screaming in terror. He felt relaxed, almost carefree. He was about to turn to the person behind him and say, "Well, I guess this is it," but before he could speak or see who the person was, his eyes snapped open.

Monday, November 12

Young hated packing. It depressed him, deciding what to take, how to fold it, where to put it in the suitcase. He never knew how much clothing he would need, and he always ended up with too much. He could never decide, for example, how many pairs of shoes he'd need, and they were so bulky they messed up the organization of the suitcase — the bundles of socks and underwear, the coiled belt, the shirts that always ended up creased no matter how carefully he folded them.

He left his bedroom, the puppy following, and walked down the hall to the kitchen. He took a bottle of Jack Daniel's out of the cupboard and poured himself a shot. He downed it, then stepped to the sink and turned the water on to rinse the glass. Instead, he turned the water off and walked back down the hall with the glass in one hand and the bottle in the other.

He settled on his brogues for sleuthing, his loafers for the casino, his sandals for the beach. Not that he liked beaches particularly, but he wanted to be prepared. Maybe there would be a pool. He hadn't asked the travel agent if the hotel had a pool.

He sat on the edge of his bed and phoned Priam Harvey. Harvey didn't pick up until the fifth ring.

"You up yet?"

"What time is it?" Harvey said groggily.

Young glanced at the clock radio on his bedside table. "Coming up to ten-thirty."

"What time's the flight?"

"Four. I'll pick you up at one."

"How about we take a limousine?"

"No, I'll drive. We'll leave the truck at the Park 'N Fly."

"It'd be nice to take a limousine. You can write it off as a business expense."

"I'll pick you up at one."

Back in the kitchen, Young reached into the same cupboard he kept the Jack Daniel's in. From a row of small bottles on the shelf below the liquor, he loaded a plastic screw-top jar that had once contained imported humbugs — a gift from Debi — with zinc, ibuprofen, and vitamin tablets, and with garlic, saw palmetto, and flaxseed oil softgel capsules.

A few minutes later, he was in the bedroom, bending over his suitcase, when the doorbell rang. He hurried along the hallway to the front door, the puppy bouncing along behind him.

"Hey, Poppy," his grandson said when Young opened the door.

"How come you're not in school?" Young said. "I was expecting your mother."

"I'm sick."

"You don't look sick." Young pulled the small coffee-coloured boy into a headlock. He made a fist with his other hand and gave the boy a noogie.

"Ow, that hurts!"

Young released him, and Jamal rubbed the top of his head.

"Sometimes you're too rough."

"Oh, poor baby," Young said, and kissed him on the ear.

"I wish you wouldn't do that," Jamal protested, wiping the side of his head with the sleeve of his windbreaker.

Young looked down at the puppy, who was sitting at his feet watching him. "I've got her food ready and a box of Milk-Bones and I bought her a toy to chew on. It's in the A&P bag with the leash. It's a porcupine or something."

Jamal said, "She's going to miss you. Look at the way she looks at you."

"Yeah, well, it can't be helped. By the time I get back, she'll think she's your dog. You going to be okay walking her home from here? I thought your mother was coming to get her."

"She leaves for work at, like, four-thirty in the morning."

"Yeah, I know, I guess I just —"

"She made me promise to go straight home. Anyway, it's only a couple of blocks."

"How's the new guy?"

Jamal looked up at Young blankly, but Young knew he understood the question.

"The new guy, Antwerp, or whatever his name is."

"He's okay, I guess."

"Look at me, honey."

Jamal looked up at his grandfather.

"If he ever causes any problems, or if you ever want to come over here for a while, you just let me know."

The boy nodded.

"Promise?"

The boy nodded again.

"Okay. You better run along. Don't let her off the leash, or you'll never get her back."

"Don't worry." Jamal knelt down, and the puppy came to him. She rolled on her back, and he rubbed her belly. "Have you got a name for her yet?"

"No, I don't. Maybe you'll come up with something. Just make sure it's not Fluffy or Fifi or anything like that."

Young had worked with two partners during his years with Homicide. The first had been Trick, and the second had been Lynn Wheeler.

Wheeler was still a detective constable, and when Young phoned her at eleven-thirty, she was at her desk. "Sarge!" she said when she heard his voice. "Long time no see."

"I know, I know." Young always felt awkward when he talked to Wheeler, partly because she was a lesbian and partly because he was in love with her. "How's it going?"

Wheeler looked around. She could see Big Urmson looking out the window of his office. Across from her, Tony Barkas's chair was empty. Since Young's retirement, Barkas had been her partner. "It's quiet. Tony's gone off for a Coke or something. What's up with you?"

"You and Barkas working out all right?"

"It's been almost a year now, Sarge. We're fine. He's terrific. He's not you, but he's terrific. He's fearless."

"He cover your back?"

"Yes, he covers my back. We look after each other."

"But he's not me."

"No, he's definitely not you."

Young lit a cigarette. He liked to picture Wheeler in uniform, her blonde hair bobbed above the black epaulets, her strange beautiful eyes open and welcoming — the friendly blue one, of course, which Young had always preferred looking into, but the brown forbidding one, too. "I still can't understand why they moved Urmson up to sergeant instead of you. You've got as much experience as he does, and you're ten times smarter."

"I'm a woman, don't forget, Sarge, and a dyke, and unlike Urmson, I didn't marry Staff Inspector Bateman's buck-toothed daughter."

Young smiled into the phone. "True enough."

"So what's up, or is this a social call?"

"No, nothing's up, just phoned to say goodbye."

"Goodbye?"

"Yeah, me and Mr. Harvey are off to the Bahamas. The Talmadge Cooper thing. Do me a favour and let Urmson know, will you?"

"Why don't you tell him yourself? He's at his desk as we speak. I can see him from here, staring into space."

"Just do me a favour and tell him."

"How long you gone for?"

"Six days. We're back Saturday night."

"Well, I hope it's not all business. Try and have some fun while you're down there. Have a pina colada in my honour."

"I will."

"Who's looking after the pup?"

"Debi. Well, Jamal, really. He was just here to pick it up. I thought about asking Trick — I thought it might be good for him to have the responsibility, you know how he gets — but then I remembered what happened

last time." It was while she was in Trick's care that
Young's previous dog, Reg, had swallowed a piece of
wood she was chewing in the parkette behind Trick's
building and died two days later of gastric torsion.

"I'm sure Jamal is thrilled to have her."

"Oh, he is, he is. It's just that he's never looked after
a dog before."

"She'll be fine. You know I'd have taken her."

"You couldn't take her, you've got that fat fucking cat."

"Sarge, please, if Misty could hear you —"

"It'd probably eat the puppy. Kill it and
eat it."

At noon Young was eating a hot mortadella and smoked
provolone sandwich in front of the TV when Eliot
Cronish called.

"Ah, the life of leisure," Cronish said. "Sitting at
home in front of *Jerry Springer*. I wish I could retire."

"What do you want?"

"You're eating something, aren't you? I can tell by
the muffled quality of your voice. What is it, Spam on
Wonder Bread?"

"For fucksake, Cronish."

"Fine, fine, I don't want to take you away from the
tube. What's today's theme, by the way, 'My Brother Is
Also My Dad'?"

"Goddamn it —"

"Okay, relax. I've got some news that might interest you, embarking as you are only hours from now for
sunnier climes. I've completed the autopsy on Talmadge
Cooper, and while I'm under no obligation to reveal my
findings to a mere gumshoe — in fact, strictly speaking,
I'm breaking the rules by doing so — I thought you

might be interested to know that our young musician was poisoned to death."

Young's brow furrowed. He took another bite of his sandwich.

"The external evidence — dilated pupils, flared nostrils, blood lesions all over his back and legs, dark blue discolouration — was the initial indication, which the internal examination confirmed. His liver had basically liquefied."

Young swallowed with difficulty. "What kind of poison?"

Cronish sighed. "That I don't know. We did a biopsy of the affected organs and concluded that it wasn't one of your common or garden-variety poisons — arsenic, cyanide, warfarin. But given the other evidence at the scene, the bottles of graveyard dirt, et cetera, my guess is it's some kind of voodoo concoction made from an exotic recipe — you know, eye of newt and toe of frog, that sort of thing."

"You believe in voodoo?"

"Certain aspects of it, yes. I don't believe in the witchcraft part of it, but that doesn't mean that people don't die from the real aspects of it. Poison is real. Something to think about when you're down there soaking up the sun."

Young finished his lunch and turned off the TV. He washed his dishes and left them to dry in the rack, then phoned his office.

"A-1 Investigative Consultants, Stella speaking. How may I help you?"

"It's me."

"Aren't you gone yet?"

"I'm just going out the door."

"I thought you were gone already. Why are you calling?"

"Well, to say goodbye, and to ask you to drop by the office once or twice while I'm gone to pick up the mail and check the e-mail."

"Boss," she said, "the only mail you ever get is bills and those horse racing magazines you buy for the waiting room that no one ever reads, maybe because the general public is not as interested in horse racing as you think it is, or maybe because there's never anyone in the waiting room. And as for your e-mail, I can check it from home. Someday, you know, you're going to have to learn how to do it yourself. You're back Saturday, right?"

"Right."

"Well, don't worry about anything here. Enjoy yourself. Goodbye."

Young went into his bedroom, double-checked the contents of his suitcase, closed it, set up the time-acti-vated security light in his living room, checked all the burners on the stove, picked up his keys and his suitcase and his Mets cap, locked the front door, and walked out to the street where his truck was parked. It was ten min-utes to one.

The woman working at the American Airlines counter was grim-faced. Young asked if there were any extra-wide seats. The woman said no. "Then can I have an aisle seat?" he asked. She made a face as if she'd been asked to run out to the plane herself to see if there was an aisle seat available. But Young kept his temper. Priam Harvey had warned him on the way to the airport, "Campbell, what-ever you do, don't make any jokes about bombs or mechanical malfunctions or anything like that."

Young also kept his temper when the East Indian man at the metal detector said, "You have nail clippers in your bag," told Young to fish them out, and instructed him to break off the little nail-cleaning hook. "I couldn't stab a *potato* with that," Young wanted to say, but he snapped off the hook instead and dropped it into the palm of the man's hand.

Once they had found their seats and stowed their hand baggage, and after the other passengers came aboard, and the pilot had welcomed them, and the flight attendant had explained how to use the safety equipment, and the plane had taxied onto the runway and sat awhile and then taken off, and after Harvey had consumed four Scotch and waters and began to snore, and the baby two rows in front of them had twice gone through its cycle of crying and feeding and sleeping, and after Young had read through Trick's obeah notes and dozed through a Bruce Willis movie he'd already rented from the video store at home, they landed in Miami.

He didn't even lose his temper when they were preparing to board the flight to Freeport and the woman going through the same overnight bag that contained the nail clippers told Young he was only permitted to bring one book of matches into the Bahamas.

"Only one book of matches?" Young said. "Why's that?"

"Those are the rules, sir." She had spread the half-dozen books of matches she'd found in the side pocket of Young's bag on her little inspection table. "Which one do you want to keep?"

And he didn't lose his temper when the small plane they boarded blew a nose tire during its approach to the runway, nor when he and the other passengers were instructed to get off the plane and wait on the tarmac, nor when they had to wait half an hour while a rickety crane-cum-wheelchair was jockeyed into

position to excise, like a cyst, a gigantic Bahamian
woman from the plane — she must have been pre-
loaded, Young thought, because he hadn't noticed her
get *on* the plane — nor when they'd had to board a
shuttle bus to travel a grand total of fifty yards to the
backup plane, which eventually lifted them above the
runway and the freeways and the backyard pools and
the schoolyards and the golf courses and the canals
and the hotels along the beach and carried them over
the fishing boats and the whitecaps and through the
clouds and past a towering waterspout that writhed
from the sea below them several thousand feet up to
the black hovering cloud under which they passed, a
sight that was missed by the two screaming children
across the aisle, not to mention their parents — the
grim-faced mother who said to someone, "Really, I
could write a *book* about travelling with children!"
and the doting father, whose purpose in life, it seemed
to Young, was to demonstrate to as many people as
possible his talent for parenting, a talent that involved
considerable baby talk, as well as spelling, as in
"Linda, please take the g-u-m away from S-a-v-a-n-n-
a-h" — and finally descended over lagoons and yellow
pines and thatch palms and rusting oil bunkers and
deposited them stunned and exhausted in Freeport,
where the second thing Young did after deplaning and
going through immigration and waiting for his suitcase
at the carousel, and after the taxi ride from the airport
and the business of registering at the Princess Lucaya
Hotel and figuring out how to use the credit
card–shaped key to get into the room he was sharing
with Harvey — the first thing he did was crack an ice-
cold bottle of Red Stripe he found in the mini-bar —
was phone his daughter, even though it was one in the
morning, to tell her he had arrived safely.

Sobbing, Debi told him about the crash of American Airlines flight 587 earlier that day in Queen's, New York. All two hundred and sixty passengers and crew were killed, she said, as well as five people on the ground.

Tuesday, November 13

Priam Harvey pulled a dark brown suit out of his travel bag. In sober fashion, he dressed himself in front of a wall mirror, knotting and re-knotting his tie.

Young, sitting in a chair beside the television with a bottle of Red Stripe in his hand, said, "I knew you owned a white suit, but I didn't know you owned a brown one. This all in aid of visiting the boy's mother?"

Harvey looked at Young in the mirror. "I wish you wouldn't start drinking already."

"There's the pot calling the kettle black."

"I don't want you smelling of beer when you meet her, and besides, it's only ten in the morning."

Young shook his head. "Wait a minute, I'm not meeting her. This is purely her and you. Maybe I'll meet her later to discuss terms and so on, but I don't want to be anywhere near this little reunion."

Harvey turned away from the mirror to look at Young. "I need you there ... as a buffer. Her husband's going to be there, too."

"Yeah, well, good luck." Young took a long pull at his beer. He stood up, opened the sliding door to the balcony off their room, and stepped onto it. It was a beautiful sunny day. A light breeze rattled the fronds of a majestic palm. The balcony overlooked one of the greens of the golf course that ran alongside the hotel, and a man standing on the green waited for a boy — his son, Young figured — to take his approach shot. "Not like that, try it again," the man called out when the boy's stroke stopped well short of the cup. He picked up the ball and tossed it back to the boy. "You're swaying. Don't sway. Let your arms do the work. No, not like that! Do it again!"

Asshole, Young thought. *All the kid wants to do is drive the cart.* He stepped back into the room and slid the door closed.

Harvey was still fussing with his tie. He said, "Please, Campbell, I need you there. Besides, they might say something important to the case."

"You'll be there to hear it. You can tell me whatever they say that's important."

"Why won't you come? You need to meet her at some point."

"It's messy, that's why I won't come. First of all, she's a grieving mother. I saw too many grieving mothers when I was a cop. One thing I know is mothers aren't supposed to bury their children; their children are supposed to outlive them, and when they don't it's the worst thing in the world. Doesn't matter if the kid's six or sixty. It's awful. And second, you're the absentee father, and I don't know how she's going to react to seeing your ugly mug again. And how about her husband? How's he going to react? He'll probably put some voodoo on you himself."

"He's white."

"He's white? You never told me he's white. Fine, fuck it, I'll come, but I don't know what I'm going to wear. You look so gloomy in that brown suit. I can't compete with that. I didn't even bring a tie."

"Wear your green turtleneck and your tan slacks. You'll be fine. And don't be so paranoid about the black people down here. They're wonderful. You'll see. How's my tie look, is it straight?"

"It's not the black people, it's this voodoo shit, this obeah. It makes me nervous."

"Stop worrying, it's harmless. How's my tie look?"

Young sat back down in the chair beside the television. He drained his bottle of beer and dropped it on the carpet. "I'm warning you, Mr. Harvey, if she jumps on you and starts scratching your eyes or something, you're on your own, I'm out the fucking door."

The car rental agency Young and Harvey visited offered a selection of makes and models — some of them tiny, all of them small. Young managed to squeeze himself into a Daihatsu Cuore, but once inside he could barely move. They tried a Kia Vito and a Daewoo Racer with the same result. They settled on a slightly more commodious Nissan Sunny with air and cruise.

George and Eula Francis lived in a palatial home in Fortune Cay, several miles outside of Freeport. The roof was Spanish tile, the design was Erik Christansen, there were matching Mercedes — one black, one white — on the sweeping interlock driveway, the swimming pool was big enough to have a footbridge and an island, and the view out front was a panorama of turquoise sea.

Eula Francis may have been the mother of a twenty-five-year-old, but she was still stunning. Black as ebony, she was tall and slim, her face long and sculpted like an African mask, her hair twisted as tight as a halyard and punctuated with gold clips. Her fingernails, Young noticed as he shook her hand at the front door, were long, shapely, and painted in some kind of Technicolor pattern he'd never seen before. Her grip was as strong as a man's. She wore blue jeans and a white jersey top that exposed her jewelled navel.

George Francis was slightly under medium height and pot-bellied. His thinning grey hair formed a frizzy horseshoe above his oversized ears, and he wore round, rimless glasses. His shirt was blindingly white and several sizes too large. There was a gold pin in his burgundy cravat. For a man of power and wealth, his handshake was weak. Young felt as if he had been handed a dead fish.

Harvey mumbled something to Eula, she kissed him on both cheeks, without actually touching her lips to his skin, and led him inside.

When they were seated in the living room — Young and Harvey side by side on a sofa the size of a war canoe — and after a black maid in a canary yellow dress and white apron and a little white bonnet had brought them Perrier and lime, Eula Francis came straight to the point. "Mr. Young, can you shed any light on the death of my son?"

Young cleared his throat. "A toxicology analysis was done on his body. He was poisoned."

Eula closed her eyes.

George said, "Poisoned with what?"

"They don't know yet. It's nothing they've seen before. It's not arsenic or cyanide or anything like that."

"When will they know?"

"They're working on it."

Eula opened her eyes. "We were told about the bottles surrounding his body," she said. "What was in them?"

"Some of them had water, others had dirt."

"Graveyard dirt?" asked Eula.

"All they know is it was ordinary soil. It could have come from anywhere — a school playground or somebody's backyard."

Eula began nodding her head rhythmically. "It was graveyard dirt."

Young said, "Mrs. Francis, did your son have any enemies?"

"Why would anybody kill my baby? He was the sweetest child. He was so loving and talented." She reached for a framed photo on the end table beside her chair. She looked at it for a moment, then passed it across to Young. The photo showed five young black people in school uniforms — three girls and two boys. The three girls wore plaid skirts and white blouses, white ankle socks and penny loafers, their hair in corn-rows. One of them was sitting at a piano, her head turned to the left, towards the camera. Another held two drumsticks and sat beside the first on the piano bench. The third stood behind them supporting an enormous stand-up bass. The two boys looked restless, as if they would much rather have been outside on the playing field. They wore dark pants and shoes and white shirts and skinny twisted neckties. One of them stood to the left of the girl with the bass; he was holding a trumpet. The other stood to her right; he held a saxophone. "He was thirteen when that picture was taken," Eula said. "Junior jazz band." She closed her eyes again and resumed nodding her head.

Young passed the photo to Harvey, then said to Eula, "Can you help us at all with the obeah evidence?"

She stopped rocking, opened her eyes, and said, "I grew up in a backwater community, Mr. Young. Obeah was all around me. My granny used to catch her water in a pan and toss it out the front door in the morning and out the back door at night. My mummy used to sprinkle sugar across the threshold for good luck, but all that did was bring the ants. It was all ignorance and superstition, Mr. Young, and I have separated myself from it." She looked around her spacious, beautifully appointed living room. "When George asked me to be his wife five years ago, I said to myself, 'Eula, you finally did it. You broke free of your past.' Do you know, Mr. Young, how I used to feel when white people would ask me about obeah? Insulted. It's an insult for white people to associate black people with obeah, like it was our religion. It's no more our religion than the superstitions of your culture are *your* religion — people who won't walk under ladders, people afraid of black cats or stepping on cracks in the sidewalk."

She stopped and took a moment to compose herself. "Excuse me," she said, "sometimes I become impassioned." She cleared her throat. "But why, Mr. Young, would obeah be involved in my son's murder? He was a modern, educated young man. To him the word would have no more significance than it would to you. There is something wrong about this evidence of obeah, something very wrong indeed. As I told Priam over the phone last week, obeah — in my experience — was never used to kill people. It was used to protect property or fix someone you disliked or someone who had wronged you. My mummy told a story about a woman who hired an obeah man to fix her husband's sweetheart, but the curse backfired, and the woman herself began to swell. She went to the obeah man to complain, and he told her she had to leave the island, she had to go across the sea in order for the curse to be lifted."

"Did she go?" Young asked.

Eula waved her hand in the air. "I don't know. I can't remember. It's all foolishness, and I hate it. Clytie!"

The maid came back into the room.

"Clytie," Eula said, "ask the gentlemen if they would care for another drink."

Young stood up. "No, thank you, Mrs. Francis. That's all the questions I have for now, but I'll be checking into Tal's friends and the band members and so on, and I'll get back to you as soon as I've got any news."

George said, "Mr. Young, does three hundred a day plus expenses seem reasonable?"

"More than reasonable, thank you." Young placed his empty glass on the coffee table. "Thanks for the drink. I'll be in touch."

Harvey stood up. "Goodbye, Eula."

Her hand was over her eyes. She removed it and gave a bright and brittle smile. "Goodbye, Priam," she said. She turned her head and looked up at Young. "Despite these solemn circumstances, it has been a pleasure to meet you, Mr. Young. And Mr. Young," she said, rising and taking his right hand in both of hers, "please find the monster who killed my baby. Do whatever it takes to find him. I won't rest until you do."

"That George," Young said, when they were finally in the car and driving back to the hotel, "he's quite something. He looks meek and mild, but I suspect he's sharp as a tack."

"He didn't become a millionaire by being stupid," Harvey said.

"He's like the nerdy kid who was always left till last when they picked teams in the schoolyard, and now he's got even. Money, cars, beautiful home, beautiful wife. I mean, she's incredible. She's bright, she's classy ..."

"I know," Harvey said sadly. "I sure can pick 'em."

After changing in their hotel room, Harvey and Young headed out to a beach bar called Margaritavilla, recommended by the concierge. Although the bar boasted a proper ceiling and walls, the floor was sand — clean white sand. Most people, Young noticed, kicked off their sandals at the door as they came in. Young was wearing his size-fourteen brogues. He was also wearing a powder blue dress shirt with the sleeves rolled halfway up his forearms, blue jeans, and his Mets cap. Harvey was wearing his Panama hat, an unbuttoned tropical shirt — large yellow flowers on a sky blue background — a white T-shirt, white shorts, and sandals. The cartoon on the front of his T-shirt showed a man dressed up like a coconut tree with two coconuts lying on the ground by his feet. The caption read, "I Partied My Nuts Off in the Bahamas."

While they were sitting at the bar they listened to tourists talking about which airline offered the best fares, which hotel offered the best service. Young looked around. The ceiling of the bar was covered with the scrawls of people who had signed their names in different coloured pens. One wall was covered with snapshots of women who had been persuaded to bare their breasts while visiting the bar. One whole corner of the bar was a shrine to retired Miami Dolphins quarterback Dan Marino.

After two beers and a plate of conch fritters, Young asked the barmaid, a skinny blonde who reminded him of Diane from the old *Cheers* TV show, where he might find someone who could tell him about obeah.

"You're interested in obeah?" she said.

"I'm doing a little research," Young said. "Bush medicine, folklore, that kind of thing. Sort of like scientific research."

She looked at him dubiously. "You don't look like a scientist to me."

"Really?" Young said. "What do I look like to you?"

"And if I were serious about doing research on a subject, I'd at least know how to pronounce its name. It's o-*bee*-ah, not o-bee."

Young nodded slowly. "According to my research, it's pronounced several different ways. The white Bahamians up on Green Turtle Cay, for example, pronounce it o-beer."

She narrowed her eyes. "I'm aware of that."

Young looked at her steadily.

She said, "I suppose you know bush medicine, too."

"I'm learning."

"How do you make bush tea?"

Young scratched the top of his head. "Five finger, camomile, pine bark, Sweet Margaret, lovevine, and ... oh, hell, what's the other ingredient?" He turned to Harvey.

Harvey shook his head. "Sorry, can't help you."

The barmaid said, "Stiffcock."

Young turned back to her and winked. "Yes, that's right."

Again her eyes narrowed. "Nicely done," she said. "Okay, your best bet is the Harbor Light down in Pinder's Point. The woman who runs the place knows all about obeah. Her name's Pandora." The barmaid turned to the phone on the wall behind her. "I'll see if she's there." She dialed and waited. Someone answered, and the barmaid spoke in a patois Young was unable to follow. She hung up and said to Young, "Pandora's not there today. She'll be back tomorrow. I said to tell her two white gentlemen might show up to talk about obeah."

"Thank you," Young said.

"But be careful. To get there, you have to travel through a rough area. And I don't mean the roads are rough."

Young said, "We'll be all right."

"I'm just letting you know it can be dangerous, that's all. The only white people who go down there are interested in something quite different than folklore."

As they were driving back to the hotel, Harvey said, "Where the hell did you learn how to make bush tea?"

Young shrugged. "I don't know how to make it, I just know what the ingredients are. That folder Trick gave me has enough info on obeah and bush medicine to choke a horse, and it was all in there. I studied it on the plane."

"Well, you certainly impressed the barmaid. And that business about the white Bahamians on Green Turtle Cay —"

"That was in there, too. Trick does some fine research."

Wednesday, November 14

It was two o'clock in the afternoon. Young drove while Harvey studied a tourist map they'd picked up at the hotel. They crawled slowly through the tiny hamlets of Mack Town, Hunter's, and Lewis Yard towards Pinder's Point — past the shoebox homes, the wrecked cars, the litter. One house set close to the road had two picture windows, and in each window stood a mannequin in a wedding dress. A sign on the door read, "We're open for weddings and hats."

They were midway through Hunter's when a young black man wearing large, round, red-framed glasses stepped out of a doorway and yelled at them. Young kept going, and the young man ran out into the dusty road, chasing after them and yelling.

Harvey said, "Pull over, let's see what he wants."

"I think he wants to kill us," Young said, but he stopped the car.

The man came to Harvey's window. "What's up?" he said. "Y'all lose your way?"

"This is Hunter's, right?" Harvey said.

"Yes," said the man, delighted. "Thank you, thank you."

"If we keep going we'll come to Pinder's Point?"

"Thank you, sir, yes you will." There was a pause, and then the man said, "Can I help y'all? Y'all lookin' for somet'ing?"

Harvey said, "Do you have anything to smoke?"

The man thrust his right hand through the open window and unfurled his fingers to reveal a toilet-paper-square-sized piece of plastic torn from a grocery store bag. In it lay a small amount of marijuana.

Harvey said, "Homegrown?"

"No sir," the young man said, "it Jamaican. Smell it, feel the heatness."

Harvey leaned forward into the man's palm and sniffed. "How much?" he said.

"T'irty dollar."

"No, that's way too much. Fifteen."

"Twenty."

"No, fifteen."

"All right, all right, gimme it."

Harvey took his wallet from his pants pocket and opened it, and the young man's eyes bugged out as if on stalks.

"Twenty-five dollar," he said.

"We already agreed on fifteen."

"Twenty dollar!"

"Okay, fine, twenty. But that's —"

"Twenty-four dollar!"

"What the hell!"

"Twenty-two dollar. Twenty-two. I gots to pay the man. I don't pay the man, I gets jook. Twenty-two dollar, gimme twenty-five dollar."

Young leaned over and said, "Hey, shitbird."

The man closed his mouth and stared at Young, his eyes like pink saucers inside the round red frames of his glasses.

"Twenty dollars," Young said. "That's it, end of story. Now get lost."

When they were driving again, Young said, "Do me a favour."

Harvey was exultant. "At your service, *mon frère*."

"In future, leave me out of your drug deals."

"Oh that's right, and when I roll one, you're not going to have a pull?"

"And fuck, even the dumbest tourist knows not to flash their money around. When you opened your wallet, he practically climbed through the window."

"Well, yeah, okay, that was stupid, I admit it. I forgot that piece of island wisdom. I'm a tad out of practice. I need a drink."

"His momma's probably right now trying to find her glasses. Fucking junkies!"

There were two old cars parked in the yard in front of the Harbor Light Tavern. Young pulled in, he and Harvey got out, stepped up the stairs to the verandah, and walked through the open door.

In the dim light they could see a bar with a man sitting at it and a woman standing behind it. She was saying, "When Lofton Williams' son fall nine floors off the buildin' they was workin' on, I goes to the funeral, but a week later, I seed him alive."

The man sitting at the bar said, "What you talkin' 'bout?"

"In my dream I seed him alive. He in his casket and he open his eyes and he sit right up and swing his leg out, and I say to him, 'Harry, you suppose to be dead, what you doin' alive?' And Harry say, 'No, that's all right, Pandora, I ain't dead after all. Here, I show you,' and he clamb out that casket and come after me with his arms outstretch. And that's when I wakes up. What can I do for you gentlemen?"

The man sitting at the bar turned to look at the newcomers. He looked at Young first, up at his face, then down to his feet, then back up again. He said, "Ain't you a corporation."

Young sat down on the stool next to the man.

The man nodded up at Young's cap and said, "The Mets ain't no kind o' ball team." He made a movement with his left arm, and Young was startled because the arm was a stump; it stopped mid-biceps.

Young said, "I don't like the team, I like the hat."

The man used his right hand to pour rum from a mickey bottle into a plastic cup. He added some water from a flowered china pitcher. "The Mets ain't worth shit."

Young turned to the woman behind the bar. "Two beers, please."

The woman reached behind her, opened the door to an ancient white refrigerator, and removed two bottles of Kalik.

Young said, "You're Pandora."

She looked at him levelly. "That's right, that's my name." She carefully wrapped paper napkins around the necks of the bottles and set them on the bar. "You must be the gentlemen interested in obeah."

"That's right," Young said, taking a card from his shirt pocket. "I'm a private investigator. Name's Young. This is my friend, Mr. Harvey. We're down from Canada looking into a murder."

Pandora leaned her elbows on the counter behind her. Near one elbow was a jar of pigs' feet, near the other a jar of pickled sausage. "Who dead?"

"A young man who grew up on this island. Talmadge Cooper."

Pandora's eyes widened. In the dark bar, it was as if she had flipped on the high beams of her car. "No," she said. "No, no, no."

The man sitting beside Young slipped off his stool and left the bar.

"Did you know him?"

She nodded. "I know who he be. His mummy come from around here. She growed up in Lewis Yard. I forgets her name."

"Eula."

"Eula? That's right, Eula Talmadge." Pandora shook her head. "She just a jungalist till she marry up and move away!"

On the stool to Young's right, Harvey shifted uneasily.

Pandora stepped forward and put her hand on Young's wrist. "Where this happen?"

"In Toronto, a week ago."

"How you know he moidered?"

"There were bottles around the body, and —"

"What kind o' bottles?"

"Old pop bottles, but some of them had dirt in them, and some had water."

Pandora knitted her brows. "Obeah bottles? But they be used for protectin' t'ings, like the fruits in your tree from little chirren stealin'. They don't be used for moiderin' people. One time a poyson I know very well say she want my toitle — I have a very pretty hawksbill toitle in a auditorium right here on this counter — and I say 'That's my toitle, don't touch it', and just to make sure I put bottles of dirty water in front of it, and she scared and she don't ever come back in this buildin', never to this day."

A young woman came into the bar and said hello. Pandora said, "Destiny, you watch the bar, now, honey. I be talkin' to these gentlemen." She led Young and Harvey to a table in a corner. After they sat down, she said, "Obeah just for fixin' people, not for killin' them. Preacher man over here in Hunter's catch his wife in bed with some nigger, so he beat her, so his wife buy a fix on him, and he swell up like a beachball, he just like a beachball, honey, and a month later he drive down his street and wave to ev'ybody like it a fine sunny day, and then he drive his car in the canal, and all the people jump in and dive down to save him but he have his window up, and they's knockin' at the glass, and he's wavin' at them and smilin' at them from inside his car till they have to leave him alone to die, which is what he do. But it wasn't obeah that kill him. No, it just make him swell up like a beachball. He kill himself!"

Harvey started to say something, but Pandora said, "Lady down the road here have a bridal shop, just a little house, but she got a bride in each window all dress pretty."

"Yes," Young said, "we saw it."

"One night her husband sittin' in his easy chair in the parlour, and he shoot himself in the head. Just like that. No warnin'. No message. Later on, she say, 'I didn't hear no shot, no bang. What wake me up is the blood drippin' on the floor.' And what she t'ink is somebody put a hag on him, a duppie — you know what be a duppie, it be a sperrid an obeah man make with grave dirt — and she t'ink the duppie make her not hear the gunshot, she t'ink maybe her husband have a sweetheart, and his sweetheart husband put a hex on him. But uh-uh, I know that boy, Ernest Laing, and he shoot himself for stress, not for obeah. He just a country boy from Water Cay, he can't stand the stress down here in the Point."

A tall black man came in the bar, looked carefully at Young and Harvey, and walked over to where Destiny was standing. He said something to her, and she opened the refrigerator, took a small cigar from a package, and gave it to him. He gave her some coins and walked back outside into the sunshine.

Young said, "From what I've learned, there isn't much obeah on Grand Bahama anyway. It's mostly on other islands."

Pandora nodded. "Cat Island, Exuma, Bimini, Andros, that's all where you gets the obeah. Turks and Caicos. Not here. But there's people here knows more about it than I do."

"Who?"

"I don't know who, but I know where. You goes up to West End," she said, jerking her thumb over her shoulder, "and you find out who. But be careful, honey, they strange up there, they ain't friendly with white poysons, like we is here, and don't trust ev'y-body, neither, even the ones that looks friendly, 'cause you know why?"

"Why?"

"'Cause, honey baby," and she laid her hand on Young's wrist again, "it ain't only shark does cut in the sea."

That evening, Young and Harvey went to a bar called Captain Kenny's, where Young discovered the Duck Fart — equal parts Bailey's, Kahlua, Crown Royal. It was served in a large, bowl-shaped glass with lots of ice. "A meal unto itself," he told Harvey, who was drinking Red Stripe. "I need a knife and fork for this baby."

"If we were in Canada," Harvey said, "they'd serve that as a shooter. Maximum three ounces. More likely one and a half. What you have there in front of you is a real drink. In volume, it's got to be a pint."

"It's a real drink, all right." Young raised the glass to his lips; the ice cubes rattled against his teeth as he gulped. "I might have another."

"*Garçon*," Harvey said, raising his hand, "another Duck Fart for my friend."

Young said, "What's a jungalist? Pandora said Eula was a jungalist."

"Yes, I wasn't too happy about that."

"Why?"

"It's a local word. It basically means 'slut.' She was saying that Eula had a reputation when she was younger. That was back when I knew her, a long time before she married George."

"Oh well," Young said, "it's not like *you* don't have a reputation."

Back at the hotel, Young stood on the balcony outside their room and watched the sprinklers water the golf green below him.

"What are we doing tomorrow?" Harvey called from inside. He was rolling a joint on the coffee table.

"We're going to West End," Young replied.

"Oh yes," Harvey said, "where we will once again risk our lives in the pursuit of justice."

He came outside with the joint. He lit it and drew hard. He offered it to Young, who took three quick tokes.

Harvey said, "That was cynical of me."

"What was?" Young asked, holding his breath.

"That comment about the pursuit of justice. I'd forgotten for a moment that it's my son's murderer we're pursuing."

They finished the joint and stood side by side on the

balcony watching the sprinkler. After a while, Young said, "Have you got your son's CD with you?"

Harvey said, "I thought you had it. Didn't you borrow it from me?"

"No, I asked you where I could buy a copy, and you said it was hard to find or something. I forget exactly what you said. But then you said you'd lend me yours."

"If you promised to return it."

"That's right, if I promised to return it."

"Right, you were going to get Trick to burn a copy for you."

"That's right."

"So where is it?"

"That's what I'm asking you. I'm asking you if you have it with you."

Harvey closed one eye. "So what you're saying is I never gave it to you?"

"That's right, you were going to, but you never did, so I thought if you had it with you we could listen to it now."

"Why would I have brought it with me if I thought you had it?"

Young nodded slowly. "Good point, but I didn't know you thought I had it."

"I remember now: I left it with Dexter at the bar about a week ago, and you were supposed to pick it up from him."

"But that's just it. I didn't pick it up from him. I don't have it. Maybe it's in your suitcase."

"It's not in my suitcase. Anyway, we don't have a CD player."

Young pondered. "What about the rental car? There might be a CD player in the rental car."

"I don't know, I'm not sure."

"Well," Young said, "I guess it doesn't matter whether there is or isn't since we don't have the CD."

There was a silence. Then Harvey said, "Did you get a buzz?"

"Yes, I did," Young said. "That's some pretty good shit."

Thursday, November 15

The road to West End was straight and uninteresting, relieved occasionally by a burned-out car or a dead vulture. Young and Harvey stopped briefly in the town of Eight Mile Rock for gas, and Young had to be buzzed into the station, where the cashier sat in a bulletproof booth. When he was back in the car, he said to Harvey, "Pandora was right, this is dangerous country."

After thirty miles they reached West End, where black women in tattered dresses sold conch barbeque at roadside stands. Small mountains of gutted conch shells stood pink and obscene in the sunshine.

"What do they do with those?" Young asked.

"The ones they can't sell to the tourists, they toss aside," Harvey said. "The ditches all over the island are full of conch shells. Conch shells and shopping carts."

They stopped at a bar called Mr. K's. They had to walk through a long empty room into a smaller back room where the bar itself was located. Mr. K — tall, heavy, slow-moving — served them their beers through an iron lattice. For each of them he laid a paper serviette over one of the bars of the lattice. Mr. K told them he was seventy-three years old, and when Young asked him about obeah he said he knew a little bit about it. His grandmother used to hang bottles and sticks from the branches of her mango tree to keep children from stealing the fruit.

"Was there anything in the bottles?" Young asked.

"Graveyard dirt or dirty water. Sometimes," Mr. K said, laughing, "I would untie the bottles and sticks, lay them on the ground so they couldn't hoit me, collect a armful of mango, then tie the ornaments back *on* the branches."

Young said, "Is obeah ever used to kill people?"

Mr. K shook his head. "No," he said, "just to hex them."

The next bar was called Down Home, and in an open, ramshackle hut a man with a ponytail made conch salad — extracting a conch from its shell, scoring and dicing the flesh, chopping up onion, tomato, and green pepper in a bowl, squeezing lime and orange halves into it, and adding hot sauce and several generous shakes of monosodium glutamate from a large box he kept on a shelf. When Young asked the man, whose name was Baretta, about obeah, he told a long story about the old woman who lived in the house next door to him. She was always complaining about Baretta's friends parking their cars in front of her house. She would come out and scream at him or bang on his door until the offending vehicle was moved. On several occasions she'd threatened to fix him, but if she did, he never suffered any ill effects. "I don't know much about obeah," he concluded, "but one t'ing I do know: long time after that old

woman six feet in the ground, people still be parkin' their
cars in front of her house!" Young and Harvey laughed,
as did two labourers leaning on the counter of the conch
shack drinking cans of Guinness.

As they were leaving, Young asked Baretta if obeah
was ever used to kill people. Baretta shook his head.
"No, mon, just to interfere with 'em."

The last bar they visited was the Chicken Nest. Mr.
K and Baretta had both told Young to ask for a man
named Chicken, but when he did, the woman at the bar
said Chicken was upstairs and wouldn't come down.
Her tone suggested that Chicken hadn't come down in
some time. So Young talked to a white Bahamian with
a cauliflower ear and a young black prostitute with big
brown eyes and an open sore on the back of one arm.
The prostitute told Young about a Bahamian woman
known as Crazy-on-the-Inside-Crazy-on-the-Outside
who threw rocks at Haitian people because she thought
they had put a curse on her. "She t'row one rock
t'rough the tailor man window, and he ain't even associated with voodoo." She took a sip of her Heineken
and said, "One time a man have a coise on him and he
crash his car into a skinny little tree, the car go right up
the tree, come back down again, and all the power in
Eight Mile Rock goed out!"

When Young asked if obeah was ever used to kill
people she, too, said no.

The man with the cauliflower ear said, "That's
Haitian voodoo you're talking about, my friend, where
they make dolls out of wax and stick pins in them.
That's serious business, that's lethal, that's when you
want somebody dead. This obeah" — he pronounced it
o-*bare* — "is really what you might call benign. People
use it to protect their property. You don't kill people
with it, you just mess with their heads."

The prostitute said, "Say I be your sweetheart, and I wants to fix your wife, I finds me a obeah worker, and he fix her. He ax me for somet'ing what belong to her, like a hair or a article of clothin', and then he influence her to go in a field and she can't gets out 'cause the demons won't lets her, or he spill somet'ing across her doorstep and when she step acrost it, it make her swell like she big-up, or maybe he make her widdrey up instead. Then when I t'ink your wife have enough, I tell obeah worker to stop, and I pays him, and he stop. But you know what? If I die before he stop the fix on her, she be fix her whole life!"

Young said, "So it really works."

She gave him a coy look. "It woiks for them what believes it woiks."

That evening, after Young and Harvey returned to their hotel, they stood at the edge of the public square in Port Lucaya watching a Bahamian band featuring a singer named Veronica Bishop. A few tourists and a dozen or so local children were dancing on the square. Young and Harvey were drinking bottles of Kalik.

Harvey said, "Did you notice up there in West End that nobody drank Kalik? In fact, one of the bartenders — I can't remember which — raised his eyebrows when we ordered Kalik. 'You want Kalik?' he said — I think it was Mr. K — as if we were from Mars. Even the little whore was drinking Heineken —"

"The guy with the ear was buying them for her."

"— and a lot of the black men drink Guinness. I think maybe it's uncool to drink Kalik."

Young said, "Tastes okay to me."

There was a commotion behind them, and several dozen drunken tourists in Hallowe'en costumes came bunny-hopping onto the square. Veronica Bishop's band quickly segued from a Bahamian ballad called "Blind Love" into Chubby Checker's "The Twist," which drew the drunken tourists onto the dance floor like water down a flume. A large woman dressed as a house, with her face in an upstairs window and a white picket fence made out of sticks of Styrofoam around her belly, separated herself from the group long enough to grab Harvey by the arm and haul him onto the dance floor, where she started twisting ponderously in front of him. To Young, she looked like a house during an earthquake.

When Harvey rejoined him a few minutes later, Young said, "What's with the Hallowe'en costumes? Hallowe'en was a couple of weeks ago. Jamal went out as some kind of ninja thing."

"They're from a cruise ship," Harvey said, catching his breath. "According to the lady wearing the house, there's a different party theme every night."

"Where I come from," Young said darkly, "Hallowe'en is celebrated on Hallowe'en."

"Things are different down here, Campbell. Haven't you noticed all the Thanksgiving stuff in the stores?"

"They celebrate Thanksgiving down here?"

"Oh yes. American style. Fourth Thursday in November. The grocery stores are already full of turkeys and pumpkins, and when the special day arrives everyone dresses up as pilgrims."

"How long has this been going on?"

"Beats me. All I know is anything American is picked up down here. Funny thing about the Yanks, isn't it? Everybody hates them, and everybody imitates them."

Young said, "And another thing: nobody knows how to do the Twist anymore. They were all floundering around like idiots out there."

"You should have come out on the dance floor and shown them," Harvey said. "You're the Twist machine, the Twist master."

"You and the lady wearing the house weren't bad. Did you get her name?"

"Doreen. They're from the cruise ship. Did I tell you that already? It's called the *Fantasy Adventure*." Harvey paused to belch. "I had a girlfriend named Doreen — a long time ago — down here."

"Before or after Eula?"

Harvey shook his head. "I can't remember. It had to be around the same time."

"Notice anything unusual about this particular group of tourists?"

"Aside from the Hallowe'en costumes?"

"Yeah."

"They're all fat?"

"That's right. See that one over there, dressed like half a watermelon, and that one over there, dressed like an Eat-More? You'd think they'd want to wear something that made them look thinner, not fatter, wouldn't you?"

"Not these modern fat people, Campbell. They're defiant about their size."

Five costumed women — the house, a mountain, a Volkswagen, a giant yellow tulip, and a hippopotamus — approached them. The hippopotamus spoke to Young. "You're a *tall* drink of water," she said. "Wanna boogie with my boongy?"

Young said, "What's a boongy?"

"It means 'big ass,' baby, and I got one of the biggest."

"Congratulations," Young said. "Who are you people?"

The Volkswagen said, "We're the girls from the GBB website."

"GBB?"

The hippo said, "Great Big Beauties. You should log on sometime. She leaned close to Harvey. "How about you, skinny? Wanna fuck a fat girl?"

Over the four days Young and Harvey had been in the Bahamas a pattern had emerged: they would go to bed at a reasonable hour — somewhere around midnight — and get up at nine, usually to a rich repertoire of birdsong. ("It sounds like about fifty different birds out there," Harvey said to Young on the second morning, "but it's all one bird — a mockingbird. Its song is like a sax solo, full of mimicry and variation.") They did their investigative work in the mornings and had their first drink around two in the afternoon. Young had discovered that six Coors cost twelve American dollars, whereas a litre of Ron Bacardi cost nine dollars. Young had never been a drinker of rum, but — at least when they were in their hotel room — he became one, mixing it with Coke and adding a twist of lime and three or four ice cubes. Harvey was drinking gin and tonic and kept his marijuana in an empty Pringles tube on top of the television. They took turns going to the ice machine and they took turns driving to the liquor store in the Sunny. Young swallowed his vitamins every morning, but he hardly ate. He'd skip breakfast, dabble at a plate of cracked conch and peas and rice for lunch, then maybe have some Burger King or a slice of pizza for supper. Or maybe the supper hour would drift by unnoticed. Somehow it wasn't necessary to eat. It wasn't that the weather was too hot, or that they were too busy; it was the rum and gin they drank in their room and the beer they drank in the bars that sufficed them. Just that morning Young, concerned that his calcium was in need of a boost because he wasn't eating Grape-Nuts with milk for breakfast as was his custom at home, had consumed three Kahluas and cream. When he suggested that Harvey eat something, Harvey told him he wasn't going to let food ruin his stone. After they returned to their room Thursday night — after encountering a dozen or so members of an Ernest Hemingway Look-Alike Society at a bar called Outriggers (when Harvey said to one of them, "I guess you have to know a lot about Hemingway's life and work to be a member," the reply was, "No, you just have to sort of look like him and drink a lot") — Young had a couple of pulls from Harvey's joint and sat outside on the balcony in the moonlight and watched the massive fronds of the Royal palm shifting in the wind. To Young, they looked like the heads of long-maned draught horses as they grazed, lifted, gazed serenely out at the world, then lowered, swung, and raised again.

Friday, November 16

Young and Harvey were still asleep when the phone rang.

Harvey said, "Mother of God!" and pulled a pillow over his head. Outside, a mockingbird sang *"Reefer! Reefer!"*

Young answered, and a voice said, "Good morning, Mr. Young, George Francis here. I hope I didn't wake you."

"Mr. Francis, how are you? What can I do for you?"

"Eula and I were wondering if you'd made any progress. We haven't heard from you since Tuesday."

Young had to urinate. Twice in the last hour he'd been awakened by the pressure in his bladder, but each time he'd managed to quell it. "We've been following a few leads," he said. "We've been down to Pinder's Point and out to West End, talking to people."

"Have you spoken to any of Tal's friends yet, or his fellow musicians?"

"No, but we hope —"

"Well, you should know that his rhythm section — they call themselves the Dogs of War — is providing the entertainment at a pig roast luncheon at Cardy's this afternoon."

"What's Cardy's?"

"It's a roadhouse. It's in McClean's Town, at the east end of the island."

"Well, I appreciate the information. We'll check it out."

"Am I right that you're leaving tomorrow?"

"Yes, I forget what time —"

"Stop by on your way to the airport. Tell us what you know."

Young stumbled into the bathroom and relieved himself. Then he woke Harvey up and told him about George Francis's tip. It was already 9:30, so they showered and dressed quickly.

"I've got the shakes," Harvey said. "I need some coffee."

"When we get there."

To reach McClean's Town, they had to travel for sixty miles along a straight two-lane highway, bordered for almost its entire length by yellow pine forest. They passed through several villages — New Free Town, High Rock, Pelican Point — and they passed a number of bars whose doors stood invitingly open, but they didn't stop until they reached their destination. McClean's Town was a small, picturesque fishing village. It featured a ferry that carried Bahamians and occasional tourists to several nearby cays and to Abaco, the next major island in the chain.

They found Cardy's easily, a squat white building with its garage door walls open to the elements. As Young parked the Sunny, the sound of the band could be heard. He said, "Even I know that's not jazz they're playing."

"No, my son," said Harvey, "that's rake 'n' scrape."

It was dark inside the bar, and they waited for their eyes to adjust. A large, light-skinned black woman in shorts and sandals was dancing alone in front of the bandstand. An old man wearing a captain's hat was standing to the side playing a handsaw with a screwdriver. Harvey disappeared into the crowd at the bar and returned moments later with two bottles of Red Stripe. They stood and watched the band: keyboards, electric bass, drums, handsaw, washboard, spoons. Harvey said, "See how the drummer holds his sticks up high like that? He must have grown up playing congas, and when he switched to a regular drum set he never learned to lower his hands the way American drummers do."

Young said, "How come they're not playing jazz?"

"If the situation called for jazz, they'd play jazz. The situation calls for dance music."

It was a long set. The drummer did much of the singing and all of the talking between numbers. The band played "Stealin' Love" and "Nobody's Child" and "Sweet Potato Bread." People came and went. Children chased each other around the dance floor. A sunburned white couple stuck their heads in the door, smiles pasted on their faces, then withdrew. When the musicians finally took a break, Young approached the drummer and complimented him on the music. The man, who was lean and had a short, grizzled grey beard, nodded at Young and began to make his way to the bar.

"Guinness?" Young said.

The man hesitated. "All right," he said.

Young bought two bottles of Guinness and handed one to the man. He asked if he could speak to him about Tal Cooper.

The man raised his chin. "Why you want to talk about Tal?"

"His mother hired me to find out what happened to him."

"He die, that's what happen to him."

"There's more to it than that."

The man scanned Young up and down. "Who are you?"

"I'm a private investigator." Young produced a business card from his shirt pocket.

The man led Young outside. They seated themselves facing each other at a picnic table. The man identified himself as Wycliffe Rolle and told Young he was forty-seven years old. "That's more'n twenty years older than Tal. I knowed him since he a child, though, and I play music with him since he fifteen till he go away to school. Poor boy, he were the best of us, and dead so young."

"Whenever he came back here to play, you were his drummer?"

"Sure, sure, he never let nobody else drum for him on this island." He nodded towards two other musicians, who were smoking beside a casuarina tree. "You ax them, they tells you."

"Did they play for him, too?"

"Oh yes, Tal always use Junior on keyboards and Charlo on bass, but when we play with Tal, it a Steinway Junior play on, not just a portable keyboards like that one inside, and Charlo, he use a upright bass."

Young nodded. "Did Tal use drugs?"

Wycliffe Rolle leaned back. "You cuts straight to the quick."

Young shrugged. "Just doing my job."

"He smoke a little weed, just like we all does. So what?"

"Did he do heroin or coke?"

Rolle's face went blank. "He smoke a little weed, that's all I know."

"This is important, Mr. Rolle."

"I told you, all I ever seen him do was smoke some weed."

Young took a sip of his beer. "Did he have any enemies? Were people jealous of him?"

"We *all* jealous, man, but we all loves him. No, he don't have no enemy among his music brothers."

"What about his other friends?"

"We his brothers *and* his friends." He nodded again towards the other musicians. "You ax them, they tell you everybody love Tal. Tal universally loved."

Young paused, then said, "Somebody didn't love him."

Rolle turned back to Young. "Have you talk to Keysha?"

"Keysha?"

"Keysha Groves, over to New Free Town. That's his woman. He have a chile with her, too. Rashid."

Young shook his head. "Does Keysha know he's dead?"

Rolle shrugged. "I don't know. We don't travels in the same soicles."

"Did he see her very often? Did he visit his son?"

"I don't t'ink so. I t'ink Keysha vex with him 'cause he have himself a sweetie."

"A sweetie? You mean like a mistress?"

"Mistress, girlfriend, sweetheart, it all the same t'ing. And it might be okay if his sweetie Bahamian, but she not. She American *and* she white. *And*, just in case you needs more fuels for the fire, she have a outside chile with him. Little girl."

"Where does this sweetie live?"

"In the States, I expect. I never seed her, people just talks about her. I don't even know her name. Tal meet her at that school he go to in New York. Somebody tell

me Tal say she a rich redhead. Say she a *classical* musician!" Rolle raised his bottle of Guinness to his mouth
and drained it. He said, "I gotta go back now. You see
how hard we's woik."

Young said, "I wish I'd had a chance to see Tal play
with you."

Rolle shook Young's hand. "I don't t'ink Keysha
kill him, but she might have find somebody put a
mouth on him."

"Do what?"

"Put a mouth on him. Hag him."

"You mean fix him? You think that's what happened?"

"It possible. I myself seen ghosts. I seed the ghost of
Bookie John up behind the guinep tree *before* he dead, and
he dead that same day. I seen a friend of mine make a little fire on the ground and raise it with his hand like a column of fire to his full growth, then force it back down."

"But that's obeah, isn't it? Obeah's not used to
kill people."

"That's right, but Tal didn't die of no obeah. No,
no, he had the voodoo on him."

"How do you know there was voodoo involved?"

Rolle rubbed his chin. "I hears t'ings."

"There were bottles around the body at the murder
scene, some with dirt in them, others with water, but
that's just obeah, right?"

Rolle nodded. "That's right, that's just obeah, but
that's just a confusion. I tells you he were carry down,
he were coised. His body when they find it, was it all
blue and blister up?"

Young felt a chill run down his back. "How did you
know that?"

Rolle said, "Uh-huh. 'Cause he had pufferfish in
him. Somebody try to make a zombie-slave out of him,

but they use too much pufferfish and kills him instead."

"A *zombie*-slave?"

Rolle's eyes became slits. "You don't believe me? You look up about zombie-slaves, see if I wrong. Look up the story of Clarvius Narcisse, then I *dares* you tell me I's wrong."

As Young and Harvey drove out of McClean's Town, they came upon a group of people standing at a crossroads with their arms outstretched. A middle-aged woman was brandishing a Bible. She wore a purple dress, a flowered hat, thick glasses, and white gloves.

Harvey said, "Pull over for a second."

"What for?"

"This is the real thing. I want you to see some true Bahamian culture. In ten years, this will be gone, obliterated by theme parks and McDonald's."

Young pulled over.

Harvey said, "We'll just stay a few minutes."

"They're looking at us."

"Trust me, I know my way around this island."

"They don't want us here."

"Shh. Listen."

Young sighed and turned off the ignition.

"Oh, t'ank you, Jesus," the woman in the purple dress was saying. "Oh, praise the Lord! We're so happy this afternoon that Brother Enoch and Sister Sophia was able to make the long joiney from Eight Mile Rock to bring their scripture and their testimony to our meetin'. We are soldiers in the army of the Lord, cherished ones, and I pray in the name of Jesus that the enemies of the Lord shall be driven from His sight — ex-pecially those agents of the devil who is sellin' drugs to our chirren right here in McClean's Town!"

Her audience consisted of a dozen well-dressed men and women who were spread out across the intersection, sporadically waving their hands or clapping them, and calling out "Hallelujah!" and "T'ank you, Jesus!"

A woman in a sand-coloured dress caught Young's eye and held it. She beckoned to him. Young smiled and shook his head. She began to walk towards the car. "Come and join us!" she called. She was a big woman, and beneath the bodice of her dress her chest moved.

Harvey said, "Okay, I think we've seen enough. Let's go."

Young didn't move. He watched the woman advancing on him.

"Come and feel the sperrid of the Lord," the woman said. She reached out her arms. Her skin was black and gleaming.

"Start the car," Harvey said.

Young was mesmerized. He couldn't move.

"Campbell, start the car."

Another five or six men and women were drifting towards them, arms outstretched, singing: "The longer I serve Him, the sweeter He grows; The more that I love Him, more love He bestows; Each day is like heaven, my heart overflows; The longer I serve Him, the sweeter He grows."

"It's like *Night of the Living Dead*!" Harvey said. With one hand, he reached over and turned on the ignition. With the other, he waved to the advancing crowd. "Thank you!" he called. "Gotta go!"

"You see why I fell in love with this place," Harvey said, "all those years ago?" They were safely back in Freeport, in a bar called the Winston Garden Club. It was happy hour: two Kaliks for five dollars. "You can disappear down here. You can stay drunk all the time, and nobody says anything. It's an accepted lifestyle choice down here among the disenfranchised, the expats, the broken, the losers, the lost, those who are seeking, those who are finding, and — not to be forgotten — those who are hiding."

"Please, Mr. Harvey," Young said, "don't go getting all philosophical on me. It makes me edgy."

"The women are so beautiful —"

"Excuse me, have you forgotten Hippopotamus Woman and Mount Vesuvius Woman and the woman wearing the house?"

"I'm talking about the *black* women. The way they do their hair ..."

Young nodded. He thought about the woman in the sand-coloured dress. "Yeah, it's tempting all right, but you know what?"

"What?"

"There's something about the place I don't like. There's garbage everywhere, there's all these half-finished mansions and abandoned hotels. Half the roads don't go anywhere. I was in the Pantry Pride yesterday to buy some mix for my rum, and this guy standing at the checkout — I thought he was a bag boy — asked me if I was looking for a party. He said, 'You want some smoke, you want some blow, I got blow. Girls, you want girls? Nice and quiet. No fuss. I send 'em over in a cab.' This is a scary place, Mr. Harvey. All the white people who live here are drunks or crazy or both. I would be too. We don't belong here. We're Conchy Joes, isn't that what they call us?"

"The term refers to white people who were born here."

"Whatever. I bet they don't feel at home here either — not completely." He paused and took a long drink of his beer. "Besides, we gotta go back. Well, I do. You do as you want."

"Why do you have to go back?"

"Because Eula Francis hired me to find out who killed her son. Your son. Tal wasn't the victim of obeah or voodoo or anything like that."

"But didn't your musician friend back at Cardy's say something about pufferfish?"

"Oh, Tal was poisoned, all right, but the killer fucked it up. He wanted to make the murder look like voodoo, but he made it look like obeah, and obeah's not about killing people." Young paused. "The killer thought all voodoo was the same, and he expected us to think the same thing. Which leads me to believe that the solution to the mystery is probably just the opposite."

"The opposite of obeah?"

"Yeah, the killer wanted to distract us from the most obvious reason why Tal was murdered."

"Which is what?"

"I don't know yet, but I'll bet it has something to do with him being the next John Coltrane."

It was their last night in the Bahamas, so they visited the casino at the Princess Hotel, where Harvey had worked twenty-six years earlier.

"I'm surprised I'm not experiencing withdrawal," Harvey said, as they walked across the parking lot towards the entrance. "I haven't gambled since we got here." His T-shirt proclaimed, "Do the Macarena!"

Inside, the place was large and spacious, but practically empty. Young bought himself and Harvey a hundred dollars each of tokens and — over a period of an hour — they lost them at the slot machines. Young thought he had won the jackpot at a machine called

Stampede when three Stampede symbols lined up across his screen: lights began to flash, and whinnying and mooing sounds emanated from several different speakers. Young looked around for one of the attendants to come to his assistance. *They'll probably have to take me into their office*, he thought. *They'll have to write me a cheque.* But after all the mooing and snorting and yee-haws faded away and the lights died down, he won only six dollars. *Plink, plink, plink*, they sounded as they dropped into the tray under the machine. *Plink, plink, plink.*

Later, he sat down at a blackjack table. He had the dealer — a young woman whose name, according to the nameplate on her blouse, was Ferrice — all to himself. He didn't like to play blackjack when there were other people at the table. They always played too fast for him, and he always felt that he was too deliberate, that he was holding up the proceedings. But Ferrice let him go slow and easy. After twenty minutes he was up a hundred and fifty dollars; fifteen minutes later he was down a hundred.

"Ferrice," he said, lighting a cigarette, "do you know anything about obeah?"

Ferrice was tall and formal. She gave him a stony look. "I only suppose to talk about blackjack."

"Please? There's only the two of us here. You've already won all my money. We have to talk about something."

She looked left and right. "Obeah's where you puts some jumbey t'ing in you pocket and carries it around."

"Why?"

"Why? To hoits somebody, that's why."

"To kill them?"

"No, no, that's voodoo, that's black magic. Obeah's just to hoits them."

"What about bush medicine?"

"That's different. That's good for you, but it's old, all right, don't nobody but grannies use it no more. Onlest time I seen it … yes, one time when I little I gets the browncurtis, and my aunty — she a bubby ogly woman — she berl up some bush tea and she make me drink it, and the pains is sharp, all right, sharp as darts, and I cascate, but I gets better, true-true."

Young took a breath and said, "Thank you, Ferrice."

He found Harvey at the bar, drinking a Kalik. He ordered one, too.

Harvey said, "I haven't met a solitary person who was working here when I was. Not one. Not a croupier, not a … well, what the hell. I shouldn't be surprised, should I? It's a transient business. High turnover." He sipped his Kalik.

Young said to the bartender, "Pretty quiet around here tonight."

The bartender widened his eyes like he was looking at a lunatic, leaned back, laughed loudly, shook his head, and said in the heartiest of voices, "Oh no, mon, you be here tomorrow night, it be jumpin', jumpin', jumpin'!"

Young finished his beer in two swallows and got up off his stool.

Harvey said, "What's your hurry? Relax."

"No, it's time to go."

"Come on, man, let me buy you a —"

"Don't you hear what I'm saying? I've had enough. It's time to go home."

Dreaming, Young saw the preacher woman in the purple dress. She was holding a cigarette in one white-gloved hand and a black bottle of Guinness in the other. Her followers were all around her, laughing and chatting, smoking and drinking. A thickset man was playing a handsaw with a butter knife. The woman in the sand-coloured dress separated herself from the group and walked towards Young, who was rooted to the ground like a tree. "I'm Sister Faith," she said, her breasts swaying heavily under the thin material of her dress. She reached out her shining black arms. "Come and join us."

Saturday, November 17

Clytie in her canary yellow uniform opened the door and ushered Young and Harvey through the house to the pool deck. Eula Francis was sitting on a chaise longue talking on a cellphone. She was wearing a lime green sarong, gold sandals, a gold turban, and gold-framed Oakleys. When she saw the two men, she waved them forward and motioned them to sit down at a small glass-topped table a short distance from her. Clytie asked if they would like anything to drink. Harvey said beer and Young said water. A moment later, Eula folded up her phone and said, "I've been expecting you. What time's your flight?"

Young said, "Four."

Eula nodded. "I hope you've had a pleasant stay."

"We have. Is your husband here?"

"No, that was him on the phone. He's on his way to lunch with a client. Why?"

"I need to ask you a question before we leave, and I thought he might have something to say on the matter."

Eula removed her sunglasses and looked directly at Young. "You sound very serious, Mr. Young. What's the matter?"

"Mrs. Francis," Young said, "when me and Mr. Harvey visited you on Tuesday, you provided us with a lot of information, but you left out certain other information which we've found out since, and which may prove useful to us, and I'd like to know why you didn't tell us in the first place."

Eula's expression was blank. "I'm sure I have no idea —"

"Tal had a son." Young took his notebook from his shirt pocket and flipped several pages into it. "With a Bahamian woman named Keysha Groves. Son's name Rashid."

Eula swallowed. "She's a domestic who worked for me several years ago. She seduced my son, got pregnant by him in the belief that he would marry her, which he offered to do — that's the kind of man my son was — but I intervened. The woman receives an allowance for the care of the boy, but she has no claim on us."

Young nodded at his notebook, then looked across at Eula. "You're aware your son has another child in the States, by another woman?"

Eula's eyes widened. "That's not true. That's impossible."

"Why is it impossible?"

Eula reached for her cigarettes. "I would have known. I would certainly have known."

"Apparently, the mother's a musician, too. According to our sources, Tal met her at Juilliard. Are you sure you don't know anything about this?"

Eula fumbled with her lighter. Harvey leaned over, took the lighter from her hand, and lit her cigarette for her. "I would certainly have known," she repeated as she slid her sunglasses back into place, "because Tal told me everything."

"One last question, Mrs. Francis, if you don't mind. Did your son drink much, or use drugs?"

"Certainly not. He enjoyed a beer occasionally with George and me, but he never touched drugs. He said they destroyed the mind."

"I don't want to argue with you, Mrs. Francis, but I spoke to one of his band members, and he said Tal smoked marijuana."

"That's ridiculous! That's just jealousy talking. They were *all* jealous of Tal." She turned away, leaned back in her chaise longue, and lifted her face to the sky.

Young checked his watch. "We have to get a move on, Mrs. Francis. I'll be in touch in a few days."

Harvey stood up. "Goodbye, Eula," he said.

Eula didn't move or speak. She looked like a wax figure whose posture and clothing — sandals, sari, sunglasses, turban — made her lifelike.

As Young and Harvey passed back through the house, Clytie emerged from the kitchen with a tray of drinks. "Thanks anyway, Clytie," Young said, "we can't stay, but I'm sure the missus will have hers."

Outside at the car, Harvey said, "Where to now? The airport?"

Young squeezed himself in behind the steering wheel. "One more stop," he said.

Some of the houses in New Free Town were kept up better than others, with white-painted chain-link fences around tiny green lawns, cream-coloured shutters, and

Spanish tile roofs. Keysha Groves' property, however, was ramshackle. As Young and Harvey drove up, several dogs in various stages of decomposition crawled out from under the derelict cars and trucks that littered the property. There was a late '60s Pontiac Bonneville with damage to the front end and all of its tires flat. Its hubcaps had popped and lay where they had fallen, like little birdbaths. A curly-tailed lizard had its hands up on the edge of the driver's-side front hubcap and flicked its tongue at the rainwater inside, and a Cuban Emerald hummingbird hovered over the driver's-side rear hubcap. There was a smaller car, Japanese, with both front doors flung open and a white cat asleep on the passenger seat. The house itself was an old trailer surrounded by large pots of dead and dying flowers. Lying here and there about the property were irregular pieces of sheet metal, a hospital gurney, propane tanks, a wooden dining room chair with no seat, and thousands of little coco plums fallen from the branches of the tree that overhung and rendered gloomy the entire scene. One hundred feet away was the beach, white and untrammelled, and beyond it the blue-green sea. A vast cruise ship moved slowly across the horizon like a stage prop.

Harvey said, "Maybe that's the great big beauties' boat."

A slim, dark-skinned, pockmarked woman wearing a red and white polka-dot headkerchief, a stained Old Navy sweatshirt, and a long denim skirt emerged from the trailer. She was barefoot. "I'm cleanin' my house today," she said. "I ain't receivin' no visitors." A little boy, naked, appeared behind her leg.

"Keysha Groves?" Young asked.

The woman pursed her lips. "Who you?"

"My name's Campbell Young. I'm a private investigator. I need to talk to you about Tal Cooper."

In a softer tone, she said, "Talmadge dead."

"That's right," Young said. "We're here to see if we can find out what happened to him."

The woman panned Young up and down, then turned her gaze on Harvey. "Who he?"

Harvey stepped forward. He took off his straw hat. "I'm Priam Harvey, Miss Groves. I'm Tal's father."

The woman studied him, then bent down and picked up the little boy. "What you want from me?"

During the next hour, Keysha Groves told her story. She'd grown up in the nearby village of Missile Base, dropped out of school when she was thirteen, and began to ride the bus into Freeport every morning with her mother to work in rich people's houses. She had worked almost two years for Eula Francis when she discovered she was pregnant.

"Was Tal the father?" Young asked.

Keysha had led them down to the beach. It was overcast and not too hot. They stopped twenty feet short of the surf, and Keysha put the boy down. He squatted and with one stubby finger poked tentatively at a dark red starfish in the sand near his mother's feet.

"Uh-huh. Tal half-coloured, but he still have he way with me — just like white mans do when they wife not home."

"He raped you?"

She looked up at Young. "Call it that, but it ain't. He say, 'You like to work here, Keysha?' and I say, 'Yes, sir,' and he say, 'Then you better come down to the laundry room with me.'"

"How long did that go on?"

Keysha furrowed her brow. "The second summer. When I realize I big-up, he already gone."

"Did he offer to marry you?"

Keysha tipped back her head and laughed. "You crazy? Miss Eula tell you that?"

Young nodded.

Keysha laughed again and shook her head. "Mmm-mmm, that just a lie she concoct to make she preshul baby look like some kinda prince in a story. Why, that woman buy ev'yt'ing for she son — fancy clothes, fancy car. Why, she even buy he drugs!"

"What kind of drugs?"

"Whatever he want."

"How do you know this?"

"He *tell* me! And, one time, he take me for a ride in he car out to Bootle Bay, and he give me some kind of pill. He say he mummy buy it for him. Get-better pill, he call it. Next t'ing I knows the sandcrabs have people faces, and the reef rise up out of the sea and overwhelm the woild with eels and Sergeant Major fish and yellow coral what reaches out at me like ten'acles!"

Young stared out at the ocean for a moment, then asked, "Does she give you money for Rashid?"

"Twenty dollar a month. She send it to me."

"Is that enough? It doesn't sound like very much."

"I takes what I gets."

"When was the last time you saw Tal?"

"I ain't never seen him since that summer." She looked down at the boy playing at her feet. "He never even seed he own son, and now he dead."

"Didn't he come back to the island from time to time?"

Keysha shrugged. "If he did, he never come lookin' for me."

"Did he have other women on the island?"

She shrugged again. "Expect so — they all does. But why you axin' me? Ax he friends."

"One of his friends told us Tal had a sweetie in New York."

"Mister," she said, "I don't even know what New York is."

Young wanted to ask Keysha if she knew what obeah was, but he let it go. She wandered down to the water and let it hiss over her toes. She watched the slow progress of the cruise ship across the horizon. Young smoked a cigarette. Harvey squatted in the sand with his grandson.

At the airport, Young was subjected to a full security search. The customs agent, an obese woman with a stupefied expression on her face, went through everything; her thick fingers probed his shoes and his shirts and his soap dish, even the plastic grocery bag containing his soiled socks and underwear.

Behind Young, Harvey slipped out of line and walked to the men's room. Inside a cubicle, he opened his carry-on and took out the Pringles tube. He jettisoned its diminished cargo in the toilet and dropped the tube in a trash barrel. When he was back in line, his heart was still racing. A different customs agent waved him through without searching his bags, and he was already seated on the plane and reading the airline magazine when Young, red-faced and puffing, sat down beside him.

In Miami, young men carrying machine guns and wearing baseball caps, headphones, flak jackets, and side arms patrolled Terminal C, where Young and Harvey waited for their connecting flight.

"It's a fucking war zone," Young said.

Harvey said, "So what did you think of Keysha?"

Young frowned. "She's just someone people use. Just a country girl. She didn't have Tal killed."

"You don't think Eula had anything to do with it, do you? Or George?"

"With Tal's murder? No. It doesn't add up. What Keysha said about Eula was dead on. Eula thought her son shit gold. Besides which, she got you to hire me. The investigation might never have come down here if she hadn't hired me. As for George, what's the motive?"

Harvey shook his head. "I don't know. Jealousy?"

"No, the man's got everything he wants."

Shortly after takeoff, Harvey, who had the window seat, fell asleep. Young asked an attendant for headphones so he could listen to some music. The attendant, tan and beautiful, fetched a pair from the pantry and handed them to him. They were in a cellophane bag.

"That will be two dollars, sir," she said.

"Two dollars? You're kidding, right?"

"No, I'm not kidding, sir. The headphones cost two dollars."

"But they used to be free."

"I know they used to be free, sir. We used to lend them to our passengers and ask them to return them at the end of the flight, but unfortunately quite a few people failed to return them —"

"I always returned mine."

"I'm sure you did, sir, but now we have to charge for them."

"I pay almost a grand for my ticket, and now you want two measly dollars for headphones?"

"I'm sorry, sir, but that's our policy."

Young thrust the headphones back at her. "I don't want them."

"They're reusable, sir. You can bring them on future flights. It's a one-time-only charge."

"Take them. I didn't want to buy them, I just wanted to borrow them."

Somewhere over Pennsylvania, Young asked the same attendant why dinner hadn't been served. "I'm sorry, sir, but there's a new policy. From now on, no meals will be served on non-intercontinental flights."

"Why the hell not?"

"The plastic knives and forks pose a security risk."

Young consumed six mini-packages of pretzels and four mixed-berry fruit bars and drank three cans of Sprite and four shots of Canadian Club. When Harvey woke up, it was because of the noises Young's stomach was making.

PART
TWO

PART
TWO

Sunday, November 18

When he woke up, Young was surprised to find himself in his own bed. He looked for the puppy curled at his feet, but she wasn't there. Then he remembered that she was over at Debi and Jamal's. Thinking of Debi made him think of horse racing. *I have to call Trick,* he thought, *but I have to pee first.* He stood up and made his way stiffly down the hall to the bathroom. As he urinated, he unconsciously traced the tip of his forefinger along his appendectomy scar. When he was finished, he looked for something to dab the tip of his penis against. He had thrown all the towels in the wash before leaving for the Bahamas and there was nothing at hand, so he broke off a square of toilet paper and used it. Huge and naked, he stumbled back down the hall to his bedroom, sat on the edge of his bed, scratched his belly, and dialed Trick's number.

"Arthur Trick speaking."

"It's me. I'm back."

"Have a good time?"

"Passable. Got some work done. Popped a few pops. Lost my quota at the casino."

"You and Mr. Harvey get along?"

"Oh yes. Kept him out of trouble."

"I thought I might hear from you this morning. Are we going to the track?"

"I'll pick you up at noon."

As Young hung up the phone, he looked out his kitchen window to watch the birds in the backyard, but there were none in sight. With a shock, he realized he had forgotten to top up the feeders before leaving for his trip. He threw on his windbreaker, stepped outside, removed the lid from the garbage can, scooped sunflower seeds into the plastic tub and finch seeds into the coffee mug, and hurried down the stairs to the yard. Both feeders were empty. After filling them, he stood back and whistled: *shurrrrr-tse-tse-tse*. This was his chickadee call. He whistled several times, but there was no response. As he lowered the lid onto the finch feeder and latched the roof of the large feeder, he wondered what the birds had eaten while he was gone and whether or not they would return. *They've gone elsewhere*, he thought. *Fucker let us down, so we're moving on.*

Three races into that afternoon's card at Caledonia Downs, Trick was up two hundred dollars, Young was down three hundred, and Debi was down twenty. "I like it better when we bet by committee," she said. "When we all bet the same horse."

"Why?" said Trick. The bet girl had just brought him his Daily Double winnings, and he was folding them into his shirt pocket.

"Because when we're all up or down the same amount, no one feels better or worse than anyone else."

"I told your father which horse to bet," Trick said. "I said the trey's a cinch, she can't lose."

"I know, Uncle Artie, but that's another reason we should all bet the same horse: so the winners don't make fun of the losers, and the losers don't feel bad."

"I'm not making fun of him. I'm just pointing out the facts." He turned to Young. "The idea, Camp, is to bet on the horse that's going to *win*. Then you won't feel like shit, you'll feel great like I do."

After the sixth race, Debi had to excuse herself. "That Edgar Berry who has the Carson City colt? He wants me to meet him in the lounge at a quarter past three."

"That why you're all dolled up like that?" her father asked. She was wearing a charcoal business suit with a gold pinstripe. Her shirt was blindingly white and her tie was burgundy, as was her hair.

"Is something wrong? Don't I look okay?"

"You look wonderful," Trick said. "If I wasn't your father's best friend, your honorary uncle, and a paraplegic, I'd hit all over you."

"Just be careful," her father said. "You don't know anything about this guy. He could be a snake in the grass."

"Or a multi-millionaire," Trick said, "willing to part with enough money to buy some really quality horseflesh for your barn."

After Debi left, Young said, "You know all that information about obeah you got for me?"

"What about it?"

"It was a big help. Thanks."

Trick's eyes narrowed. "Why do I smell a trap?"

"No trap. It's just that I've got some more work for you, if you want it."

"What kind of work?"

"Research. I need you to find a woman for me."

Trick nodded. "I've been trying for years to find a woman for you. You're not the easiest guy to shop for."

"No, I'm serious. I need you to find a woman who might be involved in the case."

"Who is she?"

"I don't know her name. All I know is she was Tal Cooper's girlfriend, and she had a baby by him — a daughter."

"That's not much to go on."

"It's all I got. Oh, and she was a student at that music college in New York."

"Juilliard?"

"That's the one. And she's got red hair."

"Do you know what type of music she was studying?"

Young began to shake his head, then said, "Classical comes to mind."

"Okay, I'll see what I can find out. Anything else for me?"

"Yeah, as a matter of fact, I want you to see what you can find out about a guy called ..." Young pulled his notebook out of his shirt pocket and flipped several pages into it, "... Clarvius Narcisse."

"How do you spell that?"

Young showed him the notebook.

Trick studied the name. "What's so special about Clarvius Narcisse?"

Young closed the notebook and replaced it in his pocket. "Apparently, the guy was a zombie."

Jamal greeted Young at the door. "We were starting to wonder."

"Who's we? Your mom's still at the track."

"Me and Cujo."

"Cujo?"

"That's the name I gave her."

Young leaned forward and kissed the boy on his forehead.

"Poppy, haven't I asked you not to do that?" Jamal said, wiping his face with his shirt-sleeve.

The puppy appeared at Young's feet and growled up at him.

"You too big now to let your grandfather kiss you?" He put the boy into a headlock.

The puppy started biting Young's pant leg.

"Hey!" Young said, looking down. He shooed the puppy away. "She's defending you."

"Yeah," the boy said, extricating himself from Young's hold, "we bonded pretty good while you were away. We're pretty tight."

"I'll bet you don't want her to leave."

"That's okay, you're only a couple of blocks away."

Young pulled his wallet from the right front pocket of his jeans. "Now, let's see, what do I owe you? How's ten bucks sound?"

"For the whole week?"

Young paused. "Yeah, I guess that's not very much. How about two bucks a day, times six, that's twelve, make it fifteen bucks."

"That's still not very much."

Young stood with the wallet in his hands. "Well, why don't you tell me what you think's fair. Hell, when I was your age —"

"Don't get mad. It's different now than when you were a kid. Inflation and everything. Five bucks a day would be fair. Times six. Thirty for the week."

"How old are you?"

"Twelve."

"You're a hard-nose for twelve. You're gonna go places."

Young heated himself two Michelina dinners and ate them in front of the TV. The puppy wouldn't settle down. She wandered around the apartment, crying. When Young gave her a treat, she ate it, then resumed crying. "You big baby," he said. He found her chew toy and tossed it to her, but she ignored it. He even lay down on Reg's old blanket with her, but still she whimpered.

At nine-thirty, Young sat down in his breakfast nook and phoned Wheeler.

"Welcome back," she said. "Successful trip?"

"Yup. Popped a few pops, asked a few questions."

"Get a few answers?"

"A few, yeah."

"When'd you get in?"

"Last night."

"Last night, and you didn't call till now?"

"Wheeler, please don't start."

"Don't start what?"

Young lit a cigarette. "You know, pretending like we're boyfriend-girlfriend."

"Okay, fine, you don't give me a moment's thought, but let me ask you a question. You just lit a cigarette, right?"

"Yeah, so?"

"Did you use the Zippo I gave you for your birthday?"

"Yeah, so what?"

"So *what*? I gave you that lighter. It means we're close. It means we're special to each other."

"Wheeler, you know it makes me crazy when you talk like this."

"Talk like what?"

"When you make fun of my feelings for you. You don't know how you get."

"How do I get?"

"You get mean."

There was a pause. "Do I really?"

"Yes, you do, you get mean."

"Maybe it's because I really do love you, but I know it's impossible because I'm sexually orientated towards women, not men, especially three-hundred-pound men with kinky red hair."

"Not that you give a shit, but I'm two-eighty-five, and as for my hair I could shave it off and be a skinhead if that would make you happy."

"Sarge, I do love you, but you're just not my type. You know I love you."

"Never mind, forget it."

"Did you get to the track today?"

"Of course I got to the track today, it's Sunday."

"How much did you lose?"

Young inhaled. "Three hundred, thereabouts."

"Three hundred! Yikes."

"Wheeler, for fucksake —"

"Okay, I won't say another word. Have you got a name for the puppy yet?"

"Jamal wants to call it Cujo. I was thinking maybe Reg, or Reg the Second."

"No, you can't call her Reg. I thought up one you might like."

Young tapped the ash off his cigarette. "Really, what?"

"Thelma and Louise."

There was a pause, then Young said, "That's two names."

"If you name her after the characters, you're right, it's two names, but if you name her after the movie, it's only one."

"Susan Sarandon was in it, right?"

"Yes, she was, and —"

"Remember that scene in *Atlantic City* where she's washing herself with a lemon, and Burt Lancaster —"

"Which one did Susan Sarandon play, Thelma or Louise? And who played the other one?"

Young shook his head. "You know we don't allow chick flicks when we're playing movie trivia."

"She played Louise, and Geena Davis played Thelma."

"Well, fuck, you didn't even give me a chance to think about it. What if I included sports movies? I'm sure you'd bitch about that, or at least you'd want a minute or two to think about your answer."

"Like what sports movie?"

"Well, I don't know." He held his cigarette in one hand and massaged an ear with the other. "Like that Kevin Costner one where he's a minor league catcher, and Susan Sarandon plays a groupie."

"They're called baseball Annies, and the movie was *Bull Durham*, and since when have you had this fixation on Susan Sarandon?"

"*Bull Durham*, right, I knew that, but the point is you can't call a dog Thelma and Louise. You have to choose."

"Have you picked her up yet?"

"Yeah, I stopped by earlier. She's with me now, but she won't settle down. She's pacing all around and making these whining sounds."

"She probably misses Jamal. She's been with him for a week, right? Do you have something you can give her?"

"I gave her Reg's blanket, and that didn't work. I gave her a treat, and that didn't work. I gave her her chewy, and that didn't —"

"Her what?"

"Her whatchamacallit. Her chew toy. Her porcupine."

"You said chewy."

"So what?"

"Stay away from that word, Sarge. You're a big, big man, way too big for a word like chewy."

"Maybe you should chew my shorts."

"All I'm saying is it's not a good look for you."

Monday, November 19

It was 8:00 a.m., and Young was sitting in his breakfast nook finishing up his Grape-Nuts when the phone rang.

"Welcome back," Cronish said. "Are you tan and svelte?"

"Nope," Young said. "Fat and ugly, as usual." He lowered his cereal bowl to the floor. "What's new?"

"You'll recall our conversation the day you left when I told you I'd completed the autopsy."

"I remember." Young watched the puppy leave off chewing the rubber porcupine and begin slurping the leftover milk in the bowl.

"I told you all the physical evidence suggested Talmadge Cooper had been poisoned."

"Right, but you didn't know what kind of poison."

"Exactly. Well, while you were toasting your toes in the tropical sun, I was busily researching tropical poisons."

"How'd you make out?"

"Very well indeed. I found several that looked promising, but I've narrowed it down to two. The poisons I discounted included, for your delectation, oleander juice and the venom of the many-banded krait. But the two that caught my fancy warrant serious consideration."

"I'm listening." Young sat up straight. His cigarettes and ashtray were still on the table from the night before. Normally he resisted smoking before noon, but on this occasion he decided to allow himself one.

"The first is called ciguatera. It's a toxin ingested by small fish when they eat certain types of algae. When those fish are eaten by larger fish, the larger fish become carriers of the poison. Barracuda and blackfin grouper are two examples. That's why people in the Caribbean are very careful when they clean barracuda and grouper. I read on the Internet that a fisherman who catches a barracuda will cut off a tiny piece of its flesh and drop it on an anthill. If the ants eat the meat, it's safe for human consumption."

Young used his Toronto Maple Leafs lighter to light his cigarette. He inhaled mightily. "How does this tie in with Tal Cooper?"

"The contents of Mr. Cooper's stomach included undigested fish, and the undigested fish turned out to be among certain salt water types that include barracuda."

"So it could be barracuda, but you're not sure."

"That's right, but what I am sure about is that the fish in Mr. Cooper's belly was infected with ciguatera."

"Bingo."

"Not quite. Ciguatera poisoning is rarely fatal — only about five percent of the time — but Mr. Cooper's blood revealed the presence of the other, far more lethal poison. It's called TTX, and it comes from various species of rockfish, among other things. The Japanese love rockfish, and Japanese chefs take special courses so they know how to clean the fish properly before cooking and serving it. Even so, several hundred Japanese restaurant patrons die every year after paying the equivalent of several hundred dollars for the privilege of eating it. If even a pinhead's amount of poison is ingested, it's fatal fifty percent of the time."

Young tapped the ash off the end of his cigarette. "And Tal Cooper's blood had TTX in it?"

"That's what I'm telling you."

"So he had two poisons in him."

"So it appears. Somebody fed him bad barracuda and somehow introduced TTX into his system as well."

"You said rockfish earlier. Are rockfish related to pufferfish?"

"They are indeed. They're one and the same."

Young examined his cigarette. "Fellow in the Bahamas told me about pufferfish venom, said it was used by these witch doctors or whatever you call them to turn people into zombies."

Cronish cleared his throat. "Right, well, one theory has it that TTX powder is fed to the victim — ground up in his porridge, perhaps — and another claims the 'witch doctor,' to use your term, makes a cut in the victim's flesh and rubs the powder into the wound. In either case, the effect is a kind of paralysis. The victim appears to be dead, and in fact may even be pronounced dead by a normally reliable physician and may even be buried, only to be dug up and revived a few nights later by the witch doctor, who is able to keep the zombie, who seems to remain in a state of stupefaction for an indefinite period of time, as his personal slave."

Young ground out his cigarette in the ashtray. "And that's how you make a zombie."

"Well, there is one other way."

"There is?"

"Rum, fruit juice, grenadine, triple sec."

"Very funny. Where would the killer get the poisons?"

"Lots of poisons are readily available to the consumer. I'm sure voodoo poisons are, too."

"Where?"

"Wherever voodoo supplies are sold, I imagine."

Young phoned Stella at home. "I'm back."

"Well, hallelujah. Listen, can you call me back in half an hour? I've got Nicky in the tub."

"Can you just tell me if there was any mail, or e-mail, or whatever?"

"If there's any mail, I wouldn't know about it, because I haven't been to the office, and as for e-mail, you didn't get anything work-related, just a bunch of junk mail offering you — among other things — a bigger penis overnight."

Trick was sitting at his computer. His search on the Internet for Clarvius Narcisse eventually led him to a website for a magazine titled *California Wild* and specifically to an article that had appeared in its summer 1998 issue. The article was written by William Haugen Light, whose author's note suggested that he knew a lot about biology, zoology, geology, something called polychate systematics, and — of special interest to Trick — toxicology.

Although the story of Clarvius Narcisse took up only a fraction of the article, Trick thought it might be just what Young needed, so he printed out the entire article and, with a yellow highlighter in his left hand, shakily marked those sections he considered important.

... first surfaced in 1982, when Wade Davis, a Harvard graduate student in ethnobotany, noticed a similarity between the reported experience of voodoo "zombies" and victims of *fugu* poisoning. He was investigating the strange case of a man claiming to be Clarvius Narcisse, a Haitian man who was pronounced dead by physicians in 1962. According to the man's account, he was merely paralyzed. He claimed he heard himself pronounced dead, and remembered being placed in a coffin and buried. He was later dug up, beaten, and forced into slavery under a voodoo "zombie master."

Two years later the zombie master was killed, according to the account, and Narcisse and his fellow "zombies" escaped. Still fearing the vengeful brother who had allegedly contracted his zombification over a land dispute, Narcisse wandered about the country for the next 16 years. When he learned of his brother's death, he returned to his native village where he convinced his sister and other villagers of his identity by revealing details that only Narcisse could have known.

Davis was conducting the investigation at the request of his professor at Harvard, Richard Schultes, the "father" of ethnobotany, who had been contacted by a Haitian psychiatrist. He found that bokor use a toxic powder to create zombies. This powder is made of ingredients from a number of plants and animals, including porcupinefishes (*Diodon hystrix* and *D. holocanthus*) and pufferfishes, including *Sphoeroides testudineus* and *S. spengleri*, all of which are known to contain tetrodotoxin in their tissues and to have caused human poisonings.... Davis notes that zombies are not randomly created out of innocent victims in Haiti. Rather, zombification is a sentence imposed upon perceived wrongdoers and malefactors by the secret societies — a direct offshoot of similar powerful societies in West Africa. Narcisse stated that he had been condemned in such a trial and his cousin confirmed that he was given a powder ... which appeared to induce his paralysis....

Davis emphasizes that there is no assembly-line production of zombies in Haiti, and the successful creation of a zombie is an exceedingly rare phenomenon. Since the effective dose is essentially the same as the lethal dose, most victims must simply be killed by the procedure, or else suffer minimal or no ill effects. But as pointed out by Davis, one success would establish a bokor's reputation for all time.

Trick did some additional research and typed out three definitions on his word processor:

1. Bokor — (singular and plural) a voodoo sorcerer or practitioner.
2. Fugu poisoning — a sometimes fatal poisoning resulting from eating fish infested with tetrodotoxin.
3. Tetrodotoxin — "one of the most potent toxins known to science"; found in the "ovaries, liver, skin and other tissues of many pufferfishes of the family Tetraodontidae ... particularly in species of the genera Fugu and Sphoeroides"; commonly known as TTX.

Trick also typed out several questions:

1. Although Camp believes that T. Cooper's murder was made to look like voodoo, is it possible that it really was voodoo?
2. If so, is it possible that someone was trying to turn Cooper into a zombie?
3. If so, is it possible that Cooper is not dead, but in a state of paralysis (such as C. Narcisse described)?

A prickle ran across Trick's scalp. He phoned Homicide and asked Desk Sergeant Gallagher to put him through to Big Urmson.

"Urmson," he said, "this is very important."

"Trick?"

"Yes, it's me, listen —"

"Long time no see, how the hell are you?"

"Urmson, listen, Talmadge Cooper's body —"

"What of it?"

"Is it still intact?"

"Huh?"

"Is it still in one piece, or has it been buried or cremated or something?"

"All I know is Cronish did an autopsy on it. We're supposed to ship it back to his mother when we're done with it."

"An autopsy."

"Yeah."

Well, Trick thought, *that answers question number three.*

"Listen, Trick, I've been meaning to call you."

"What about?"

"Well, I was talking to Sarge before he went away, just trying to pick his brain, you know, about this murder, and he said I should talk to you, that you were working on it for him. I think he said you were doing some research."

"That was over a week ago, Urmson. What have you been doing in the meantime?"

"Don't worry about that, I've been making a few inquiries of my own, but I was hoping you might be willing to share your findings with us. After all, we're all on the same team."

"If I come across anything important, I'll let you know, but you have to remember, I don't work for Homicide except on a contract basis, and right now I'm not on contract. If you want the fruits of my labour, offer me a contract. As it is, I'm working for Camp."

"How much is he paying you?"

"Nothing, but the benefits are good. He hauls my crippled ass out to the track every Sunday and we go drinking together, which is more than I can say for my other former colleagues, for whom it seems I no longer exist. I know people feel awkward around me, I know I'm at best an inconvenience and at worst an embarrassment —"

"Geez, Trick, I didn't know you felt like this. I didn't know you had all this bitterness bottled up —"

"It's okay, Urmson, I'm just yanking your chain." Trick hung up and dialed Young at home.

Young picked up on the third ring. "What?"

"It's me. I've got all the dope on Clarvius Narcisse."

"Like what?"

"You're right, he was a zombie, and there's this poison called TTX that's used to turn people into zombies. I printed out an article —"

"Read it to me."

Trick read the article to Young, and the definitions of bokor, fugu poisoning, and tetrodotoxin, and when he was finished Young said, "Cronish said people can buy this TTX stuff at voodoo stores."

"Voodoo stores?"

"That's what he said."

"I've never heard of a voodoo store."

"Maybe you could ask some of your friends if they know where there's a voodoo store."

"You mean ask some of my *black* friends?"

"Right."

"Camp, you amaze me."

"What?"

"I may be black, and I may or may not have black friends, but that doesn't mean they're any more likely to know about voodoo or the whereabouts of voodoo stores than my white friends would."

"I thought I was your only white friend."

"I was born right here in Toronto, Camp, not in Jamaica or Haiti or Alabama. I have plenty of white friends."

"And you have plenty of black friends, too, right? You've told me so. And lots of those black friends were born in places where voodoo is practised. Like Jamaica and Haiti. And it stands to reason there's a better chance *your* friends know something about voodoo stores in Toronto than *my* friends, right? Besides, it wouldn't be such a big deal if a black man was snooping around one of these voodoo stores."

"Why's that?"

"Well, my guess is that the people who run these voodoo stores are more likely to be black, or do you want to argue that one, too?"

Trick was silent for a moment. "It's more likely, I'll grant you that."

"Thank you. Cronish told me the autopsy on Tal Cooper showed he had TTX in his blood. So we've got to find out if the killer got hold of the TTX in a voodoo store in Toronto. Maybe they have to keep records of who buys what poison."

"Right, but still —"

"Well, you tell me then. Isn't the guy in the voodoo store going to be a bit suspicious of a big old white boy pawing through his merchandise and asking questions about who bought TTX? Wouldn't it be better to send in a black guy?"

"I hope you're not thinking —"

"Why not? You're black, plus you're in a wheelchair."

"Why is me being in a wheelchair an advantage?"

"It makes you hard to say no to."

"Camp, where have you been? Most people have no trouble at all saying no to me."

"I do."

"Yeah, well, that's because you're a little light in your loafers."

"Come on, be a sport."

"I don't know about this."

"Just see if you can find a voodoo store."

Trick sighed. "All right, I'll do that much."

"Thank you, brother."

There was a buzzing sound at Trick's end.

Young said, "What's that?"

"Front door," Trick said. "Hang on while I buzz her in."

"Buzz who in?"

"Miss Leventhorpe."

"Miss *Lev*enthorpe? Who's Miss Leventhorpe?"

"She's my caregiver. Haven't I told you about her? She's six feet tall and strong as an ox. She's a Southerner, Camp, from North Carolina, and she's got the sweetest drawl you ever heard. She calls me Ah-thuh."

"Good-looking?"

"Not in the conventional sense, but *I* think she's gorgeous."

"What's she do for you?"

"She bathes me and exercises my arms and legs."

"I'm glad to see my tax dollars at work."

"Oh, she's not from Health Canada."

"She's not? Where's she from?"

"The Red Garter Escort Service."

Young laughed. "You're shitting me, right?"

"No, I'm not shitting you."

"What else does she do for you?"

"Like I'm going to tell you that."

"I just want to know my man's looked after."

"No fear there. How about you, you looked after?"

Tuesday, November 20

Young said, "What time is it?"

"Half past nine," said Trick. "Did I wake you?"

"I'm not sure. Half-and-half. I must have been dozing. What's up?"

"I talked to a friend of mine last night, and he gave me a name and address. He says it's the only voodoo store in the city."

"Well, I didn't expect a chain. When are you going?"

"That's why I'm phoning. I can't go. My friend knows I'm mobility-challenged, and he warned me there's a long flight of stairs up to the store. You're going to have to either go or find someone else, someone whose legs still ambulate."

"Fuck."

"Anyway, I have to chase down the Juilliard girl-friend."

"Fine. Where am I going?"

"It's above a bookstore in Greek Town."

"Strange place for a voodoo store."

"Well, as a matter of fact, the owner's Greek."

"A Greek black guy?"

"No, a Greek white guy, but according to my friend he's got dreads, if that makes you feel any better."

"Fine, I'll talk to you tonight. McCully's?"

"Sounds good."

"Pick you up around eight."

"See you then." Trick hung up, checked his notes, and dialed a long-distance number.

"The Juilliard School," a female voice with a thick Bronx accent announced. "How may I direct your call?"

"Registration, please," Trick said.

"One moment."

A male voice answered. "Registration. Gary Garvin speaking."

Trick explained that he was an investigator affiliated with Metro Toronto Homicide, that he was working the Talmadge Cooper murder case, and that he had been asked to prepare a list of names of the friends Cooper had made while he was a student at Juilliard.

"*Who* Cooper?" Gary Garvin said.

"Talmadge," Trick said.

"Oh yes," Garvin said, "Talmadge. I remember the name. Caribbean boy?"

"That's right."

"Jazz saxophone if I'm not mistaken."

"Right again."

"You say he's been murdered?"

"Yes, in Toronto, two weeks ago."

"How dreadful."

Trick listened to the clicking of computer keys.

"Yes, here he is. Talmadge Harvey Cooper. Class of '98."

"Specifically, I'm looking for a young woman Cooper was friends with. She was a student there, too. I don't know if she was in the same year he was."

"I've been registrar here for thirteen years, and I'm very good at my job, but I'm going to need a tad more information than that."

"She was studying classical music."

"Well, that narrows it down a bit, but it could be anything from oboe to opera singer."

"The only other thing I know is she had red hair."

There was a silence on the other end of the line. "I wonder," Garvin said. "There was a very beautiful young woman here around the same time Mr. Cooper was ... very beautiful ... a veritable *explosion* of red hair. If I'm not mistaken, she played cello. I remember because of that Altman film — I'm sure you know the one — there was a girl in it who played cello, a real cello player, and she reminded me of this girl, except that the girl in the movie, whose name escapes me, was much taller. I'm afraid I've reached that age where I not only fail to remember the titles of movies, but when I say, 'Oh, well, you know the one I mean, it starred —' then I can't remember the names of any of the actors either. However, I'm much better at remembering — or at least tracing — former students and, if I'm not mistaken, she was Jewish, her surname began with an F, I think, something like Feinstein." The quiet clatter of computer keys resumed. "*Voila!* Here she is, this is the girl I remember — Amy Feldman!"

Trick said, "You wouldn't happen to have an address for her."

"Not a current one, I'm afraid, but her next of kin, as of September 1997, were, let's see ... Dr. and Mrs. Sidney Feldman, of Monroe, New Jersey."

With his erratic left hand, Trick began to print "Feldman, Monroe NJ" on a pad of paper he kept on the arm of his wheelchair.

"As I recall, Miss Feldman pretty much vanished from sight before she even began her sophomore year. Gossip had it she was in the family way — courtesy of Mr. Cooper — but I can't confirm that. She did disappear, though. We don't know what became of her, there's no forwarding address, and in my capacity as editor of the 'What Are They Up To Now?' column in the alumni news, I can assure you that if she *is* up to anything worth reporting, she hasn't told her alma mater about it."

Trick thanked Garvin, hung up, and phoned directory assistance for Monroe, New Jersey.

The phone rang just as Young was sitting down with a slab of lasagne to watch *Investigative Reports*. He picked up the receiver and said, "What?"

"I've got a name for you."

"Who?"

"The Juilliard girlfriend. Her name's Amy Feldman. I just talked to her father. He and his wife have the little girl. He confirmed she's mixed race."

"Does he know where Amy is?"

"No. Somewhere in New York, he thinks. He says she's a heroin addict."

"How long since he's seen her?"

"She borrowed his car three months ago to drive into New York, and nobody's seen her since."

"What's she doing for money?"

"Dr. Feldman said he and his wife gave her money for a long time, but then she stopped asking them."

"How long ago was this?"

"Just before she disappeared."

"Maybe she'd saved up a little nest egg and decided to buy herself a party. She's probably hooking now. Did you ask her father if maybe she's hooking?"

"No, I didn't."

"You have to ask, Trick, otherwise you don't find out shit."

"I'll give you his number, you can ask him yourself."

"All right, don't get your nose out of joint. The fact that she hasn't tried to see her kid in three months is definitely a bad sign."

Trick paused. "Maybe she's in a hospital somewhere —"

"Or she's hooking or she's dead."

"Maybe she found herself a sugar daddy."

"My money says she's dead." Young sighed. "Okay, good work." With his fork, he cut loose one corner of his lasagne. "I'm going down to that school, snoop around a bit. Maybe I'll pay a visit to the Garden State, as well."

"I thought you were going to snoop around the voodoo store."

"I am, this afternoon. This other I'll do towards the end of the week."

Trick said, "Another thing. You're a movie buff, right?"

"Yeah, so?"

"What's the title of the Altman movie that has a cello player in it played by a real cello player?"

"I don't know, *Nashville*?"

"*Nashville*'s about country music. Seems the wrong place for a cello."

Young glanced at the television. "Fine, well, listen, my show's starting —"

"One last thing. I was thinking about the coins in the instrument case."

"What about them?"

"According to the information you gave me, there were eleven of them, two in one group and nine in the other, depending on whether they were minted before 1973 when the Bahamas became a commonwealth."

Young looked down at the piece of lasagne on his fork. "What's your point?"

"I added them up."

There was a pause. "And?" Young said.

"They add up to seventy-four cents."

"Is that supposed to mean something?"

"I don't know. I just thought I'd tell you."

"Right, well, thanks. My show's on and my food's getting cold, I'll talk to you later."

Trick was right. It was only one flight of stairs, but it was a long one. Young could easily have missed the doorway off the street, had it not been for the signboard on the sidewalk:

RASTAMAN VIBRATIONS
Relics, Curios, Powders and Potions
Essential to the Art of Vodoun

By the time he reached the top stair, Young was puffing like a rich man climbing Everest. When he looked around, he found himself alone in a square room whose walls and ceilings were hung with all manner of trinkets, dolls, bottles, bags, postcards, posters, paintings, banners, hats, shirts, signs, slogans, announcements, and advertisements: "All Our Products Are Hand-Crafted And Consecrated!"; "Witch-Doctor Spellkits — $39.95!"; "Let Veruschka Cast Your Spell for You!"; "DNA Testing — by Mail! Who Is Your Baby Daddy? Is

This My Baby? All We Need Is Some Hair, Finger Nail, Used Tooth Brush, Etc." A doorway leading to a darkened hallway was hung with floor-length strands of beads, and from the doorway Young could hear voices rhythmically chanting, "Jer-ry! Jer-ry! Jer-ry!"

Young found an ornate bell on the sales counter and rang it. The TV sounds abruptly ceased, and a barrel-chested man with thick, grey, tube-like dreadlocks emerged from the gloom. He was wearing Nana Mouskouri glasses and brushing crumbs from his T-shirt, upon which was emblazoned a single word: "Pinstruck."

"Hello, hello," the man said genially. "I hope you haven't been waiting long."

"No problem," Young said. "This is some store."

The man inclined his head. "We pride ourselves on being the best-equipped and most knowledgeable purveyors of vodoun paraphernalia in the country."

"Vodoun," Young said. "Is that the same thing as voodoo?"

"It is the original version of the word, as coined by the Yoruba tribe of Africa, one of the first groups to practise the high art. Vodoun translates into English as 'spirit' or 'spirit of God.'"

Young cast his eyes around the room. "Myself, I'm new to voodoo."

The man smiled, revealing a gold eye tooth. "Whatever you need, we have it. We carry soaps, oils, vials, incenses, tinctures, wanga dolls, Haitian talismans, veves, loas, gris-gris sacks, books on love-cooking and egg spells, and a wide selection of spellkits."

"What exactly is a spellkit?"

The man pointed to a row of boxes displayed on the wall behind him. "Each spellkit comes with a four-inch voodoo doll and a pamphlet of incantations. Depending on your individual needs, we can

sell you a money spellkit, a love spellkit, a power-suc-
cess-prosperity spellkit, or spellkits whose exotic
applications are suggested by their names: Mojo, Get
Even, Irresistible Me, Black Cat, Uncrossing, and so
on. We also offer an all-purpose spellkit. Or, and
again this depends on your individual needs, we can
sell you a wanga doll that will cure your love or
money problems — love and money are our two prin-
cipal areas of remedy, incidentally — or we can sell
you the luck wanga doll, which is especially popular
with bingo players, or the hex wanga doll, or the sex
wanga doll, or the break-up or get-together wanga
dolls — or both for a reduced price — or the exorcist
wanga doll, or the jinx-remover wanga doll, or the
weight-loss wanga doll."

"What about powder?" Young asked.

The man looked startled. "I don't know what
you mean."

Young shrugged his shoulders. "Simple question.
Do you sell any kind of powder?"

"You wouldn't happen to be a policeman?"

Young laughed. "Do I look like a policeman?"

"Yes," the man said, "as a matter of fact, you do."

"Well," Young said, "I'm not." He placed his
right hand over his heart. "Scout's honour. Now what
about it?"

The man smiled thinly. "Yes, we have a variety of
powders. What type are you interested in?"

Young paused for effect, then carefully pronounced,
"Tetrodotoxin."

The man's eyebrows rose. "You may not be aware
of this, being new to vodoun, but TTX is illegal. There's
a law against selling it. It's what's used to create zombies, and in the hands of beginners it can be fatal. It's
like a book of matches in the hands of a child."

Young took his wallet from his right front pants pocket. "Just for the sake of argument, Mr. uh ...?" Young looked up.

The man hesitated, then said, "Georgiadis."

"Just for the sake of argument, Mr. Georgiadis, how much TTX would a C-note get me — if it was legal to sell it, of course." He placed a hundred-dollar bill on the counter within inches of the man's ringy fingers.

"I would guess something in the neighbourhood of a thimbleful."

"Would that be enough to kill a man?"

"It would be enough to kill ten men, maybe more."

"I see." Young slowly moved his hand forward to reclaim the money.

The man snapped the bill off the counter. "Wait here," he said. He disappeared through the doorway and into the darkness of the hall. Young surveyed the counter. He slipped a Rastaman Vibrations business card from a small stand beside the cash register into his left front pants pocket and deposited four pennies and a dime that he found in the same pocket into a Mothers Against Drunk Driving donation box.

When he returned, the man, wearing surgical gloves, dropped a small twist-tied baggy containing a few pinches of brown powder onto the counter in front of Young. "I could be arrested for this," he said. "So could you. If anything happens, I've never seen you in my life."

Young slid the bag into the pocket of his windbreaker. "You asked me earlier if I was a policeman, and I said no. It's true, I'm not. But I was." Again he extracted his wallet, removed a business card, and handed it to the man. "Where it says Campbell Young, that's me. And where it says Investigative Consultant, that's me, too." He shoved the wallet back into his pocket. "I've still got a lot of friends on the force, and if I took it into my head to do such a thing, I could have you shut down in five minutes. Shut down for good."

The man watched Young's eyes. "What do you want?"

"Did you hear about a musician being murdered at the Sutton Place Hotel?"

The man fingered his dreadlocks. "I don't listen to the news."

"Couple of weeks ago. Jazz musician."

"I may have heard something about it. What —"

"TTX was found in his bloodstream, and the barracuda in his belly was full of" — and again Young pronounced carefully — "ciguatera."

"What's this got to do with me?"

"I want to know," Young said slowly, "who bought the TTX."

"I haven't sold any TTX."

"You just sold some to me!" Young leaned powerfully across the counter. "Now I don't know if you keep records of your sales, I don't imagine you do, but it really doesn't matter because if you don't start singing three things are going to happen: one, I'll arrange for a search warrant to be issued within the hour; two, your inventory — including your motherlode of TTX — will be confiscated; and three, you'll end up out of business and nailed with a hefty fine, or, worse, a stretch in maximum security if it's proven you're accessory to murder. So if I were you, Mr. Georgiadis, I'd start singing."

The man shook his head. "I've already told you. I haven't sold TTX to anyone. Not even you. If I'm asked, I'll say you got it somewhere else." He held up his hands and waggled the fingers, which were still encased in plastic. "And don't bother dusting that baggy, you won't find any prints. And when your friends on the force come back with a warrant, they can search high and low, but they won't find anything illegal on these premises."

Ursula Drown was pounding, without success, on the door of her husband's soundproof basement studio.

Ever since his teens, when he'd discovered jazz, Buddy Drown had wished he was black, and for a time he had affected black mannerisms and figures of speech and styles of dress that he hoped would make him fit in with the black musicians he began hanging around with in his early twenties. Sometime in his late twenties he accepted the fact that he was white; after all, Zoot Sims was white, and so were Stan Getz and Gerry Mulligan and a number of other great sax players. He'd eventually married a white European woman, which in the fifties and sixties had been a very black thing to do, a thing done by many black musicians when they realized not only that the racism they faced every day in America would never go away, no matter how admired they were by the liberal white population, but that they were revered — idolized, in fact — in France and Germany and Scandinavia, where they were regarded as exotic geniuses.

Ursula was Swedish. She had met Drown in Stockholm eight years earlier when she was an art student and he was a non-soloing member of the reed section of a swing band. He brought her back to Canada, set her up in an apartment, divorced his first wife — a dressmaker who had a close personal relationship with cocaine — married Ursula at City Hall, and settled her into a rented bungalow. He gave her money to buy art books and supplies. She took several courses at the Art Gallery of Ontario, but as time passed she lost her inspiration and abandoned any hope of being a painter.

Late one afternoon three years into their marriage, she packed up all her oils and brushes and canvases and transported them by public transit — she didn't drive — to a mall, where she deposited them in a dumpster behind a Wal-Mart. She kept her books, however. In her spare moments, which were plentiful, she would study the plates: still lifes, seascapes, nudes. One book in particular — *Modern American Painting* by Peyton Boswell Jr., which she had discovered in a used bookstore — became her staple. She spent hours poring over the composition and detail of the paintings, the artists' use of shade and colour and perspective. Her favourites included Benjamin West's *The Death of Wolfe*, John McCrady's *Swing Low, Sweet Chariot*, Frederick J. Waugh's *The Big Water*, Winslow Homer's *Prisoners from the Front*, and everything by Thomas Hart Benton. She loved paintings that told stories, or at least hinted at them, such as Benton's *Persephone*, in which — according to the notes — "the mythological goddess of nature is a realistic Missouri girl about to be violated by a local farmer."

As her dreams of an artistic career faded, Ursula as well lost her starry-eyed attitude towards her husband and gradually stopped attending his gigs. Instead, she resigned herself to a quiet, childless life.

Drown, whose temper was unpredictable and violent, frightened her. As his star failed to rise, his moods darkened, and their lovemaking, which at first had been frequent if unimaginative — he had never let her take the lead — became sporadic and cold. For him, it seemed, sex had become an outlet for his anger. He forced her to perform acts that she might have enjoyed, might even have initiated, had she been given a chance, had they been acts of love instead of hostility. This degradation, too, she grew to accept. She felt, variously, like a drudge, a slave, a hostage, a murder-waiting-to-happen. She wasn't stupid — she could have run away if she'd wanted to — but something in her nature told her she was doomed no matter what she did. Her decision to paint had been foolish, based as it was on no appreciable talent; her decision to follow Drown to Canada was likewise a mistake. He didn't love her, he never had. He was enamoured only of her pale skin, her long, flaxen hair, her boy's body. She had loved him at first, but she realized now that it had been a superficial love. His thick torso and bald head had reminded her of her father, who died when she was six.

More than once she thought to herself as she ironed his shirts or prepared his supper, *One of these days he's going to kill me.*

But at this moment, as she hammered her small fists against the locked door of his basement studio, she was unusually animated. And when at length her persistence filtered through the big, bold Coltrane sounds that filled Drown's ears as he practised the master's changes in "Dear Lord," he removed his headphones, laid down his Selmer, hit "stop" on the CD player, and unlocked and opened the door. Because she knew better than to disturb him, he was more alarmed than angry.

"What is it?" he said.

She was breathing quickly, scared. "A man on the telephone says he must speak to you."

"I'm busy. You know better than to disturb me when I'm down here."

"I know, Buddy, I'm sorry —"

"Did you tell him I was busy?"

"Yes, yes!" Now she was in tears. "But he tell me if I don't want to see you dead I should bring you to the telephone."

Drown brushed past her and climbed the stairs to the kitchen. He lifted the receiver off the counter. "Who is this?" he demanded.

"It's me," a heavy voice said. "The Greek."

Drown chewed his lip. "What do you want?"

"We have to talk."

"Why?"

"Because I had a visitor."

"I don't know what you're —"

"This visitor said that somebody who happens to be in the same business as you are is dead, and they found TTX in his blood —"

"Quiet! Not over the phone."

"So it's true."

"I told you, not over the phone. I'll meet you someplace."

"Where?"

Drown pressed two fingers into his forehead. "The Black Swan. Tomorrow night."

"Why not tonight?"

"I'm busy tonight."

"What time tomorrow night?"

"Late. I've got a gig, a retirement party. Eleven o'clock."

"I don't trust you. You'd better be there."

"I'll be there. I'll explain what happened. How'd you get my number? How do you even know my name?"

The Greek laughed. "Don't you remember? You had no cash, you paid with MasterCard. And your phone number's in the white pages! Now that you've taken up a new line of work, you may want to get yourself unlisted!"

After he hung up the phone, Drown turned and saw Ursula watching him from the door to the basement.

"What is it, Buddy?" she said. "Is there something wrong?"

He shook his head, pushed past her, and went back down the stairs. Ursula heard him close and lock the door of his studio, and a minute later she heard the muted sounds of his saxophone.

"Wheeler," Young said, "it's me."

"Hiya, Sarge." She wedged the phone between her cheek and her shoulder. The cat on the kitchen counter meowed at her, and she picked it up. "How goes the battle?"

"Got a question for you. Movie trivia."

Wheeler turned away from the counter and looked at the clock on the microwave: 8:17. "Why aren't you at McCully's?"

"Just going out the door. What's the name of the Robert Altman movie with a cello player in it? A woman. She's a real cello player in real life."

"*Short Cuts.* Lori Singer is the real name of the real cello player."

"Excellent, thanks. Bye."

"I love you, too."

Young pushed Trick past the bar at McCully's. They said hello to Priam Harvey, who was sitting on his usual stool, and to Dexter, who was filling a pint glass at one of the taps.

They settled themselves at a table, and Jessy appeared in front of them. "What a sorry pair," she said.

Young said, "Do you sell beer in this dive?"

"Excuse my friend," Trick said. "You are the well that never goes dry."

When Jessy returned with their drinks — two bottles of Blue for Young and a bottle of Tuborg and a glass for Trick — she said, "Want me to pour it for you?"

"I can do it," Trick said, and she left.

Young studied Trick for a moment, then said, "I've noticed you've been drinking your beer out of a glass lately."

"I've always drunk it out of a glass."

"Bullshit. Back when you used to drink the beer of the common man, you didn't need a glass."

Trick nodded at the bottle in Young's hand. "That stuff you drink you could drink out of an eavestrough, it wouldn't make any difference."

"But now that you drink that yuppie European shit, you have to have a glass."

"I *like* it out of a glass. It's more flavourful."

"It's more *flavourful*!" Young lisped.

"Fuck you."

Young laughed. "So tell me about Miss Leventhorpe. I want to know all about her."

Trick shrugged his left shoulder. "I like her. She's straightforward."

"What's her personality like?"

"She's nice. And she's strong as an ox."

"You told me that yesterday. What else?"

"She's got tattoos."

"Tattoos of what?"

"One of Dale Earnhardt on her — let's see — her right arm. Like a portrait. The Winston Cup on her left arm. Chevy emblem on her ankle."

"What about the small of her back?"

"Two checkered flags, crossed at the staves."

"Nice. What about her breasts?"

"Nope, nothing on her breasts."

They drank for a while.

"So," Trick said, "your turn. What happened at the voodoo store? You went this afternoon, right?"

"Yeah, well, I talked to the owner —"

"Hey, Artie!" a woman called. She was sitting two tables over, wearing a cowboy hat and a tight white sweater.

Trick turned towards her. "Hey yourself," he said.

Young said, "Friend of yours?"

"Not really. Just someone I had a conversation with."

"Oh, really. Where was I?"

"Beats me. Must have been when you were in the Bahamas. If memory serves, we talked about cats. Or, rather, she talked about cats."

"You came here by yourself?"

"I am not completely dependent on you."

Young nodded and lit a cigarette. "How'd you get here?"

"Taxi. Boum-Boum picked me up."

"Who pushed you when you got here?'

"I had my automated."

"You brought that big mother in here?"

"It's no trouble for Boum-Boum. He had the van with the lift." Trick looked at Young. "I have to be able to manage without you, you know."

They sat in silence until Priam Harvey wandered over to their table and sat down.

Trick said, "Mr. Harvey, do you know what your son's middle name was?"

Harvey scrutinized Trick's face. "I wasn't aware that he had one."

"He did: Harvey."

"Are you serious?"

"I am."

Harvey shook his head slowly. "I don't know what to say about that."

Young said, "Tell Mr. Harvey about the coins."

"It's probably nothing."

164   *J.D. Carpenter*

"Tell him, for fucksake."

Trick looked at Harvey. "I added up the coins that were in the saxophone case at the murder scene."

"Yes?"

"Well, I don't know if there's any significance, but they totalled seventy-four cents."

Harvey tilted his head.

Young said, "What?"

"'74 Miles Away,'" Harvey said.

"What is?"

"It's the title of a Cannonball Adderley tune. '74 Miles Away.'"

"Who the fuck's Cannonball Adderley?"

"Alto sax player. Very big about thirty years ago. His quintet actually had a hit on the pop charts. 'Mercy, Mercy, Mercy.' Made it to number eleven in '67, I think it was. But a real jazz man nonetheless."

Behind Young a man's voice said, "Which one of you's Artie?"

Trick and Harvey looked up. Young twisted in his chair. The voice belonged to a tall, skinny man standing a few feet away. He had spiked blue hair, a muscle shirt, and tattoos down his arms.

Trick said, "That would be me."

The man said, "You stay away from my girl. Nobody talks to Kelly Ann without I say they can, least of all a cripple. You understand me?"

"Spider, don't," the woman in the cowboy hat said, pulling at his arm.

"You understand me?" he repeated.

"Go fuck yourself," Trick said.

As the man dove across the table at Trick, Young reached out and caught the cuff of his jeans. The man slid through the grove of bottles and glasses and into Trick's lap with such force that the wheelchair — its brakes locked — was knocked over on its back, spilling Trick onto the floor. Young, still hanging onto the man's cuff, was pulled backwards and fell on the table, which collapsed, splay-legged, like a poleaxed steer. He rolled onto his hands and knees and crawled after the man, who was punching Trick in the face. The woman in the cowboy hat leaped onto the man's back and began screaming, "No, Spider, no!" Young pushed the woman aside and threw his bulk across the man's shoulders. He locked the blue head in the crook of his arm and levered with his right knee at the base of the man's spine. Trick, on his back, blood gleaming against his black cheek, shouted, "Bring him here! Give me a shot at him!" Young was dragging the man towards Trick when Dexter appeared. "Let him go!" he yelled. Young cranked the blue head one more notch — the man's back bent like a bow — released the headlock, rested his weight on his left arm, grasped the man's head like a volleyball with his right hand, and bounced it off the floor.

"Get out of here, Sarge," Dexter said. "The both of you."

Young, his ears filled with his own panting, struggled to his feet. He righted the wheelchair and picked Trick up like a rag doll. From his arms Trick shouted, "Show me his face, Dexter! Show me his face!"

Dexter rolled the groaning man onto his back. His mouth and chin were red with blood, bubbles forming in his nostrils and between his lips, and his nose was flat.

"How do you like it now, motherfucker?" Trick said.

Young deposited Trick in his wheelchair and pushed him quickly towards the door. As they passed the bar, Harvey, who had retreated to his stool during the melee, said, "Enjoy the rest of your evening, boys."

Wednesday, November 21

As Young walked down the hall to his aunt's room, two of the Alzheimer's ladies were shuffling towards him, arm in arm like schoolgirls. When they saw him they stopped. One of them reached a shaking hand towards him, touched his wrist, smiled up at him, and said, "You're my boyfriend." Then her eyes grew frightened, she clutched his sleeve, and in a barely audible voice she said, "I can't find my lunch money. Teacher will be angry." The other woman began to sob. She was the one, Young remembered, who had been waiting forty years for her husband to come home from work.

Aunt Gladys was sitting alone in the loveseat watching *Jeopardy*. "I have a list of chores for you, Nephew. I hope you don't mind."

"What, water your plants?"

"Well, yes, I need you to do that, of course, but I also need you to wash my glasses and trim my fingernails. I know it's a bother, but the girls are so busy I hate to ask them. Oh, and I need you to fill my flask and straighten the blinds."

Young looked at the blinds. "What's wrong with them?"

"They're not even. The one on the left is lower than the one on the right —"

"Maybe a quarter of an inch, Aunty."

"— and they're not tilted at the same angle. I want you to turn that twisty thing."

Young pulled three cans of Labatt Blue from the pockets of his windbreaker and set them on the coffee table. "Where's Petergay?"

"One of the girls took her for her walk. Now, if you don't mind …"

Young went to the windows and adjusted the blinds. When he had them the way she wanted, Gladys said, "Thank you, dear, now please open my closet door so I can see inside."

Young opened the door, and Gladys craned her neck towards it.

"Are there any hangers with nothing on them?"

Young did a quick search. "Yeah, a few."

"Wire or plastic?"

Young removed them and held them up for her to see. "One plastic, three wire."

"Throw the wire ones away, and hang my white crepe pants on the plastic one."

"Your what?"

"My white crepe pants. They're on the same hanger as the navy crepe pants."

"These ones?"

"Those aren't crepe, dear, those are joggers."

A few minutes later, Young was in Gladys's bathroom filling her flask from a litre bottle of Appleton Gold.

"I hope you don't think I drink too much," she called. "It seems every time you visit I need you to do that."

"I wish I had a funnel."

"Well, buy one, I'll pay for it."

"Half of it's going down the sink."

"Well, be more careful!"

"Just kidding."

He returned to the main room.

"Make sure the top's not on too tight."

"It's not." He let her test it, then placed the flask in the top drawer of her bedside table.

She turned her attention back to the television. "I hope you don't think badly of me, but a warm toddy helps me sleep. Does my breath smell?"

"No, Aunty."

"Because I can't brush my teeth very well. Would you bring in some Listerine next time you come?"

"Yes."

"It seems like ages since I've seen you."

"I know, I'm sorry, I've been busy."

"Tell me about Florida. Did you win any money on your horse races?"

"I didn't go."

With some effort, she turned her head to look at him, but before she could speak the door to the room swung open and Petergay appeared — small, bird-like, leaning on the arm of an immense attendant. The attendant said, "Gladys, please back me up on this. Petergay not only won't use her walker, she won't use her cane! She's going to fall down and break her crown."

Petergay, who was watching the progress of her feet, said, "Just steer me to the couch and spare me the sermon. Have you got the TV on, Glad? It's almost time for *Coronation Street*." She looked up and saw Young. "Well, look who's here. How was Florida?"

"He didn't go," Gladys said, "and I know why. He stayed to help his friend."

"The one what lost his child?"

"That's right. Now come and sit with me and we'll pull this quilt up over our knees. Nephew brought us a refreshment."

The attendant backed Petergay towards the loveseat, then lowered her until she was sitting. Petergay sighed and said, "Thank you, whatever your name is, now please let go of me."

The attendant straightened up and put her fists on her hips. "My name is Melissa, as you very well know. Not only are you a stubborn old woman, but you're rude, too. You very well know what my name is." She marched out of the room and closed the door with more force than necessary.

"Why should I know her name?" Petergay said.

"She has sweet little hands," Gladys said, "for such a big woman."

Petergay said, "Is one of those for me?"

Young snapped the tab on a can of Blue. "I'll get the cups," he said. When he had retrieved the plastic cups from his aunt's drawer and poured some beer into each and placed them in front of the women, he said, "Petergay, remember you told me about your grandson? The one in Millhaven?"

Petergay held her cup to her lips with both hands and tipped her head back slightly. She gulped loudly as she drank. After she returned the cup to the coffee table, she emitted a long muffled belch. "Bad as I am with names," she said, "I phoned my daughter and she reminded me of it. Claude Johnson." She belched again. "I wanted to have it ready for when you come back to ask me for it." She belched a third time, a tiny one. "Anything you need to know 'bout black magic, he know the answer. What I don't know is if he be willin' to talk to you. He not very friendly at the best of times, not even with my daughter, and I expect he have even less motivation in talkin' to police."

"I'm not police anymore, I'm an investigative —"

"Oh, you police, all right."

Young nodded. "Can I tell him you sent me?"

"No, thank you. He too dangerous for that. Just make sure you tell him the murder you tryin' to solve be a *black* man's murder. That might gain you some ground." She turned her attention to the TV screen. "Now hush. Me and Glad gots to watch our show."

When Young arrived at McCully's it wasn't quite happy hour, and only one stool at the bar was occupied. The occupant was Priam Harvey.

"Afternoon, Mr. Harvey," Young said, as he settled in beside him.

"Afternoon," Harvey said.

Young glanced up at the TVs above the bar, one of which showed a talking head in front of a racetrack backdrop. "How you doing?"

Harvey rapped his knuckles on the bar. "I made a few ill-advised wagers, but then I got lucky on the feature. Six bills."

"Very nice. Who was the unfortunate donor?"

"Ringo."

"Shame on you. Man has a family."

"Then he should know better than to make book with a shark like me."

Two hours later, Young and Harvey were still sitting at the bar, all the other stools were occupied, and the air was full of smoke and laughter. The two men had discussed hockey, politics, pickup trucks, where to get the best sausages in the city, the previous night's fight with the blue-haired man, the extent of Trick's injuries ("Bloody nose, that's all," Young said), Louis Armstrong, and dogs. At one point, Harvey said, "Oh, I almost forgot," reached into his suit coat pocket, and extracted a copy of his son's CD. "At long last," he said, and presented it to Young with a flourish. "*Goombay Bop*. The Talmadge Cooper Quintet. With my compliments."

"Thank you," said Young, studying the cover. "I'll look forward to this."

Dexter passed their way behind the bar, and Young said, "Dexter, do you know how to make a Duck Fart?"

Dexter pursed his lips in thought. "Squeeze it?"

Young shook his head. "Wrong kind of duck. I'm talking about a drink me and Mr. Harvey discovered in the Bahamas."

"Never heard of it. What's in it?"

"Equal parts Kahlua, Bailey's, Crown Royal. Served over ice in a glass the size of a cereal bowl."

Dexter's eyebrows rose. "Expensive. I make that up for you with just one ounce of each, and it's like nine dollars."

"Right, and to do it properly — to make a meal of it — it should be at least two ounces of each."

Dexter took his *Mr. Boston: Official Bartender's and Party Guide* out from under the bar and flipped through it. "It's not in here."

"Trust me," Young said, "it's a real drink. Just because it's not in there don't mean jack shit."

Dexter leaned towards Young. "Tell you what," he said in a low tone. "I'll make it with two ounces of each, and it'll cost you ten bucks. But this is a one-time-only offer, Sarge, and if you ever tell anyone, especially the boss, I'll deny it."

"I won't breathe a word."

"You, too, Mr. Harvey."

"My lips are sealed."

"I suppose you want one, too."

"No, thanks. I prefer my own poison."

Dexter scooped ice into a large glass.

Young lit a cigarette.

Harvey slid off his stool and headed towards the men's room.

Young said, "Jessy off tonight?"

Dexter filled a shot glass with Bailey's Irish Cream and upended it into the glass. "She's always off on Wednesdays, you know that."

At the retirement party, the Buddy Drown Trio played "In the Mood," "Mood Indigo," "Ain't Misbehavin'," "Embraceable You," "I Get a Kick Out of You," "Take Five," "Dear Lord," "Nancy with the Laughing Face," "Smoke Gets in Your Eyes," "Straight, No Chaser," "Take the 'A' Train," "Hello, Dolly!," "Auld Lang Syne," and "For He's a Jolly Good Fellow." At 11:30, after one encore — "In a Sentimental Mood" — Drown leaned into the microphone and said, "That's it, folks. We had a great time. Enjoy your retirement, Stan! You guys make sure he gets home okay. Good night!" The crowd chant-ed, "More! More! More!" Drown's drummer and bassist were surprised that he refused to do a second encore, and further surprised when he declined to join them for a drink. Drown could always be counted on for a drink and a few stories about the good old days when he'd rubbed shoulders with Miles and Dizzy and Bird. But not tonight. He told them he had to run, hurried out to his aging Grand Am, locked his sax in the trunk, drove up Sherbourne and east on Bloor, crossed the viaduct, and parked on a side street north of Danforth Avenue, a block from the Black Swan.

Peter Georgiadis was sitting at a small table in the corner. There were two bottles of beer in front of him, one full and one nearly empty. "You're late."

Drown could tell he was drunk. "I'm here now," he said. He pulled out a chair and sat down. "When we talked on the phone, you mentioned a visitor. Tell me about this visitor."

"He's a private eye." Georgiadis jammed his thick fingers into his shirt pocket and produced Young's business card. "Huge man. Big as a fucking house."

Drown examined it. "May I keep this?" he asked.

Georgiadis shrugged.

Drown tucked the card into his own shirt pocket. "So what did you tell this visitor?"

Georgiadis cleared his throat. "I didn't tell him anything. I never mentioned the TTX."

"Well then," Drown said, "what's the problem?"

Georgiadis smiled, revealing the gold tooth. "No problem, unless I *do* mention the TTX."

"I don't follow."

"It's like insurance. You pay me —"

"You bastard."

Georgiadis made a mock-innocent face and held a hand to his chest. "Me? A bastard? What about you? You're a killer."

"Shh!" Drown looked around, but the few patrons at the bar were absorbed in a hockey game on the big-screen TV. He regarded Georgiadis. "How much do you want?"

"Oh, how's a grand sound?"

Drown nodded slowly. "I guess I can —"

"Per month. After a few months, we'll talk again."

Drown stood up. "Okay. I'll make sure you get it."

"Aren't you going to have a drink? I haven't finished my beer."

"No, I have to go."

"One drink. As a gesture of good faith, I'll buy."

Drown paused. "All right. One beer."

"Good man. No hard feelings, I hope. Strictly business. Whenever opportunity knocks, I open the door."

"I understand. Just don't bleed me dry."

"I'll just bleed you a little bit, how's that?"

Twenty minutes later they left the bar. On the street, Georgiadis put his arm around Drown's shoulders. "You know," he laughed, "for a killer you're not such a bad guy."

Drown said, "How did you know I was in the same business, as you put it, as the dead man?"

Georgiadis squeezed his shoulder. "Once I knew your name, I asked around. You're famous! You know, I play a little myself. Guitar, mandolin —"

"But you didn't mention my name to this private eye?"

"No, no, I assure you." Georgiadis stopped in front of a subway entrance. "This is where we say goodbye, my friend. Now remember," he laughed, wagging a finger in Drown's face, "in future, be very, very careful where you use your credit card!"

Drown said, "I'm taking the subway, too."

Georgiadis threw his arms in the air. "It's kismet!"

As they passed through the turnstile, Drown kept his head down. They descended the stairs side by side, Georgiadis singing something in Greek. The station was empty except for a homeless man asleep on a bench. Drown and Georgiadis stood a few feet from the yellow warning strip at the edge of the platform. Georgiadis had smuggled a bottle of beer out of the bar and drank from it. Drown heard the noise of a train approaching. He stepped away from Georgiadis and said, "How far do you go?"

Georgiadis stopped singing. "Woodbine. What about you?"

The train emerged from the tunnel and entered the station. As the shrieking of the brakes began, Drown stepped towards Georgiadis and offered his hand. "Well, goodbye!" he shouted over the din.

Georgiadis smiled, moved the bottle of beer to his left hand, and extended his right. "But aren't you coming, too?" he shouted back.

Without taking Georgiadis's hand, Drown took one step sideways and, palms outward, double-straight-armed Georgiadis at the shoulders. Georgiadis staggered backwards, arms windmilling, eyes wide, beer bottle arcing upward into the darkness. He disappeared beyond the edge of the platform just before the train swept by. Drown turned and, as he jumped back up the stairs, almost collided with a young couple hurrying down from the street. "Hey, asshole!" the boy shouted, and spun to go after him, but the girl pulled him by the hand, saying, "Cody, come on, we'll miss the train!"

Young knocked several times before he heard footsteps approaching.

A voice whispered through the door, "Who is it?"

"It's me."

There was a brief silence. "You've got some nerve, big guy."

"Let me in."

"I haven't seen you in months, and now you think you can just —"

"What do you mean, I see you all the time at the bar."

"At the bar! I'm talking about one-on-one — like a date? Do you even know what a date is?"

Young laughed through the door. "I don't do dates." He paused, then said, "I've got something for you."

"Yeah, I'll bet you do."

"I do."

"Are you drunk?"

"I had a couple, but I'm not drunk."

"It's late, I was in bed."

"Sorry. Did I wake you?"

"I was watching Leno. What have you got for me?"

"I can't tell you, but I'll give you a clue: it's about the size and shape of a submarine sandwich."

Young heard her snort. "And probably just as soft."

"Well, we can fix that, can't we? You've still got my blue pills, don't you?"

"They're probably expired by now!"

"Aw, come on, Jessy —"

"Besides which, they're not good for you. They're bad for your heart."

"Not if I just take a half."

"You get all red in the face."

"Come on, let me in."

"No, I told you, I was already in bed."

"I'll read you a bedtime story."

"No, fuck off. Go away."

"I'm not leaving. I'll make noise and wake up the people downstairs — the whatchamacallits, the Hungarians."

"They're Ukrainians, and if you wake them up, I'll kill you."

Young laughed again. "I'm not leaving till you let me in."

He heard her sigh through the door. "All right, but only for a few minutes." She unbolted the door and opened it. Her red hair was uncombed. Her green eyes were tired. "This is just a visit, mister. No funny business."

Young said, "Got anything to drink?"

Thursday, November 22

"You've got a call!" Stella yelled from her desk in the reception area. "It's Trick!"

It was ten o'clock in the morning, and Young was sitting at his desk eating Grape-Nuts. He kept a carton of milk and a few other essentials — a loaf of bread, a jar of pickles, packages of mortadella and provolone, a six-pack of Blue — in the mini-fridge beside his filing cabinet. The puppy was lying at his feet, sucking on an empty. "How you doing? How's the old schnozzola?"

"I'm fine," Trick said, "healing nicely. But listen, the other night just before the fight, you were about to tell me what happened at the voodoo store."

Young ladled a spoonful of Grape-Nuts into his mouth. "Yeah, well, I talked to the owner for a while —"

"Peter Georgiadis?"

"That's right. Got him talking about TTX. Flashed

178   J.D. *Carpenter*

some money in front of his nose, and he went for it like fish to frog."

"He sold you some?"

"He did indeed. I dropped it off for analysis yesterday morning, and the lab called me a few minutes ago. It's the real deal." He took another spoonful of cereal. "So there's a very strong chance he was the source of the TTX that killed Tal Cooper. Only voodoo store in town, right?"

"Did Georgiadis mention anybody else who bought some?"

"Obvious next question, right? I asked him point-blank, and he insisted I was the only one."

"So you don't have a name?"

Young loaded his spoon again. "That's what I'm saying, but now that I know the powder's for real, I'm going to pay him another visit this afternoon, squeeze him a little harder, see what I get."

Trick grunted softly. "Won't matter how hard you squeeze."

The spoon stopped in mid-passage. "Why not?"

"He's dead."

"Georgiadis?"

"Last night about midnight. That's why I'm calling."

"What happened?"

"Run over by an eastbound subway at Broadview Station. According to the subway driver, he was pushed."

"No shit." Young's spoon completed its journey. He chewed and swallowed. "Any other witnesses?"

"Homeless guy sitting on a bench. Two kids who say the killer practically ran them over running up the stairs."

"So we should be able to get a description. How'd you get all this?"

"Urmson called me half an hour ago. When he got the Suspicious Death report and then found out the dead guy ran a voodoo store, he thought we should know about it. I guess he tried to get you at home, but you were already gone. Doesn't he have your office number?"

"Probably lost it."

"Anyway, he called me. I figure whoever bought the powder caught wind that we were snooping around, so he made sure Georgiadis couldn't talk."

"That or Georgiadis tried some blackmail and it didn't go over very well."

"Urmson's all excited, wants you involved. That's another reason I'm calling. If you want a word with the witnesses, Urmson's got them all coming in to Homicide at eleven o'clock this morning."

Young lowered his cereal bowl to the floor. "I'll be there."

"You sure this is kosher?" Young asked Big Urmson an hour later as he shook off his windbreaker. "Have you let your own boys at them?"

"I will when you're done. They're waiting for you."

"They're not all together, are they?"

Big Urmson chuckled. "Come on, Sarge, I wasn't born yesterday. Homeless guy's in number three, the kids are in five, subway driver's in six."

Young nodded. "I'll do them in that order. I won't be long."

"Share the wealth, right, Sarge?"

"Of course, Urmson. And Urmson, will you please for fucksake stop calling me Sarge. I'm retired, remember? I'm not your sergeant anymore."

Shortly after noon Young stuck his head into Big Urmson's office. "All done. You can send in the troops now."

Big Urmson stood up. His desk was littered with Burger King wrappers, and as he cleared them away a telephone was revealed, as well as framed photos of Staff Inspector Bateman's buck-toothed daughter and an elderly couple standing in front of a motorhome, a paperweight in the shape of an apple, a pencil sharpener in the shape of a duck, and a file folder labelled *Georgiadis*. "How'd it go?"

"Good. We're looking for a Caucasian male, late forties or early fifties, stocky build, slightly under average height, five-foot-eight or thereabouts, two hundred pounds, bald as a baby, reddish complexion, long grey overcoat."

Big Urmson smiled. "Sounds like the witnesses were happy to do their civic duty."

"Not really. I had to get the homeless guy a week's lodging at the Good Shepherd, and the two kids want front row seats for the trial. The subway driver didn't need any persuasion — just counselling. This was his third death in five years of driving. The other two were suicides, but this one was definitely a murder. He saw it plain as day. Said it looked like the two men were shaking hands, then the one guy shoved the other guy off the platform right in front of the train."

"Since I'm coming back Sunday morning, I figure I'll leave the puppy here at my place, save her from getting used to your place and then having to come right back and get used to my place again, and you can stop by after school tomorrow afternoon and tomorrow evening and Saturday morning and Saturday evening and Sunday morning and let her out and feed her and make sure she's got enough water."

"I'll take her for a walk, too."

"Even better. I gave you a key, right?"

"Yup, I already put it on my chain."

"And you know where the leash is and the bag of food and her treats?"

"No problem. Same wage as last time?"

"What?"

"Same wage as last time. Five bucks a day."

"Fine. Let me talk to your mother."

"She's gone to bed already."

"All right, well, give her a kiss for me when you see her in the morning and tell her I'll see her at the track on Sunday. Will you do that for me?"

"She'll be gone before I get up."

"Well, hell, when you do see her give her a kiss and tell her I'll see her Sunday. Will you do that for me?"

"No problem. And this one's on me."

"You're not going to charge me for giving your mother a kiss?"

"That's right, it's a freebie."

"Are you serious?"

"Of course not. You need to chill, Poppy."

Before going to bed, Young let the puppy out. He had picked up his plane ticket at the travel agency; packed a small suitcase containing three shirts, three pairs of socks and underwear, and extra pairs of slacks and shoes; arranged for an airport limo to pick him up at 6:00 a.m. Friday; and phoned Trick to explain that his flight would leave at 8:20 a.m., he would be in New York before lunch, visit Juilliard, rent a car, drive down to Monroe, New Jersey, to find Amy Feldman's parents, maybe catch a card of standardbred racing at the Meadowlands, find somewhere to sleep, drive back into New York City Saturday morning, snoop around some more, go to an art gallery to see some paintings of race-horses that Priam Harvey told him he should see, attend the afternoon thoroughbred card at Belmont, do some bar-hopping Saturday evening, find somewhere to sleep, drive out to the airport Sunday morning, return the car to the rental agency, fly home on the 9:05 flight, and be back in Toronto in time to join him and Debi for lunch at Caledonia Downs. Then he bid Trick good night, hung up, poured himself a nightcap, chain-smoked two cigarettes on his balcony, let the puppy back in, brushed his teeth, and went to bed.

Buddy Drown drove his Grand Am along the curving streets of Town & Country Estates, the suburb he and Ursula called home. It was almost midnight, and the streets were lamplit and deserted. He turned into the staff parking lot of Town & Country Elementary School, stopped the car, turned off the engine, opened the glove box, and removed his cellphone. He dialed and gazed idly at the darkened windows of the school until a voice answered. "It's me," Buddy said. "I've got something for you. Tomorrow night. Now listen carefully, I'm going to tell you where to meet me…. Tomorrow night, that's right…. You're what? Well, get yourself un-busy, Otis, because what I have in mind will take you no more than half an hour and will be worth every minute of your time. I'm talking serious junk…. Yes, it's a job, of course it's a job…. No, no, the reason *I* won't do it is not because it's dangerous, it's because I lack the skills required to do it, skills which you, through some accident of birth, happen to possess…. What's that? My fucking Jesus, Otis, how many times do I have to tell you? Tomorrow night! I'll meet you at eleven o'clock *tomorrow night* in front of the Wheat Sheaf. And make sure you're straight when you show up, because you obviously aren't right now."

Friday, November 23

Young's flight to New York City was short and sweet. The seat beside him was empty, so he was able to sprawl a bit; he read the sports pages and dozed until the plane landed at JFK. He waited patiently at the baggage carousel for his suitcase, then hurried out of Arrivals, flagged a taxi, and told the driver to take him to the Juilliard School. Twenty minutes later, the yellow cabs were swarming around each other like wasps as they raced up the Henry Hudson Parkway. Young's cabby drove so fast that Young clutched his suitcase to his chest and closed his eyes whenever he saw a collision taking shape. The cab screeched to a stop at the Lincoln Center Plaza, and Young found himself disgorged and trembling on the sidewalk.

The Juilliard School was large, square, and impersonal. Tiny Chinese girls carrying enormous instrument cases struggled across the lobby like ants bearing loads several times their size. Young waited for the uniformed woman sitting at the reception desk to acknowledge him. Finally, without looking up from her magazine, she said, "Uh-huh?" and Young said, "I'm here to see Gary Garvin. I have an appointment for eleven o'clock." The woman glanced at a clipboard by her elbow and said, "Through the turnstile, second floor, 226. Here's you a badge."

Gary Garvin greeted Young at the door to his office. "Come in, come in!" he said. "How nice to meet a Canadian. I love Canadians!" Garvin was a small, balding man in his fifties. He wore a magenta bow tie, a white shirt, and a magenta blazer over grey slacks. He motioned Young to a chair in front of a large, busy desk and took a seat behind it. Music played softly in the background. "Now," Garvin said, clasping his hands in front of him, "I could begin with my usual patter, you know, 'The Juilliard School, originally the Institute of Musical Art, has been in its present location since 1969, blah, blah, blah, and all about Augustus Juilliard, and how he was a wealthy wine merchant —"

"That's *Kind of Blue*, isn't it?" Young asked.

Garvin appeared startled, then said, "Why yes, yes it is. Too loud? I can turn it down." He swivelled towards a console behind him.

"No, no, it's just that I recognize it."

"Well, I didn't realize I was dealing with an afi-cio*nado*!" He patted his hands together, and Young wondered if he was being mocked. "All aspiring jazz musicians, I'm sure you'll agree, should study *Kind of Blue*. The ideas in it are so wonderful. And the playing, well, my goodness, Mr. Davis's trumpet in 'So What,' as I like to tell my friends, is like a good riesling — crisp and tart, yet fruity! Lip-smacking. And then Mr. Coltrane comes in honking and braying like a donkey.

And Mr. Adderley sounds like the Pied Piper, all flutey, leading the children through the forest." He chuckled. "Oh, and Mr. Evans's piano? *So* sombre. He sounds like he's been locked up in an attic for twenty years! And then Mr. Chambers's bass line takes them all away — like a group of mental patients off to their beds!"

Young said, "Yes, well, the reason I'm here —"

"Reputedly," Garvin said, waggling a finger, "reputedly, it's great music if you're in the mood for love." Garvin giggled. "Or so I've been told." He gathered himself. "But you're not here to talk about Mr. Davis, are you? You're here to talk about Mr. Talmadge Cooper."

An hour later Young climbed into another taxi and told the driver to take him to a car rental agency. Soon he was entering the Lincoln Tunnel in a forest green Mustang, leaving behind him the chaos of New York: the blaring horns, the rat-a-tat-tat of rock drills, an argument between a caned and limping East Indian man and a black cabby who was trying to reverse onto 5th Avenue — "I said sorry, what else you want from me!" — the dog walkers, women in furs, homeless vets with their tours of duty painstakingly printed on placards, and the massive work force — cellphoned and surgically masked — striding down the sidewalks, still striving, still New Yorkers despite the horror ten weeks earlier.

As Young headed south on I95, he thought over Gary Garvin's last few comments. "Your Mr. Cooper was a very, *very* promising musician. He had more talent than we'd seen come through here in years. But he developed a taste for the good life. Rumour had it he was into cocaine, and that poor girl, well, he ruined her. There's no other way to put it. She was so sweet, she had so much potential herself, but by the time he was done with her, well, she was done with herself. Sucked the juice out of her, then cast her adrift. Pardon the mixed

metaphor. And then it was heroin for her, or so I've
heard. If you find her parents, Mr. Young, be gentle with
them. And if you find Miss Feldman herself, and if she
still has her faculties intact — as Mr. Salinger might say
— please remember me to her."

The attendant at the gatehouse of the Regency at Monroe
Adult Active Community in Monroe, New Jersey, was fat
and affable. "The Feldmans? Yes, sir, number twenty-nine
Arnold Palmer Place, third left off the main drag. Be careful of the traffic calmers, sir, they're probably more'n
you're used to."

As Young moved the Mustang slowly forward, he
saw before him a completely fabricated town. The
streets and houses were spotless and unvaried, the rises
and dips in the landscape were manufactured, the twen-
ty-foot maples in front of every fourth house were
implanted, the lawns had been trucked in and unrolled,
and the mailboxes were regimentally alike — white
with black lettering, an American flag decal in the
upper-right-hand corner. He thought of *Pleasantville*,
and he thought of *The Truman Show*. Four small bill-
boards — two on the left, two on the right — greeted
him as he neared the first intersection: 'Regency at
Monroe: Where Neighbours Turn Into Friends'; 'Tennis
Anyone?'; 'Are You Ready To Relax?'; 'Get Into the
Swing!' Checking the street signs, Young discovered
that he was on Billie Jean King Parkway. He crawled
past Jack Nicklaus Lane, mounted and descended a
speed bump the size of an ocean swell, passed McEnroe
Court, paused at a golf cart crossing, mounted and
descended a second speed bump, and turned left into
Arnold Palmer Place. He parked on the street in front
of number twenty-nine.

At the front door, he pressed the bell and waited. In time, the door opened and a small, grey, sixties-ish man stood there, a rolled magazine in one hand. He looked up at Young anxiously. "Yes?" he said.

"Dr. Feldman?" Young said.

"Yes, I'm Dr. Feldman. If it's a problem with your teeth, I'm sorry, but I'm retired. The best I can do is refer you to Dr. Jacobs, who bought my business. If you'll wait a moment, I'll get his card for you."

"No, it's not about my teeth. My name is Campbell Young, I'm an investigative consultant in Toronto." He produced his wallet and handed Dr. Feldman one of his business cards. "I'm working a murder up there, and I've come down here to follow a few leads."

"Toronto? But that's in Canada. Why do you want to talk to me?"

"I need to talk to you about your daughter."

Dr. Feldman raised his chin. "My daughter? My daughter's dead."

Young paused. "I'm very sorry to hear that, sir. I didn't know."

"Why do you want to talk about Amy?"

"A man named Talmadge Cooper was murdered in Toronto, and I'm —"

"Murdered? He's dead?" He smacked the magazine against his thigh. "Well, that's good news." He turned into the house. "Miriam!" he called. "He's dead! The bastard's dead!"

As Dr. Feldman steered Young by the elbow into the living room, Mrs. Feldman emerged from the kitchen, a tea towel in one hand, a large glass ashtray in the other, and a cigarette dangling from her lips. She was even shorter than her husband, but overweight; her face was white, and there were dark circles under her eyes. She placed the ashtray on an end table, removed the cigarette from her mouth, and said, "How did he die?"

Dr. Feldman said, "Please sit down. I'm sorry, I've forgotten —"

"Young."

"Mr. Young."

"How did he die?" Mrs. Feldman repeated.

Young faced her. "He was poisoned."

She nodded slowly and sat down on a brown settee. Her husband sat down beside her and together they listened as Young, who had lowered himself into a wing chair barely wide enough to contain him, summarized the Talmadge Cooper murder case and his investigation so far. After ten minutes, Mrs. Feldman said, "Would you like some coffee?" and disappeared into the kitchen.

Dr. Feldman said, "From what you've told us, Mr. Young, it would seem that his murder has nothing to do with us, or with Amy."

"When I decided to come here," Young said slowly, "I didn't know Amy was dead. My partner spoke to me on Tuesday and told me he'd been talking to you, and that as far as you knew, Amy was still alive."

"Ah yes, Arthur Trick, was it? I remember the conversation; however, a lot has happened in the interim. Amy's body was found Wednesday, and she was buried Thursday. Yesterday. We Jews dispense with our dead as quickly as we can, Mr. Young." His gaze surveyed the living room. "You would never know it from looking around this house that someone had just died."

Young said, "I knew there were problems with drugs, and I thought if I could talk to her, she might be able to tell me if Cooper had any enemies, drug dealers, for example, who he might have owed money to. Maybe" — and here Young glanced towards the kitchen

— "this is a good time for me to ask about the circumstances of Amy's death."

Dr. Feldman bowed his head and ran his fingers through his hair. Then he looked up at Young. "She was living with us. She and the baby. One morning about three months ago, she asked to borrow the car to drive into the city. She said she had an interview for a job. She had us believing she was clean and sober and that she was attending her meetings and maintaining regular phone contact with her sponsor. So I gave her the keys, she drove away, and, well ... she basically vanished." He paused, leaned forward, and ran his fingers through his hair again. "After not hearing from her for two days, we reported her missing. We provided photographs of her and a description of the car. Six weeks later, they found the car in front of an apartment building on the upper west side — judging from the tickets under the wipers it had been there for almost a month — and then on Wednesday we got a call from the police saying her body had been found in the Pine Barrens."

"The Pine Barrens?"

"It's a state park in central New Jersey, about thirty miles from here. It's where the Mafia dumps its bodies, so they say, and it's where Amy's body was dumped. She died of a heroin overdose, most likely in New York. She was a tiny thing — like her mother was, once upon a time — and somebody stuffed her into a garbage bag and left her on a riverbank near a place called Jenkins Neck."

Mrs. Feldman stuck her head back into the living room. "How do you like your coffee?"

"Just sugar, thanks," Young said. When they were alone again, he said, "Where's the little girl?"

Dr. Feldman tilted his head towards the hallway. "She's in her bed, blissfully unaware of the tragedies that surround her. We'd just put her down for her nap when you arrived."

Young looked around the living room. There was an upright piano against one wall, with a framed photograph on top. He stood up and walked over to it. The girl in the photo had long red hair. She was wearing a white summer dress and standing in a garden. Young peered closer. She was slim and serious.

Mrs. Feldman entered the living room, smoke curling from the cigarette in her mouth, and placed three steaming mugs on the coffee table. She walked over to where Young was standing and took the cigarette from her lips. "That was taken on her eighteenth birthday," she said softly. "October 31, 1997. She was two months into her first term at Juilliard. She was already walking the same halls as the man who would destroy her."

"A-1 Investigative Consultants, Stella speaking. How may I help you?"

"Yes, may I speak to Mr. Young, please?"

"He's not in at the moment. May I take a message?"

"This is Sears calling. I've got a package in the truck for him, but the address is his office from the looks of it."

"What kind of package?"

"It's a side-burner barbeque. The reason I'm calling is I'm guessing he'd rather have it delivered to his home than his office."

"A barbeque?"

"That's right, a side-burner barbeque."

"I'm sorry, but like I said, he's not here right now and unfortunately I won't be able to reach him till Monday."

"I understand. What general area of the city does he live in, if I may ask?"

"East York."

"No kidding. East York's on my route today, as a matter of fact, but let's see ... well, that's too bad: I won't be back in East York again till *next* Friday."

Stella thought about it for a moment, then said with a laugh, "Oh, what the hell," and recited Young's home address.

Without really thinking about it, Young found himself turning left, south, as he departed Regency at Monroe Adult Active Community. South towards the Pine Barrens. He searched in his suitcase on the seat beside him and found the CD Priam Harvey had given him two nights earlier at McCully's. He slid it into the slot in the Mustang's dashboard and for the next half-hour listened to the talent of a dead man whose short history, as it was slowly being revealed, caused Young to consider Tal Cooper not only a pampered son, a user of hard drugs, and a despoiler of women, but a fine musician as well.

By the time he reached Four Mile, New Jersey, at the top of the Pine Barrens, Young had listened to "Caribbana Man," "Blues for Bird," and "Conch Salad." He pulled into a parking lot in front of a roadhouse. Inside, the barmaid was talking about contractions to a woman drinking Corona. Sitting at the bar, a long-haired man in a headkerchief was doodling on a napkin. Young ordered a Rolling Rock and leaned against the bar, not far from the man. After a few minutes Young asked the man how far it was to Jenkins Neck.

Without looking up from his artwork, the man, who was wearing a muscle shirt and whose tattoos were in evidence, said, "Ten minutes."

Young said, "I heard a body was found down there the other day. Woman in her twenties?"

The man looked up for the first time, assessed Young, and said, "What of it?"

Young shrugged. "I heard this area is a dumping ground for the Mafia, being so close to New York and all, and I just wondered if it was a Mafia hit."

The man shook his head. "Drug addict, what I heard. Connie," he said, "that body they found down to Lester Wainwright's place, it was a drug addict, right?"

The barmaid interrupted her discourse long enough to say, "Uh-huh."

"Thought so," the man said. "Weren't no Mafia hit." He smiled at Young, snaggle-toothed, then returned to his doodling.

Young drove south on 563 towards Jenkins Neck. He listened to "Perdido" and "Freetown High Times" and failed to notice the similarity between the forests of pitch pine and scarlet oak on either side of him and the yellow pine forests of Grand Bahama Island.

Jenkins Neck had a cranberry bog in it and a canoe rental business and a convenience store. Young found Lester Wainwright's mailbox without having to ask anyone.

Wainwright lived alone in a tarnished Airstream trailer inside of which Young felt like a tinned sardine. The place was filthy — dirty dishes piled in the miniature sink, soiled clothing in a heap by the door, a row of dusty feed caps lining the top of the pullout sofa — but Young sipped gamely at the coffee he had been given.

"She were in the cedars down on the bank," Wainwright, who was lean and grizzled, told him. "M'dog found her." He nodded at an old mongrel asleep on a mat by their feet.

Young said, "I heard she was in a garbage bag."

Wainwright nodded. "Yes, sir, but one arm was flopped out, y'see, one arm was flopped out, that's how I knowed it were a person."

"What did you do?"

"I rode my bicycle down to the store and told Mrs. Buzby, and she phoned it in. Highway patrol come right quick, and a doctor come, too. I watched them lay her out on the bank. She were a blue colour, and she had scabs all up the inside of one arm, and she had one o' them drug paraphernalias stuck in her butt." He nodded again.

"Can you show me where you found her?"

Wainwright stood up. He was wearing farm overalls, but he was barefoot and shirtless. The dog roused itself from the mat.

Young followed Wainwright through the woods to a steep bank that ran down to a narrow river. The tea-coloured water was deep and fast-moving.

"Show the man, Buster," Wainwright said. "Show the man."

The dog crept halfway down the bank, sniffed the pine and cedar litter, lifted one forepaw, and barked twice.

"That's right where she were at, where Buster's at."

Young imagined her there, the girl in the photo — her red hair, her blue skin. "Anything else you can tell me?"

Wainwright thought for a moment, then said, "I don't know why they didn't just th'ow her in the river and let her get swept away. That's the Wading River, sir, and it would'a carried her all the way t' Atlan'ic City."

Young nodded. "Why do you suppose they dumped her so close to your trailer?"

Wainwright shrugged his narrow shoulders. "Blame it on me, I reckon."

* * *

The drive from Jenkins Neck to the first roadhouse he came to — in Tabernacle, New Jersey — took Young twenty minutes. He was so preoccupied by his visit with Lester Wainwright that he paid no attention to "Last Man Best Bone" and "Goombay Bop," the last two cuts on Talmadge Cooper's CD.

He ate a plate of spaghetti at the Village Pump in Tabernacle, watched a middleweight fight on the bar TV, drank six Rolling Rocks, and rebuffed the advances of a martini-drinking golfer named Neil who said, "We're all just so happy you're having a nice time in our little town, and I want you to know that you're sitting in an authentic south Jersey redneck bar." Before last call, Young escaped to the Mustang — glittering greenly in the moonlight — patted its fender, said, "Take me home, girl," and fell asleep in his clothes in a by-the-hour motel room in Red Lion, New Jersey, that came with a mirror on the ceiling but no bathroom door. At one point during the night he dreamed he was buried alive in a cigar tube–shaped Airstream trailer just large enough to contain his body. The inside of the trailer was illuminated, and he was lying on his back watching the skin of his arms turn blue.

The intruder climbed the steps from the backyard to the balcony. There was no screen door to contend with, just the kitchen door itself, and by using a palette knife and a slot screwdriver, he was able to open it. He put the tools back into the gym bag he was carrying, took out a flashlight and a Smith & Wesson .38 Special, tiptoed along the darkened hallway to the bedroom, and swung the door inward. The beam of his flashlight revealed an unmade, unoccupied bed. The intruder proceeded to the living room, attracted by the light of what turned out to be a floor lamp. A puppy yawned on the sofa. The intruder got down on his knees and determined that the lamp was connected to a plug-in timer set to come on at 6:00 p.m. and go off at 7:00 a.m. The puppy climbed down from the sofa and padded across the floor to the intruder, who was still on all fours peering at the timer, and tugged at his pant leg. Startled, the intruder jerked up and banged the back of his head against the underside of a small round table that was part of the floor lamp. He reached around and took hold of the puppy and laid her on her back. The puppy smiled and relaxed. The intruder removed a switchblade from his hip pocket, sprang it, slit the puppy's throat, cut open her abdomen, held her motionless until she was dead, and rolled her onto her stomach. Then he took eleven glass bottles from the gym bag and stood them around the carcass. He walked into the kitchen, stumbled over a dog dish, and washed his hands and the switchblade at the sink. He found a tea towel in a drawer, dried his hands and the knife with it, tossed it in the general direction of the dog dish, undid his fly, urinated on the linoleum in front of the stove, zipped up, washed his hands a second time, found another tea towel in the drawer, dried his hands again, and dropped the towel on the puddle of urine. Finally, he opened the door of the refrigerator and looked inside. When he left the apartment a few minutes later, he was carrying the gym bag with one hand and a tray of Nanaimo bars with the other.

Saturday, November 24

Jamal unlocked the front door of his grandfather's apartment. "Cujo!" he called. He was surprised the puppy wasn't there to greet him. Friday morning and again Friday afternoon, the puppy had somehow anticipated his arrival and was scratching at the inside of the door even as Jamal was inserting the key in the lock.

"Puppy!" he called, but there was no response.

He walked down the hall towards the kitchen. What caught his eye was a puddle in front of the stove with a dishtowel in the middle of it. "You're supposed to pee on the paper," he said. "You know better than that." Then he saw the dog dish upside-down near the breakfast nook and pellets of puppy chow broadcast across the floor. A jolt of fear coursed down his arms and into his hands. He hurried back down the hall and into the living room, and there, in the centre of the black and red carpet, was the puppy. "Oh, there you are," Jamal said with relief. "Still asleep, you fat thing?"

The puppy didn't move, and a second jolt travelled up Jamal's spine like a scalpel. As he rolled her onto her back, a small purple mass of entrails slid onto the carpet.

Jamal ran back along the hall towards the door. He was screaming and waving his hands in the air. He didn't remember having closed the door, but he must have. He wouldn't have left it open with the puppy running around. His hands were shaking so violently he tried three times before he could grasp the knob.

He ran down the front steps of his grandfather's building and along the sidewalk in the direction of the house he and his mother and Ant'wawn lived in. Not until later that afternoon would he ask himself whether he really had seen an arrangement of pop bottles around the puppy's body. Old glass bottles with something in them.

Young was back in New York City by mid-morning. During the drive from New Jersey, he considered catching an early flight back to Toronto, but eventually decided to stay until Sunday as planned, even though his work was done, and see the sights. He returned the Mustang to the rental agency, made a reservation at a Best Western, took a cab to the Metropolitan Museum of Art, asked directions to the French Impressionists, and looked for the racehorse paintings by Degas that Priam Harvey had recommended, but instead found himself studying *Woman with a Towel* (1894), *Woman Stepping into a Tub* (1891), *Woman Bathing in a Shallow Tub* (1885), *Woman Drying Her Arm* (1890), and *Woman Drying Her Foot* (1886). He wandered around the second floor for two hours, and the paintings he liked best were *The Raft of the Medusa* and *Execution of Lady Jane Grey*. Outside on 5th Avenue, he bought a sausage from a vendor and watched the buggy drivers feed their horses out of red plastic buckets. Another cab took him to Belmont Park, where, over the course of the afternoon, he won fifty-eight dollars, including an exactor combining horses named Mean Trick and Debby's Hero. At Ground Zero, a bearded flutist played "Amazing Grace" while Young scanned the posters of missing people. He bought an FDNY ball cap for Jamal. For supper, he ate a full rack of baby back ribs at a place called Dallas Barbeque, then stopped in at a bar called Jimmy's Corner for shots and beer and ended up having a long conversation with Jimmy himself — Jimmy Glen, who much earlier in his life had gone eight rounds with Floyd Patterson.

At ten o'clock that night, Buddy Drown took the stage at a bar on Queen Street West in Toronto. His bald dome glistened under the lights and his blue sports coat strained against the bulk of his shoulders. "Thank you, ladies and gentlemen, thank you for your warm reception. We always get a warm reception here at the Golden Rail, don't we, boys?" His sidemen nodded, grinning. "Anyway, it's a pleasure being back after, oh my gosh, it feels like about three years. Is it that long, Jack? Has it been three years?"

The owner, behind the bar, called out, "How soon they forget! It's more like *five* years!"

Among the dozen or so people comprising the audience and chuckling at the give-and-take was Priam Harvey, nattily attired in his white plantation suit.

Drown put a hand to his brow like a visor and said, "I hate to tell you this, ladies and gentlemen, but Jack's the biggest tightwad on the circuit. My salary this evening? All the bar snacks I can eat and whatever drinks you fine folks can't finish."

More polite laughter.

"All right," Drown said, with the air of an officer about to send his troops over the top, "on with the show. We're going to start the evening off with one of my personal favourites, a composition by Joe Zawinul, long-time pianist and composer for one of my all-time heroes, the late, great Cannonball Adderley. Here we go with '74 Miles Away.'" Drown licked his lips, lifted his saxophone, and half-turned to his pianist. "One. Two. One, two, three."

At eleven o'clock, Young was sitting in the legendary Village Vanguard jazz club listening to an octet that included baritone, tenor, alto, and soprano saxophones, as well as trumpet. Among other things, the band played "Freddie Freeloader" from *Kind of Blue*, which Young recognized and which prompted him to smile knowingly at the goateed and bereted man on the stool next to him, the Charles Mingus tune "Nostalgia in Times Square," and "Last Man Best Bone," which the leader of the band, the trumpeter, a short, thick, very black man in a fire-engine red sports coat, introduced by saying, "This next one, ladies and gentlemen, was written by a phenomenally gifted young musician slash composer, Talmadge Cooper, who was taken from us two weeks ago at the tender age of twenty-five. Like the man who was *my* personal inspiration, Clifford Brown, whose composition 'Minor Mood' we'll be playing in our next set and who also died an untimely and senseless death at the tender age of twenty-five, Tal Cooper's full potential will never be realized, let alone known." He turned and nodded to his bassist. "One, two, uh one, two, three, four."

Sunday, November 25

Back in Toronto, Young rode the shuttle bus from the airport to the Park 'N Fly compound, where he eventually located his truck after a lengthy search of several seemingly endless aisles of vehicles. As he drove east across the top of the city, he smoked Marlboros and sang along to "Bad to the Bone" and "Got Me Under Pressure," which were on the radio.

He had already decided to go straight to Debi's house to visit Jamal, give him the ball cap, and pick up the puppy. Then he remembered that the puppy wasn't at Debi's — as she had been when he went to the Bahamas — she was at his apartment. Debi, he surmised, would be at the track, and it being a Sunday morning, Ant'wawn would be at church. No, that was Eldridge who went to church. *Fuck*, he thought, *what's happening to my memory? I can't remember where I left the puppy, and my daughter's boyfriends*

have become a blur. All I know is I don't like the
sounds of this Ant'wawn character. More than likely
he's stoned on the sofa, and Jamal sitting beside him
watching cartoons.

With that thought in mind, Young drove to Debi's,
parked on the street, hurried up the front walk, and
rang the doorbell.

"Wheeler?" he said, when the door opened. At first
he smiled because he was glad to see her — he was
always glad to see Wheeler, her blonde pageboy, her perfect nose — but then his smile disappeared and he said,
"Why are you here? What's wrong?"

Wheeler said, "It's okay, Sarge, everybody's fine, but
there *is* a problem."

"What problem?" Young, pushing past her, looked
around. "Where's Jamal?"

"He's in his room, but don't go in yet."

"Why not? Where's Debi?"

"She's at the track. She's got a couple of horses running today, so she asked me to come over."

Young looked her up and down. "You're not in uniform. What's going on? Where's Ant'wawn?"

"I don't know. You'd have to ask Debi."

"You said there's a problem," Young said, leaning
his head into the kitchen. "What's the problem?" When
Wheeler didn't respond, he turned his attention back to
her. His gaze was drawn to her right eye — the brown
one, the serious one.

"What happened?"

"Your puppy's dead."

It hadn't crossed his mind that the puppy could be
involved in the problem. "My puppy's dead?" he said.

Wheeler nodded. "Somebody broke into your house
and ... well ... killed her."

Young twisted his head. "*What?*"

"Jamal found her when he went over there yesterday morning."

"Jamal found her?"

Wheeler nodded again. "He's a bit traumatized by the whole thing."

"I'll go in and see him."

Wheeler put her hand on his arm. "He's asleep. Let him sleep awhile longer."

Young was rocking ball to heel. "Why would somebody kill the puppy?"

Wheeler looked down. "I don't know. I sent a crew in — I hope you don't mind, but we didn't know where you were staying in New York, and because you don't carry a pager or cellphone we had no way of contacting you. Anyway, they came up empty for fingerprints. The best we got was a urine stain."

Young stared at her.

She cleared her throat and said, "Seems the guy took a piss in your kitchen."

"Mother*fuck*er!" He thought for a moment. "Can we get DNA out of piss?"

"We're checking that out. Anyway, we left the scene pretty much the way it was so you could look it over. We left a couple of pop bottles, too."

Young stopped rocking. "Pop bottles?"

Wheeler nodded solemnly. "Just like with Tal Cooper. Eleven pop bottles placed around the body of the puppy."

Young said, "Did it cross your mind that whoever murdered the puppy maybe didn't know I was away?"

Wheeler looked up at him. "Yes, it crossed my mind."

"That whoever murdered the puppy was there to murder *me*?"

He turned and walked down the hall to Jamal's room. The door was closed. He knocked quietly. There was no answer.

He turned the knob and eased the door inward. Jamal was asleep on his bed. Young stepped carefully across the clothes-strewn carpet. He eased himself down beside his grandson and patted the dark, damp curls. The boy's eyes fluttered open. "Hi, Poppy," he said, at first as glad to see his grandfather as his grandfather had been to see Wheeler. Then his face crumpled, and he said, "We shouldn't have left her at your place!"

"It's okay, honey," Young said, "it's all right. Look what I brought you. I brought you a ball cap."

Young stopped at his apartment and looked at the pop bottles and the bloodstains on the carpet. He phoned Trick and told him he'd be right there to pick him up. He took a shower and changed his shirt and underwear and socks. His mind was churning.

Trick was waiting in the lobby of his building. Young wheeled him out to the truck, lifted him into the cab, did up his seatbelt, loaded the wheelchair into the bed, and bungee-corded it to the rail.

"Sorry about your dog," Trick said, as Young squeezed in beside him.

Young nodded but didn't say anything.

There was a light snow falling, the first of the winter, and a minute after they merged onto the Don Valley Parkway a fender-bender near Lawrence Avenue slowed them almost to a halt.

"Fuck," Young said, and rabbit-punched the steering wheel with the meat of his hand.

Trick said, "Nothing for it, Camp, we're stuck. Might as well relax and enjoy the wait. Tell me about your trip. What's New York City like? Believe it or not, I've never been."

Young considered nosing his way into the middle lane. He studied his side mirror. "Noisy as hell. Everybody honks their horns all the time. People shout at each other."

"Did you go to Ground Zero?"

Young nodded. "Yeah. I wanted to pay my respects, but it didn't affect me the way I thought it would. It just made me feel kind of numb."

"Maybe it was just too awful."

Young nodded. "Maybe."

"What about the New Yorkers themselves? What did they say about it?"

"Didn't come up."

"It didn't come up? How could it not come up?"

Young inched into a small gap in the traffic beside him. "I talked to lots of people, but nobody mentioned it, so I figured I shouldn't either." A driver honked angrily at Young; Young gave him the finger and nudged the truck fully into the middle lane. "It was like if you meet somebody on the street — an acquaintance, like — and their wife's just died of cancer or something, you don't say anything because you figure they don't want to talk about it. That's what it was like."

They drove in silence for a while, then Young said, "So, you and Miss Leventhorpe still getting along?"

"Yup," Trick said. "I asked her to marry me."

Young did a double take. "You're kidding, right?"

"Yes. I'm kidding. I wouldn't impose myself on my worst enemy, let alone somebody I love."

"You *love* her?"

"Yeah, I do. I've told her so. She says, 'Ah-thuh, it wouldn't work out. I'm a white girl from Kannapolis,

North Carolina, my daddy and Dale Earnhardt went to school togethuh, and I'm a great-great-granddaugh-tuh of Confederate General Collett Leventhorpe who fought at Gettysburg. Meanwhile, you're a nigruh. It wouldn't work out.'"

By the time they got to the racetrack and parked, and by the time Young unloaded the wheelchair, loaded Trick, traversed the parking lot, paid their admission, bought their *Racing Forms*, steered Trick onto the elevator, rode up to the clubhouse, and rolled into the dining room, Debi was fit to be tied.

"Well, it's about time!" she said. "Where have you two been?" She was wearing a black and brown striped jacket made out of what appeared to be theatre plush, black slacks, and a little round hat with a veil attached. "I have to go in twenty minutes. I've got a horse to saddle in the fifth and another in the eighth."

"Easy, girl," Young said. "It wasn't our fault. We left on time."

Trick said, "The traffic messed us up."

"I've been waiting here, by myself, for over an hour," Debi said.

"I hope you went ahead and ate," Young said.

"I did, as a matter of fact."

"Aren't you going to ask about my trip? Even your uncle Artie asked about my trip."

"Your trip? What about your dog? What about *Jamal*? What about the fact you let a twelve-year-old boy go into an apartment where a killer was lurking?"

"Now, wait a minute —"

"Don't you remember what happened when he was a baby, and him and I got kidnapped, and —"

"Of course I remember —"

"— and now you let him walk into your apartment while you're working a dangerous case, and there's some crazy person out there trying to kill you! He could have been killed! Your grandson could have been killed! You can't take chances like that with other people's lives."

Young had his hands raised like a man being arrested. "I'm sorry, sweetie, I really am. I didn't know something like this was going to happen."

"Well, you should have thought about it."

"Okay, like I said, I'm sorry, but now how about you answer a question for me? How come Wheeler's at your place looking after Jamal? Where's Antsinhispants?"

Debi took a deep breath and exhaled slowly. "I'm trying to be calm here. In the first place, his name is Ant'wawn, as I've told you countless times. Second, it's none of your business where he is. And third, I think he's left me."

"Left you? When did this happen?"

"This morning. He packed his things, phoned a taxi, and left. I think he's gone back to Jamaica." Suddenly there were tears in her eyes. She dabbed under her veil with a napkin.

"What happened?"

"He got all freaked out about the puppy's death — the voodoo part of it — and he took off. He said he was afraid the voodoo was going to catch up with him." Her chin began to tremble.

"Okay," Young said, leaning over and patting her shoulder. "There, there."

"What kind of a case is this, anyways?" she sniffed. "Something about voodoo, isn't it? And a clarinet player?"

"A saxophone player."

"Did something happen to the saxophone player?"

"He was murdered. Poisoned, actually. People in the know say he was the best young saxophone player to come along in forty years."

"What about the voodoo? Wheeler said there was voodoo around the puppy."

"That was part of the ritual. Or it was supposed to look like it, to make it look authentic. But there's something fishy about the whole thing, and I'm going down to Millhaven tomorrow and visit a convict who knows all about voodoo."

"That stuff scares me."

He laid his hand on her wrist. "I know, sweetie, I know." He paused for a moment, then said, "Look, I'm sorry we were late, and I'm sorry about Ant'wawn — although maybe it's for the best — and I'm sorry about the puppy, and I'm especially sorry about Jamal finding her. I'm sorry about all of that. But now, if you don't mind, me and Trick are going over to the buffet and get something to eat, and then we're going to order some beers — you've got time for one before you go, don't you? — and then we're going to lose some money on the ponies."

That evening, Young dialed the number of Daniel Curry, his old high school football teammate and the man who had helped him decipher the Shakespearean quotations that serial killer Lawrence Woolley had left as clues in a case Young had investigated nine years earlier, the case in which Debi and Jamal had been abducted and Trick had been shot.

Daniel's wife, Alice, answered. "Hello?"

"Yes, I'm calling on behalf of the Red Garter Escort Service. May I speak to Daniel Curry, please?"

"You're calling on whose behalf?"

"The Red Garter Escort Service."

"May I ask what it's about?"

"It's just an overdue bill, ma'am."

Alice covered the receiver with her palm, and there followed a short, muffled conversation.

Alice's palm was removed, and Daniel's voice said, "Who is this?"

"Hey, you piece of shit."

"Who is this?"

"Oh, isn't that just great. We go through the wars together, and he forgets the sound of my voice."

"Is that you, Camp?"

Daniel had retired from teaching at a community college in Toronto, and he and his wife, empty-nesters now, had purchased and were in the process of renovating a red brick farmhouse on the north shore of Lake Ontario in Prince Edward County, thirty miles west of Millhaven Penitentiary.

"Yes, it's me."

"Well, hell, I should have known." He turned away from the phone and said, "It's okay, darling, it's Camp Young." Then, to Young, he said, "My God, it's got to be five years."

"I know. Too long. How'd you like to see me tomorrow?"

Young explained the situation to Daniel, and they agreed that Young should make his visit to Millhaven first, then follow the shore road to the ferry at Adolphustown, cross to Glenora, drive to Daniel's property, have supper, and spend the night.

"We'll catch up," Daniel said.

Monday, November 26

The blue lettering leaned gracefully against the white background of the sign: "Millhaven Maximum Security Institution." Young turned into the driveway and passed a large, flat area of closely cut lawn. Three deer lifted their heads and twitched their ears. Young followed the gentle curves of the driveway past rock gardens and flower beds and eventually came upon a small cinder-block building that stood, like a sentry, in front of the main entrance. Young might have been approaching a golf course or a retirement village or a gated seaside resort, except that the whole complex was surrounded by a twenty-foot-high, double-thick chain-link fence topped by rolls of razor wire.

Young parked in a visitor's space beside the small building, and as he walked towards it, clipboard in hand, a tall, bed-headed guard opened the door and leaned his head out. "Young?" he said.

"That's me. Am I early?"

"No, we got you marked down for three o'clock, and it's a quarter to. Come on in."

Inside the building, Young had to sign in, pin a visitor's pass to his shirt, empty his pockets, and walk through an airport-style metal detector. "Sorry," the guard said, "regulations."

"What's that?" Young said, pointing at a squat machine stationed on a countertop with a computer monitor connected to it.

"Ion scanner," the guard said. "For detecting drugs. Here, I'll show you. Got a twenty on you?"

Young took out his wallet and produced a twenty, and the guard, who hadn't introduced himself but whose identification badge read "Hagerman," swabbed it with a small square of cotton cloth. He placed the cloth in the scanner, and it produced a cocaine reading of 105 on the computer screen.

"I don't use cocaine," Young said.

The guard smiled. "All it means is your twenty has been handled at some point during its lifetime by someone who did use cocaine. Just about every bill we test produces a reading for some drug or other. We can test for hash, heroin, LSD, amphetamines, methamphetamines, three different grades of THC. If the bill produces a reading over five hundred for coke, let's say, we're authorized to do a full body search, including cavities."

"What if the person doesn't have a bill on them?"

"With inmate visitors, we test watches, rings, hats — things they touch a lot."

"If the technology's so good," Young said, "how come so much stuff still gets in?"

The guard laughed. "Plenty ways to beat the system. The girlfriend wraps it in Saran Wrap, smears it with

toothpaste to fool the drug dog, and stuffs it up her wha-
zoo. Then, during the conjugal, she pulls it out, hands it
to the boyfriend, and he sticks it up his ass. That, or
kitchen staff bring it in. Or delivery men. Or medical
staff. Or even" — he raised his thumb to his badge —
"one of my less than honest brothers-in-arms."

"What about booze?"

"Oh, that they make themselves." He grimaced.
"It'll make you drunk in a hurry, that's for sure, but then
it'll make you want to die in a hurry, too. Come on,
we'll go inside."

Hagerman led Young out of the building and down
a broad concrete walk towards the prison itself. They
passed through two gates, opened electronically by one
of Hagerman's colleagues in a control tower, and
entered an open lawn area to the side of which stood a
small, boxy aluminum house.

"That's what we call the bungalow," Hagerman
explained. "It's for the conjugals. Inmate can spend a
whole weekend with his family. It's got beds and dressers
and a TV and VCR and a fridge and stove and a barbe-
cue. It's got a washer and dryer and ironing board for the
lady of the house. It's even got toys for the kids."

They climbed several steps, and Hagerman opened
the front door of the prison. Inside, they walked
through the foyer with its bulletin boards and plaques,
past a trusty pushing a mop bucket, then down a long
corridor to a large, circular area, like the hub of a
wheel, from which six more corridors extended like
spokes. A guard was standing near the gated entrance
to Corridor D.

Hagerman said to Young, "This is Norm. He'll take
you the rest of the way." Norm, who had a rifle over his
shoulder and a large belly, waved towards the hub, and
the gate slid open.

"Come on," he said, and headed into Corridor D. Young turned to thank Hagerman, but he had already walked away.

Young hurried to catch up to Norm. "Nine-millimetre?" he asked.

"Yup. We used to have shotguns, but they took them away. These things are a pissant kind of a gun. Twenty-bullet clip, but the bullets are small, eh, and wouldn't scare a baby. With the shotguns, all you had to do was crank it, and whatever bad behaviour was going on would stop pretty damn quick. Only thing with these is the ricochet is wicked."

"Ever had to use it?"

Norm looked up at Young as he walked. "No, and I'll tell you something: if one of these scum was murdering another of these scum, I might fire a warning shot, but I wouldn't shoot to kill."

"Why not?"

"I'd only shoot to kill if an officer was being attacked. See, I don't care one way or the other about the prisoners — they're just livestock to me. No, it's because once you kill a prisoner, not only will the powers that be move you to another institution, which means you have to sell your house and move your family, but if the guy you killed was connected, and his friends outside find out who you are and where you live, they'll get you." Norm stopped walking to look through a window of the corridor at several inmates pumping iron in the weight pit. "I maced a guy once, fifteen years ago, and two days later rocks come through our kitchen window, our living room window, our *daughter's* bedroom window, *our* bedroom window. We had to live in a motel for a month. That was at Collins Bay. Then I got moved here." At the end of the corridor they stopped at another gate. "This is SHU. Special Handling Unit.

Nobody gets out of their cell unless they're cuffed and shackled. What you want with Claude Johnson?"

"Information."

"I figured that much."

"I need to talk to him about voodoo."

Norm grunted. "Claude likes to talk, that's for sure, but I didn't know he was an expert on anything."

"One more question, Norm, if you don't mind: are the inmates in SHU allowed conjugal visits?"

"Hell, no. Like I said, they're cuffed and shackled any time they're outside their cell."

The gate opened, and Norm called out, "Coming down."

A voice at the far end of the corridor replied, "All clear."

"If there any are inmates outside their cells, we have to wait till they're back in. Some of these guys are like Hannibal Lector — even cuffed and shackled they'll figure a way to attack you. These guys are the meanest of the mean, the lowest of the low. What I often tell people is these guys are the animals of humanity. Come on. He's third on your left. Stay away from the bars as we walk. They'll grab at you if they can, and if they can't do that they'll spit. One guy in here used to throw his own shit, all mounded together like a snowball — that's what we called him, Snowball — but he's dead now."

They passed the first two cells uneventfully, and Young looked into the third. A bare-chested black man wearing red track pants was lying on a narrow bed with one arm folded over his eyes. White gauze around his biceps stood out starkly against his skin.

"What happened to him?" Young asked.

Norm smiled. "That's your man Johnson. He's what we call a slasher. Every few weeks, when he can't stand his cell anymore and wants to go outside for a while, he'll cut himself. He's smart, he does it just before the guard comes past his cell, which happens every fifteen minutes on the button, so there's blood all over the place, and the guard has no choice but to call for medical, and then they have to get an ambulance and take him to hospital."

"He can't be treated here?"

"Infirmary closes at four, nurse goes home, so the slashers wait till nighttime. Besides, it's not just a little cut like you could cover with a Band-Aid. Oh no, these boys go deep. One old guy, Fleck, he did it for attention. Wanted to be looked after. One whole arm was scar tissue, and his stomach was all X's. Some guys'll do it if they're in danger. If they're pretty sure the next time they have a shower they're gonna wind up with a shiv in their neck, they'll do it just to get away from whoever's after them."

Norm stepped up to the cell and ran the butt of his rifle along the bars like a boy running a stick along a picket fence. "Wakey, wakey, Claude. You got company."

The black man roused himself and sat up. "What the fuck?" he said, scratching his head.

"Someone here to see you." Norm turned to Young. "How long you need?"

"Depends on him, I guess. Ten minutes."

"Want a chair?"

"Sure."

Young and Claude Johnson studied each other while Norm fetched a battered wooden chair from an empty cell.

"I'll be nearby," he said, walked away a few steps, and leaned his back against the wall opposite the cells.

Young pulled the chair close to the bars and sat down. "Mr. Johnson," he said, "I understand you're an expert on voodoo."

Johnson reached to his bedside table, picked up a pair of black-rimmed glasses, and put them on. They gave him a scholarly look. "You a big motherfucker."

"So they tell me."

"Cop?"

"Private investigator. I'm investigating a murder, and I need your help."

Johnson laughed. "Why would I help you, mother-fucker?"

"I don't know. Why would you?"

Johnson turned his head slightly. "What's in it for me?"

"What do you want?"

Johnson reached under his pillow and extracted a knitted maroon toque. He pulled it down over his afro like a tea cozy. "I want my sentence reduced, so's I eligible for parole after fifteen, 'stead of twenty-five, which is where I sit right now."

"How long have you been in here?"

"Two years."

Young shook his head slowly. "The information I need doesn't carry that kind of weight."

"Then move me to minimum," he said. "One of them farm camps, where I can be outside pickin' cotton and singin' 'Po' Laz'rus.'"

Young said, "You're going to have to lower your expectations, Mr. Johnson, or we can't do business."

Johnson smiled. "Way I see it, you need me more'n I need you."

"You're not the only man in the world knows about voodoo."

"Then why you talkin' to me?"

"I asked around. You came well recommended."

"Mmm-hmm, I's well known insofar as voodoo is concerned. So, what *can* you offer me?"

"Anybody you'd like to have visit you?"

"You mean conjugal? We ain't allowed conjugal."

"If you say so. Where I come from, anything's possible."

"What you talkin' 'bout?"

"I mean if the product's good, the price goes up." Young took a pen from his shirt pocket and held it over the clipboard. "What's the lucky lady's name?"

"Well, let me think a minute, they's so many to choose from. I guess Shaneeka. Shaneeka Wilson. She got one of my kids." Johnson shifted to the end of his cot, closer to Young. "You really think you can get me the bungalow?"

Young was writing down the name. "Like I say, it all depends on how good the information is."

"You get me the bungalow for a weekend, you get me that, I'll tell you anything you want to hear."

"I just want some information to help me find out who killed a jazz musician — guy called Talmadge Cooper."

Johnson nodded. "I heard about him. Brother, right?"

"That's right. He was murdered in a hotel room and his body was surrounded with voodoo. Some people think the voodoo was real, some people think it was fake, to send the cops off in the wrong direction."

Johnson wrapped his fingers around the bars of his cell. "Go ahead and tell me 'bout this voodoo. I tell you if it's real or not."

For the next five minutes, Young summarized the case. As he spoke, he referred to notes on his clipboard — Tal Cooper's background, details of time and place — but mostly he concentrated on the evidence found at the scene. Johnson listened raptly, and when Young was done he shook his head and said, "That ain't voodoo.

That just a mishmash. That just somebody who don't know what they doin' did that. Somebody fake it to look like voodoo."

Young said, "That's pretty much what we figured."

"Who this 'we'?"

"A couple of people did some research for me."

"Then what you need me for? You just stringin' me along, motherfucker?"

"No, I needed you to confirm what they said. But there's one more question I have to ask you."

"I'm listenin'."

"Is there such a thing as a voodoo store in Toronto?"

Johnson smiled. "Not only do I want the bungalow for the weekend, and Shaneeka, but I want a dozen T-bone steaks and a case o' wine."

"I'll see what I can do."

"Okay, then, the only voodoo store in Toronto is run by a Greek guy on the Danforth."

Young turned his clipboard so that Johnson could read what was on it and pointed to a notation.

"That's right," Johnson said. "Rastaman Vibrations." He looked at Young. "If you already knew, why'd you ask?"

"I wanted to make sure it was the only one. So far, you haven't told me anything worth a hamburger, let alone a dozen steaks."

"Okay, listen to this. You said the body had zombie powder in it. That's where your killer got it. The Greek imports it direct from Port-au-Prince."

"Used to import it. He's dead."

Johnson lifted his chin slightly. "Say what?"

"Last Wednesday. The Broadview subway chewed him up and spat him out."

Johnson lowered his chin and scratched it. "I never made the Greek for a jumper."

"He didn't jump. He had help."

Johnson looked at Young. "You full o' news, motherfucker."

"I keep my ears open. What else you got?"

Johnson pursed his lips. "I got a name."

Young poised his pen over the clipboard. "I'm ready."

Johnson shook his head slowly. "You deliver Shaneeka and the meat and the wine, then I tell you."

Young smiled. "You don't have a name." He stood up.

"Wait," Johnson said. "Okay, but you better come across."

Young sat down again.

"And I want tobacco. Motherfuckers chargin' two hunnert a bag in here. And I want rollin' papers — real ones."

"Don't you have a bible? I hear onionskin works real well."

"It works okay — I'm halfway through Leviticus — but it don't tear straight, and I got no gum. If I had some envelopes I could use the gum off 'em."

"Okay, I'll get you tobacco and papers and I'll see what I can do about the rest. Now what's the guy's name?"

"Otis Mayhew," Johnson said. "Used to play trumpet, but he lost his chops. Also happens to be a fellow voodooist, like me. Not as fine as me, but he knows a thing or two."

"Where do I find him?"

"Hangs around the clubs in Toronto. Spadina and Queen. Up around College. Just ask any of the brothers. They'll know."

Young stood up again.

"Don't forget what you promised."

"I didn't promise. I said I'd see what I could do."

Johnson squeezed the bar on either side of his head. "What your name, motherfucker?"

Young nodded at the gauze on Johnson's arm. "Take care of yourself."

Johnson's brow furrowed. "What your name?"

Young turned to Norm, who was cleaning his fingernails with a jackknife. "All done," he said.

"What your name?" Johnson repeated, as Norm and Young started towards the gate.

In the corridor, Norm said, "Get what you came for?"

"We'll see."

"What's he want?"

Behind them Johnson called, "What your *name*, motherfucker?"

"Tobacco and papers."

"That all?"

"And a weekend in the bungalow with his girlfriend, a dozen steaks, and a case of wine."

Norm laughed. "Like that's going to happen."

Young said, "What's he in for?"

"You don't want to know."

"Tell me."

"Okay," Norm said, "you asked. He was a janitor in a school in Windsor. Took a ten-year-old girl in the boiler room and strangled her. Raped her first, of course. Then burned the body. Probably would have got away with it if he hadn't kept her panties in his locker."

Young's eyes went hard. "I remember the case. I didn't associate the name." He paused. "Well, I know one bungalow Mr. Johnson will never see the inside of."

They walked along. Distantly, they could hear Johnson bellowing, "*What your name, motherfucker!*"

Young said, "I was at least going to get him the tobacco and papers for answering my questions, but fuck that, too."

* * *

As Young drove back out to the highway he looked for the deer, but they were gone. He passed through the small towns of Bath, Sandhurst, Conway, and Adolphustown until the road stopped at a wharf. He smoked a cigarette and watched the ferry approach. The *Quinte Loyalist*. When it arrived, it disgorged two pickup trucks, four cars, and a horse van. A ferryman waved Young on. He was the only traveller heading west. The passage lasted ten minutes, and then he was in Prince Edward County. He followed the directions he'd scribbled on his clipboard, and in a disappointingly short time — disappointing because he found himself suddenly happy to be on the road, and part of him wanted to keep going — he pulled into the driveway of Daniel and Alice Curry's red brick century farmhouse.

Young trudged up the steps to the verandah, and Daniel met him at the door.

"You old shoe," Daniel said.

They embraced manfully, at the shoulders.

"You look good," Young said. "Slim and trim."

"I joined a health club in town. I play a lot of squash."

"Retirement agrees with you."

"Same back at you. You're retired, too, don't forget."

"I know," Young said, as Daniel led him inside, "but I haven't quite gotten into the rhythm of it yet."

"You miss the structure, perhaps."

Young took off his windbreaker, and Daniel hung it in the hall closet.

"I guess so. I don't get out of bed till I want. I eat when I want. Sometimes I don't even know what day it is."

"An enviable state."

"But sometimes I feel ... I don't know ... uncon-nected."

"What you need is a job."

"I've got a job. What I need is a drink."

"Hello, Campbell," a voice said, and when Young looked around he saw Alice framed in the kitchen door-way. "Are you hungry?"

"Always," Young said, feeling a warmth like home wash over him. "I'm always hungry."

"I've made pot roast, and there's scalloped potatoes and green beans. And apple pie made with Macs from our own little orchard."

"Got any of that good red wine you guys always have on hand?"

Daniel said, "It's already decanted and awaiting your pleasure. If you'll make your way into the dining room, you'll see several of its brothers standing at atten-tion on the sideboard, should they be needed."

"Oh," Young laughed, rubbing his hands together, "they'll be needed."

After supper Alice went upstairs. "She's involved with a group that helps street kids," Daniel explained, as he and Young cleared the table, "and that means she spends most of her evenings on the phone or sending e-mail." They rinsed the dishes and glasses and cutlery and filled the dishwasher. They scoured the pots and wiped the harvest table and blew out the candles.

"Congratulations," Young said. "You've turned me into a woman."

"Working in the kitchen is good for the soul," Daniel said. "I've got some Scotch, if you're interested."

"Okay if I smoke?"

"We'll go outside."

They stood on the verandah with several fingers of Johnny Walker Black. It was a clear night and starry, but too cold to sit down. They listened to the chugging and belching of the cement plant across the bay. "Sometimes it's quite loud," Daniel said, "other times you can hardly hear it."

"Depends which way the wind's blowing?"

Daniel nodded. "Some mornings we'll go out to the car and it'll be covered with cement dust. And it doesn't just wash off either. You have to take vinegar to it."

"Trouble in paradise."

Daniel laughed. "I guess I shouldn't complain, should I, if that's as bad as it gets."

A car drove by.

"We're so remote, some nights only one car will go by. In the nice weather, we'll be sitting out here for hours and there'll be no traffic. I mean *no* traffic. It's so different from the city. We love it. Eventually a car will go by, and Alice and I will look at each other, and one of us will say, 'Well, time for bed.'"

"It's not too quiet a life?"

"Oh no, it has its moments. Just last week we were sitting out here — it was still light, and it was cold but we were bundled up — and it was peaceful and quiet, and we were dimly aware that a car was approaching. We couldn't see it beyond the trees, but we could hear the hiss of the tires. And then — bang! I thought it was a blowout. We watched, and the car rolled into sight and stopped in front of the house. A man got out and walked to the front of the car. I called out to him. He shouted back that he'd hit a deer. I walked across the grass towards him and looked back in the direction he'd come. The deer was lying on the shoulder of the road. The collision had done a lot of damage to one side of the guy's car. It was a not-very-old Nissan Maxima. We invited him inside, and he phoned his insurance company and the police and thanked us for letting him use the phone and walked back out to his car and drove away. Alice and I went out to the road and looked at the deer. It was on its side. Its eyes were open and its legs were in a running position. A small amount of blood had escaped its nostrils. It was a beautiful animal. We had seen deer tracks on our property, but we'd never been up close to one. We studied the cloven hooves. Its eyes — already glassy, as if a taxidermist had replaced them — were the size of baseballs. I leaned down and touched its flank. It was still warm. Alice touched it, too. We walked back to the house and washed our hands. A few minutes later, we heard a vehicle brake sharply in front of the house. We thought maybe it was the police. We hurried outside and watched a skinny little man about sixty years of age lower the tailgate of his half-ton, then he and a big woman with white hair leaned down and picked up the deer — the woman took hold of the hind legs and the man the forelegs — and swung it up and into the bed of the truck. They acted quickly and furtively, like two people committing a crime. No wasted motion. No looking around. Then they hopped back in the half-ton and took off. It made Alice cry to see how they threw the deer in the truck."

Young walked down the steps to the grass. He dropped his cigarette and crushed it under the toe of his shoe. He bent down, picked up the butt and deposited it in the pocket of his jacket. "This was last week?" he asked.

Daniel nodded. "About a week ago. Last Monday or Tuesday."

Young looked up at the stars. "They're probably still eating it."

Tuesday, November 27

When Young woke up in the guest room of Daniel and Alice Curry's farmhouse, he didn't know where he was. As he groggily retrieved his bearings, he became aware of a low-grade hangover making itself comfortable in the guest room of his brain. He got up, made his way to the bathroom, urinated, showered, dressed, made his way downstairs, discovered his host and hostess preparing breakfast, was informed that Grape-Nuts was not a staple of the Curry household, drank two large glasses of orange juice, ate three eggs over hard, half a pound of bacon, and four slices of whole wheat toast, and swallowed three ibuprofens. He drank two cups of coffee, said his goodbyes, climbed shakily into the cab of his truck, and drove a hundred and thirty-five miles to Toronto.

His first stop was the city's tenderloin.

After parking at a meter on Spadina Avenue north of College, Young took a stroll and soon encountered a junkie known as Twist-Me-One whom he had known years earlier when he walked a beat. Twist-Me-One was a burned-out hippie. In the old days, he used to braid leather bracelets for the tourists, and, out of pity, Young had bought two. He had given one to Tanya — they were still together at the time — and one to Debi, who had only been seven or eight years old. Tanya hated hers — she was afraid she'd catch something from it — but Debi loved hers and wore it until it unravelled.

Twist-Me-One was huddled in a sleeping bag on the sidewalk in front of a branch of the Bank of Montreal.

"Twister," Young said, "is that you?"

The man looked up. His eyes were bleary and vague.

"Don't you remember me? Campbell Young."

Twist-Me-One narrowed his eyes in concentration. "Cop?"

"Used to be, that's right. I would have walked right past you, but you're still wearing your Leafs toque."

"Leafs are my team, man."

Young took a handful of coins from his pants pocket and dropped them into the cardboard coffee cup Twist-Me-One was using as a donation box. Then he hunkered down beside him. "How you doing? Still making bracelets?"

Twist-Me-One shook his head. "Can't do it no more. My fingers are fucked." He withdrew his hands from the folds of his sleeping bag and showed them to Young. The fingers were swollen and red, and the nails were black-rimmed and cracked.

Young said, "Sorry to hear that, Twister, but listen, I'm glad I ran into you. Maybe I can help you out a bit."

"How you going to help me out? Buy me a townhouse?"

"I need some information. You're a pretty savvy guy, you know the streets. There's twenty in it for you."

Twist-Me-One slid his hands back inside the sleeping bag. "What do you want to know?"

"I'm looking for a guy named Otis Mayhew. Do you know him?"

"Maybe. What's he done?"

"I don't know yet. Maybe nothing."

"Try Nugent's."

"What's he look like?"

"Skinny little black guy. Buggy eyes, like a frog."

"Thank you, my friend." Young stood up, extracted a twenty-dollar bill from his wallet, and folded it into the coffee cup. "What are you on these days, Twister? Last time I saw you you'd quit booze."

"I do junk when I can get it. Mostly I do coffee and cigarettes."

Young retraced his steps and turned right on Spadina. He crossed the road and stepped from the sunshine of the sidewalk into the gloom of Nugent's Tap Room.

Young scanned the bar stools, but only two were occupied — neither by a black man. The bartender, fat and bald in a dingy white shirt, nodded at Young. As Young continued to survey the dark interior of the bar, his gaze came to rest on a cigarette machine in a corner to his right, beside which squatted a skeletal black man with protruding eyeballs.

As Young approached the cigarette machine, he said, "Otis Mayhew?"

The man watched him warily.

Young said, "Me and you need to talk."

The man launched himself sideways. Young was ready for him and caught him by the arm. He was surprised how small Mayhew was, how slight. "You're just like a bird, Otis. Where you flying to?"

"I ain't done nothin'!" Mayhew protested, trying to pull free. "Lemme go!"

"Friend of yours said I should look you up," Young said. "Said you might be able to help me."

"I don't know nothin' 'bout nothin'! Lemme go!"

"Friend told me you're the man I should talk to."

"What friend? I ain't got no friends."

"He says you played trumpet once upon a time. That right?"

Mayhew stopped struggling and took a breath. "So what? I did, and now I don't. What friend you talkin' about?"

"Claude Johnson."

Mayhew's face froze, his bulbous eyes red-veined and yellow, and he stood stone still.

Young frowned. "Something I said?"

Beads of perspiration appeared on Mayhew's brow. "He still in stir, ain't he?"

"Yeah, he can't hurt you."

"That man evil." Mayhew trembled in Young's grip. "He know everything about a man. He know what your *thoughts* even!"

"He told me —"

"You *seen* him?"

"Yeah, I paid him a little visit, we talked about obeah and voodoo, about a murder case I'm investigating, and he said —"

"What your name?"

"Young, why?"

Mayhew looked away.

"What's wrong, Otis? Why're you so nervous all of a sudden?"

"It wasn't my idea. He *made* me do it."

"What are you talking about?" Young's eyes widened. "Wait a minute, you're the one that killed my dog?"

Mayhew tried to pull away. "Lemme go!"

Young tightened his grasp on Mayhew's arm. "Look at me," he said, but Mayhew wouldn't, so Young pushed him against the cigarette machine, lifted his arm, laid it across the top edge, and said, "I'll break your arm, you little cocksucker. Look at me!"

Mayhew looked at him.

"Why'd you do it?"

Mayhew's eyes rolled in his skull, and he began to blubber, "Please don't, please don't."

"Talk," Young said, and changed his grip to the one children use to crack Popsicles.

"He *made* me do it," Mayhew moaned. "He said he'd kill me if I didn't."

"Who?" Young demanded. "Who made you?" He lifted the arm six inches above the hard metal edge of the cigarette machine.

"Please don't —"

"Who made you do it?"

The bartender, who had been watching from the safety of the bar, said, "You there, what's going on?"

Without taking his eyes off Mayhew, Young said, "Take a walk."

"I don't want any trouble in here."

"Take a walk!"

The two men at the bar got off their stools and went outside. The bartender said, "I'll be in the kitchen. You got thirty seconds, then I call the cops." He disappeared behind a swinging door.

Young said, "Who made you do it?"

Mayhew licked his lips. "Buddy."

"Buddy who?"

"Don't hurt me."

"Buddy who?" Young snarled.

"Buddy Drown."

"Buddy Drown? The sax player?"

"That's right. He said he'd give me some smack and drove me to the place. He give me a piece and a knife and told me your name. I went inside and I was reading the names at the intercom and I found yours, but then I heard some people talking, so I went outside around back and figured out which apartment was yours. I went up the stairs to the balcony and got in that way. Buddy said you was a big man and I better be careful, but you wasn't there, but this dog was, and I killed it with the knife. I put the voodoo bottles around it, just like Buddy said to do —"

"He gave you the voodoo bottles?"

"He gave me a bunch of old glass bottles. I made them up to look like voodoo."

"But they were supposed to go around *my* body, right?"

Mayhew swallowed and said, "Then I come back outside and we drove away."

"Did you do the bottles for Tal Cooper's murder, too?"

"Who? I don't — "

"You did more than that, didn't you? You're the one that killed him."

"No! I swear —"

"Then who did?"

"I don't know! Maybe it was Buddy!"

Young took a deep breath. "You killed my dog, you miserable little fuck. You pissed on my floor and you killed my dog." Young raised Mayhew's arm another four inches.

"Please don't hurt me, I'm beggin' you, please don't hurt me!"

"You were looking for me. Buddy hired you to kill me. Why didn't you just leave when you saw I wasn't there?" Young squeezed tighter. "Why'd you have to kill the dog? My grandson found it! My *grandson* found your mess!" Young's heart was racing. He didn't know which to do first — find Buddy Drown or punish Otis Mayhew. He decided quickly. Against the hard edge of the cigarette machine, Mayhew's forearm snapped like kindling.

Priam Harvey was sitting on his usual stool at McCully's. The stools on either side of him were occupied, so Young tapped him on the shoulder from behind and said, "I need to talk to you."

Harvey swivelled ninety degrees and, wobbly as a bobblehead, said, "Well, the prodigal son returns." He was smiling like a man whose life has been one long disappointment. "Rumour has it you've been visiting our neighbours to the south. Now sit down here beside me and tell me about your travels."

"There's someone sitting there."

Harvey turned to the bottle blonde beside him. "Excuse me, Cynthia," he said, "but we need your stool."

Young made room as the woman — drink in hand, chin high, eyes averted — squeezed past him.

"Now," said Harvey, as Young eased one haunch onto the stool, "tell me where you've been and who you've seen and the secrets you've uncovered."

Young leaned into Harvey's ear. "I know who killed your son."

Harvey's smile disappeared. He took a moment to compose himself. "Who is it? Is it someone I know?"

"The name I'm about to give you is the name of the man who either did the killing himself or contracted it out."

Harvey nodded. "I understand."

Young said, "I shouldn't even be telling you this. Are you sober enough to keep it to yourself?"

Harvey nodded again. "Who is it?"

Young studied the grief in Harvey's eyes. "Buddy Drown."

Harvey pulled his head back. "You can't be serious."

Out of the corner of his eye, Young caught Dexter signalling to him. He was holding up two fingers. Young shook his head, then said, "Oh, I'm serious all right. He's definitely the mastermind, maybe the trigger man, too. It's possible he got somebody else to do it, but I doubt it. Tell me something, did they know each other, him and your son?"

Harvey was staring at his cigarette pack. "I'm sure they knew *of* each other, but I don't know if they ever met."

"There was no sign of a struggle in the hotel room. Whoever the killer was, Tal knew him well enough to let him in."

"But I don't understand. Why would he do it?"

"I'm guessing jealousy," Young said. "You told me yourself that Buddy Drown is the main man around here on saxophone."

"He *used* to be the main man on saxophone, that's true, and probably thinks he still is. He's definitely got a high opinion of himself."

"Maybe he was afraid Tal was going to knock him off his throne."

"I remember what you said in Freeport — that the murder might have something to do with Tal being the next Coltrane — but Tal was just passing through. Lots of sax players pass through Toronto. Buddy doesn't kill *them*!"

"Maybe there's more to it."

Harvey picked up his cigarette pack. "It doesn't seem possible. Buddy Drown?" He struggled with the cigarette pack, then lowered his head. "It all seems so unreal ... but if you're convinced..." He looked up at Young. "Are you convinced?"

"No doubt about it."

Harvey nodded slowly. "Okay then, what happens next?"

Young took the cigarette pack from Harvey's trembling hands. "That's where you come in. I can't just have him arrested, because I don't have any hard evidence that he's the killer or that he had anything to do with it. All I've got is the word of a dopehead Buddy Drown hired to kill me, but since I wasn't home, he killed my dog instead."

"Somebody tried to kill you?"

"It's possible the dopehead killed Tal, too, but I doubt it." Young shook a cigarette loose and pointed it at Harvey. "Tal was poisoned by something he ate. I think he had dinner with whoever poisoned him, maybe in his hotel room, and you can be sure it wasn't the dopehead. But it very likely could have been Buddy Drown."

With shaking fingers Harvey lifted the cigarette to his mouth. "Why would Buddy Drown want *you* dead?"

"It must have been when I left my business card with Peter Georgiadis —"

"Who?"

"The guy who sold the TTX to whoever killed your son. And who, if I'm right about Buddy Drown being the killer, or at least hiring the killer, told him about me snooping around the voodoo store." Young nodded to himself. "He must have shown him my card, or given it to him. That's how Drown knew where I lived."

"Your home address is on your card?"

"No, but my home phone is. He must have traced it somehow." Young paused. "And my money says Buddy did Georgiadis, too."

"What do you mean, 'did Georgiadis'?"

"Someone tossed him under the wheels of a subway the day after I paid him a visit. Maybe he tried to squeeze Buddy, I don't know. All I know is Buddy had something to do with it."

Harvey was searching his pockets for matches. "This is all very disturbing."

Young pulled at one ear. "I'm starting to change my mind. I'm starting to think the missing piece of the puzzle — the answer to why Buddy killed Tal, or had him killed — has something to do with the dopehead."

"Why do you say that?"

"I'm starting to think it has more to do with drugs than jealousy."

Harvey shook his head. "You're losing me."

"The dopehead told me Buddy promised him some smack."

"What does that prove?"

"It proves Buddy has access to drugs."

"*All* musicians have access to drugs."

"Don't take this wrong, Mr. Harvey, but according to the people I talked to when we were in the Bahamas, your son was a drug user."

"So what? I'm a drug user! Even *you*, on occasion —"

"I'm talking serious drugs. My guess is there's more than a musical connection between your son and Buddy Drown."

"Okay, but answer one more question for me: two minutes ago I asked you what's going to happen next, and you said, 'That's where you come in.' What did you mean by that?"

Young flipped open his Zippo and ignited it. He held the flame to the tip of Harvey's cigarette. "Simple, really. I have to set a trap for Buddy Drown, and you're the bait."

PART THREE

PART
THREE

Wednesday, November 28

Young spotted Twist-Me-One sitting in the window of a diner on College Street, hunched over his coffee like a freezing man over a fire. He tapped on the window, and Twist-Me-One's head in its blue and white Leafs toque jerked up as if on strings. Twist-Me-One watched nervously as Young entered the diner, walked towards his table, pulled a chair out opposite him, and sat down.

"Where's your sleeping bag?"

Twist-Me-One shrugged. "Wherever I left it."

Young nodded. "I found Otis."

Twist-Me-One leaned forward, glanced left and right, and whispered, "Why'd you break his arm?"

"Word travels fast."

"No, seriously, why'd you break his arm? If he finds out I put you onto him, he'll come after me. He'll do some of that voodoo shit on me."

"He doesn't know you were involved."

"I shouldn't even be talking to you."

"He killed my dog, that's why I broke his arm."

Twist-Me-One took a breath. "He killed your *dog*?"

"He wanted to kill me, but I wasn't home at the time."

"Lucky for you."

"No, lucky for him. Listen, I've got a couple more questions. If I like the answers, there's another twenty in it for you, and I'll be out of here in less than a minute."

Twist-Me-One nodded. "Okay."

"When you're flush, where do you get your junk?"

Twist-Me-One inhaled the steam off his coffee. A crafty look entered his eyes. "Why aren't you in uniform?"

"I'm retired."

"Then why should I tell you anything? If I tell you what you want to know, I lose my supply."

"If you don't, then I tell my friends who *aren't* retired to bust your sorry ass."

"For what?"

"They don't need a reason, you know that."

"I could use a vacation — warm bed, regular meals."

"Then don't talk, and I'll let Otis know who put me onto him. Is that what you want?"

"Why are you threatening me? Didn't I help you —"

"Look, Twister, I may not be a cop anymore, but I'm still in the business. I'm private now and working a case, and I'm not after a dog-killer, I'm after a man-killer."

Twist-Me-One sat up straight. "Who got killed?"

"A musician, a young man who happened to be the son of a very good friend of mine."

"This the one at the Sutton Place?"

"That's right."

Twist-Me-One considered. "Was he a user?"

"So I've been told."

"And you think he was killed over drugs?"

"That's one theory I'm running with. I think his supplier killed him, I think I know who his supplier might be, but I need your help to find him."

Twist-Me-One nodded, as if to confirm something in his own mind. "I get what I need from a dealer name of Poor Paul, but that's all I can tell you. He's just penny ante, just a street hustler. I don't know who else goes to him, and I don't know where he gets his stuff."

"What about Otis? Do you know who his dealer is?"

"No idea. There's a dealer for every junkie, just about."

"Where do I find Poor Paul?"

Poor Paul did business out of a body shop at the end of a laneway behind a convenience store on Eastern Avenue. He was of Italian descent, second-generation Canadian, medium height, dark-haired, wiry. His hands, face, and navy blue coveralls were smeared with engine grease. As he stood with Young in the sunshine outside his garage, he held a cigarette in one blackened hand and a soiled red shop rag in the other.

"I need to know two things from you," Young said after a minute of introduction. "Who's your supplier, and where do I find him?"

"I don't know what you think you got on me, man —"

"Hey, we both know what I got on you, and unless you want Narcotics picking through your garbage and checking under your bed, you better talk."

Poor Paul dropped his cigarette on the gravel and crushed it under his shoe. "You're full of shit. You're not even police."

"Listen, guinea," Young said, turning and grabbing two fistfuls of coverall and lifting Poor Paul onto his toes, "I know who your customers are, and I know how easy they squeeze. You've got five seconds to tell me what I want to know before I start rearranging the land-scape. Four. Three."

"Okay, okay! There's this ladies' wear shop on Queen West. Kuka's or Kiki's, some shit like that. He operates out of the basement."

Young set Poor Paul back down on the ground. "Your supplier operates out of a ladies' wear shop?"

"Isn't that who we're talking about?"

"What's his name?"

"I don't know."

"You don't know his name? What's his street name? What do you call him?"

"I don't call him anything."

"You must call him something."

"No, I'm telling you —"

Young took hold of Poor Paul's coveralls and lifted him onto his toes again. "Two. One."

"Mr. D! People call him Mr. D."

The store was called Kuka's Fashions. Outside the entrance, two mannequins so lifelike Young mistook them for real people appeared to be enjoying the sun-shine. He lowered his head and turned sideways to pass through a beaded curtain and found himself not only set-ting off a jangling of small bells but struggling to see in the dim orange light of the interior. As he made his way towards the counter, he did his best not to knock over any of the racks of clothing that crowded the tiny shop. There was a smell in the air — incense or potpourri — and there was some sort of eastern music playing.

He waited while the salesgirl attended to a customer. When the customer left, Young and the salesgirl were alone in the store, and as he walked towards her, she looked up at him and smiled. "May I help you?" she said. She was older up close than she had seemed from a distance. Mid-forties maybe. She had a big ball of frizzy yellow hair on her head and not much meat on her bones.

"Nice music," Young said.

"Yes," the woman said, "I find it very restful."

"Who is it?"

"Ravi Shankar."

Young nodded. "Are you Kuka?"

"No," the woman laughed, "this is Kuka." She patted the head of a ginger cat lying on the counter. "How may I help you?"

"You the owner?"

The woman's smile faded slightly. "Yes, I am."

"I'm looking for a friend of mine."

The woman's smile disappeared, but she continued to look steadily up at Young. "Does your friend have a name?"

Young leaned down into her face. "Well, he prefers just to use a short form. Calls himself Mr. D."

The woman stepped back but kept her eyes on Young's. "There's no one around here by that name."

"Is there a back room to this building," Young said, straightening up and looking around, "or a basement or someplace where a man might carry on the kind of business that could land anybody he associated with in shit so deep she might drown in it?"

The woman's eyes went hard, her mouth set.

"The man's street name is Mr. D," Young continued, "and what you need to know is he's not just a drug dealer. That would be okay — you could live with that, couldn't you, and whatever junk he tosses your way, or maybe he rents the basement from you. Is that it, does he rent from you, it's all on the up and up? No, the problem is that besides being a drug dealer," Young leaned back down towards her, "he's a murderer, too."

Young heard the bells jangling behind him. In a mirror on the wall behind the woman, he watched two shoppers enter the store and begin to browse. He returned his attention to the woman. "Talk," he said.

The woman regarded him coldly. "Who are you?"

From the breast pocket of his shirt, Young removed a business card. He handed it to her, and she read it.

"You're not police?" she said.

"Funny thing, people keep asking me that, and I keep explaining that no, I'm not, but I was, and I'm still very well connected."

The woman looked across at the customers. "May I help you, ladies?" she said brightly.

"Just looking," one of them replied.

Young reached across the counter and tapped the woman's wrist. "Don't try that shit with me," he said. "I'm not going anywhere. I'll wait right here till they're gone. I'll be here when you close up, if I have to."

The woman looked up at him with something like pleading in her eyes. "He hasn't been here all week."

"When do you expect him?"

"He keeps his own hours. I never know when he'll show up."

"What about his customers? Isn't it a little awkward when a bunch of junkies start lining up at your front door?"

"He doesn't sell to junkies, he only sells to dealers, and they know better than to show up when he's not here."

"How do they know when he *is* here?"

"I don't know. He puts the word out."

"And you never know when he's going to show up?"

She shook her head.

Young straightened up again and scratched his neck. "If you don't mind me asking, what's his hold on you? Why do you let him use your place?"

She looked down, her jaws working, but didn't speak.

"Listen, I don't want to have to play hardball with you, but I can have the boys in blue down here in ten minutes, a warrant in an hour, a search of the premises, and by closing time tonight you'll not only be out of business but looking at five years in a correctional facility full of two-hundred-pound crack whores who're dying to meet you."

She raised her eyes to his. "My name is Madeline Drown. The man you're talking about is my ex-husband."

Young stopped his truck at the end of the laneway, turned off his engine, and waited in semi-darkness for Poor Paul to close up shop for the night: he watched him roll his tire rack inside, strip off his dirty coveralls and pull on a yellow and black full-body leather motorcycle suit, turn off the garage lights, close and lock the bay door, lock the office door, and start walking with his helmet under his arm towards a Kawasaki Ninja leaning on its side-stand at the corner of the building.

Young started his truck and eased it forward into the apron area in front of the garage. When Poor Paul turned around at the sound of the motor, Young leaned out his window and said, "Little late in the year, isn't it?"

Poor Paul just stared at him.

"Come on," Young said, "hop in here with me. It's toasty."

Poor Paul cast a glance back to his bike, as if considering a Steve McQueen–style escape, then observed that Young's truck was blocking the mouth to the laneway, puffed his lips twice, and carefully placed his helmet on the Ninja's seat.

When he was sitting in the cab of Young's truck, he said, "I told you everything I know."

"Not quite," Young said, lighting a cigarette. "There's one more little detail."

"What?"

"When's Mr. D going to be back in the shop to do some business?"

Poor Paul shrugged his shoulders. "I don't know."

Young gave him a dead look. "When *will* you know?"

"I ... I get a phone call."

"You due for one?"

There was a pause. "Soon. Sometimes it's Thursday."

Young nodded. "Tomorrow's Thursday. Who phones you?"

Poor Paul looked away. "Mr. D."

"Good." Young reached into his shirt pocket and pulled out a business card. "Here's my number. You phone me when you get the call. Night or day. And don't fuck with me, Paulie, your neck's on the line. You can warn Mr. D and get sent down with him or you can help me nail him, in which case I'll make sure you're looked after. And if your lawyer's any good, you'll get immunity. Worst-case scenario, you go to trial and get time served for dealing."

"I don't get it," Paul said. "If I tell you when the next meeting is, but I don't go to it, he'll know something's —"

"Oh, you're going to the meeting, don't worry about that. So will me and a whole lot of my friends."

Buddy Drown poured several ounces of Wolf Blass Yellow Label into his goblet, picked up his fork and steak knife, and began his assault on the strip loin that lay like a burn victim on his plate.

"I'm sorry it's overdone," Ursula said. "I had to answer the door. You were downstairs."

"Who was at the door?" Drown asked evenly as he sawed into the meat.

"Jehovah's Witnesses. Two women. They drove right into our driveway —"

"What did you tell them?"

"Well, I didn't want to be rude —"

"You didn't want to be rude?" Drown laid down his cutlery and looked at his wife. "You didn't want to be rude to a couple of strangers who knock on our door at suppertime?"

"I told them I was busy, but they just kept talking. You know how they are. They asked me if I question why there is suffering in the world."

Drown took a deep draught of his wine. He swirled it against his palate, then swallowed. "Oh, the reason for suffering is plain as day. Do you know what it is?"

"You always tell me greed is the root of all evil."

"This isn't about greed, this is about disobedience. Do you think those women are disobedient to their husbands?"

Ursula frowned at her empty wine goblet. "I don't know. I don't even know if they're married. The one woman was older, maybe sixty —"

"A woman's job is to be obedient to her husband. *Your* job is to be obedient to me." He picked up his knife and pointed it at her. "And one way to show your obedience is to fix my supper the way I like it, and what I like is my steak rare. Blood rare."

"You're a much better cook than I am, Buddy —"

"Damn right I am. I should do *all* of the cooking in this house, and if I wasn't so busy practising and playing ..." He looked down at his plate, his upper lip curling in disgust.

Ursula watched. She knew the signs: the brittle calm, then the vitriol, then the body language. To speak would only make matters worse, but sitting in silence — like a woman in the path of a tornado — was no better. "Please, Buddy," she said, "please don't be angry."

He stood up from the table, lifted his plate, stepped to the sliding glass door that opened onto the deck, opened it, and threw the plate and its cargo of meat, scalloped potatoes, and French cut green beans into the darkness of the garden.

Ursula stood up and began to back away.

Buddy strode across the kitchen, seized her by her braid, and dragged her along the hall towards their bedroom.

"It's me."

"Sarge! What a surprise!" At first Wheeler's voice was joyful, but then it turned serious. "Everything all right?"

"Yes, everything's fine —"

"How's Jamal?"

"Jamal's fine, but listen, I have to talk to you."

"Okay, I'm listening. You had me worried there for a second. Your tone of voice —"

"In person. Not over the phone."

Wheeler surveyed her surroundings. "There's nobody here but Misty and me and, let's see, Alex Trebek, but he's only here in a cathode ray kind of a way, so we can talk right now if you want to."

"No, in person. You never know who's listening."

"We seem a little bit paranoid this evening." She started to hum the theme music to *The Twilight Zone*.

"Wheeler, for fucksake —"

"Okay, where?"

"McCully's, half an hour."

When he came out of the bedroom and walked down the hall to the kitchen, Buddy was dressed to go out. He was wearing his electric blue sports coat and he was carrying his saxophone case.

Ursula was sitting at the kitchen table turning the pages of *Modern American Painting*. Her braid was undone, her hair dishevelled. Her housecoat was open, and her breasts looked like two small animals whose hiding place has been discovered.

"I won't be long," he said, sliding the knot of his tie up to his neck. "Ray Hamill wants me to sit in at the Blue Spot."

She slowly lifted her head and looked at him. Her eyes were dark beneath, and there was red swelling over one cheekbone. "All right," she said, and returned her gaze to the painting she had been studying when he came in. It was Thomas Hart Benton's *The Jealous Lover of Lone Green Valley*, the focus of which is a barefoot woman in a pink dress who has just been stabbed in the chest by a man in a black hat.

Young was standing outside McCully's Tavern smoking a cigarette when Wheeler walked around the corner.

"What's up?" she said. "You sounded kind of scary on the phone."

Young leaned down close to her. "I'm setting a trap for a man named Buddy Drown. He's the guy that killed Tal Cooper, he's the guy that killed Peter Georgiadis, and he's the guy that tried to have me killed."

Wheeler was red-cheeked in the cold air. She took off her tam and shook out her short blonde hair. "How do you know all this?"

"I'll explain inside, but before we go in I have to tell you what's going to happen tomorrow."

"Why do you have to tell me what's going to happen tomorrow?"

"Because you're going to be there."

"Where, exactly, is 'there'?"

"The basement of a ladies' wear shop on Queen West."

"Really. What's happening there?"

"That's where we take down Buddy Drown."

Wheeler raised her eyebrows. "Have you talked to Urmson about this yet?"

"No, that's why I'm talking to you, so you can brief him."

"In case you've forgotten, Sarge, you're not on the force anymore. I know it's just a minor technicality, but I'm not sure you have the authority —"

"It would be better if he wasn't there. Tell him you've got everything under control, but you want Barkas with you. And don't tell him I'm going to be there."

"This is hardly by the book —"

"Come inside. I'll tell you all the details and answer all your questions. I'll buy you a Shirley Temple."

As he drove down the Don Valley Parkway, Buddy Drown hummed along to a tune on the jazz station, Bennie Wallace's cover of Monk's "Ugly Beauty." The Grand Am hummed along too. His saxophone case lay on the backseat like a black Lab.

He parked on a side street and walked out to Spadina. A few minutes later, he dropped a quarter into the pay phone inside the front door at Nugent's. He waited, drumming his fingers against the top of the phone. "It's me," he said, after the voice at the other end announced itself. "Tomorrow. Usual time, usual place."

He hung up, then made four more calls.

When he was done, he started towards the bar — *a bourbon sour would go good right now*, he thought — but there was Otis Mayhew, one arm in a sling, eyeballing him from the bar, so he turned and left the building. He hurried to his car, drove back up the parkway, passed his exit, and continued all the way to the northern suburbs of the city. He exited the parkway, drove to a strip mall, and parked in front of Casanovas, a lap dancing establishment where he was well known and where the girls went out of their way to be friendly.

After one drink with Wheeler, Young returned home to watch *Cold Case Files*. It was about a girl who'd gone missing in Colorado some years earlier and whose long brunette pigtail was found several years later. Young had already seen the episode and knew that a photograph the killer took of himself — he used the dead girl's camera, aiming it at a dresser mirror as he lay across the bed of a motel room, a prostitute lounging in the background — would appear later in the program.

The phone rang, and Young picked it up. "What?" he said.

"Tomorrow night," a voice said. "Ten o'clock. Downstairs at Kuka's. There's a back entrance you go through."

"Good," Young said. "How many others will be there?"

"Usually there's five others."

"That include you?"

"No."

"Mr. D?"

"Yeah, five others including Mr. D."

"People pack at these shindigs?"

"I don't know about anybody else."

"So you do."

"Fucking right."

"Well, you're not packing tomorrow night."

"What?"

"You heard me. No piece. And one more thing. I want you to tell Mr. D you've got a new customer for him."

"Now hold on, I got a right to protect myself —"

"You'll do as I say, Paulie, or the deal's off, and you know what that means."

"I didn't murder the guy!"

"Paulie, you don't help me with this, you'll wish you were never born."

Young listened as Poor Paul lit a cigarette. "Who's the new customer?"

"He'll wait outside while you go in. You tell Mr. D about him, tell him he's got twenty-five hundred he wants to spend, and he's got it on him. Then you come back outside and let him in."

"What if Mr. D says no?"

"He won't say no."

"What if he does?"

"He won't."

Poor Paul drew on his cigarette. "What's the guy's name?"

"Never mind his fucking name. I'll pick you up in front of your garage at nine-thirty tomorrow night."

"You know what, you can handle this without my help."

"Don't fuck with me. Just be there." Young hung up, then picked up the TV remote and flipped to the weather channel to check the time. 9:44. He dropped the remote to his lap, picked up the phone again, and held it far enough from his face that he could make out the number pad. The sequence of numbers he punched was more familiar to him than his own.

"McCully's," Dexter said.

"It's me. Mr. Harvey there?"

"That you, Sarge? I thought you were here."

"Mr. Harvey there?"

"Just arrived, as a matter of fact."

"Put him on. Wait — is he drunk?"

"Mr. Harvey," Dexter called, "Sarge wants to know if you're drunk."

There was a muffled reply, then Dexter said, "He's coming."

Young waited as Dexter handed the phone to Harvey. Harvey said, "No, I'm not drunk. Everyone at the bar's laughing, thank you very much, at my expense."

"You been drinking tonight?"

"I went to see a film, if you must know, and, sad to say, the sale of spirits is still prohibited at the Odeon. You're a film buff, right?"

"What of it?"

"Just thought you might like to hear my critique."

"No, listen —"

"I can't remember the title, but it had Tom Hanks in it. The most interesting character was a volleyball."

"Listen, I need to talk to you tonight, and I need your full attention."

"I'm all ears."

"No, I need to talk to you in person. I'll be there in fifteen minutes."

"Oh, I see — a delicate matter. What's it about, if I may ask?"

"You."

"Me?"

"Yes. You as bait."

Thursday, November 29

————————————

Young was sitting at the desk in his office, spooning Grape-Nuts into his mouth with one hand and holding the phone with the other. A few Grape-Nuts and several droplets of milk clung to the red and white checkered bib Stella made him wear whenever he ate at work.

On the other end of the phone, Trick said, "Why are you telling me this? It's like telling someone who used to love dancing but who's crippled now and can't dance anymore that you're going out dancing."

Young said, "I'm telling you because you're part of this operation, you've been part of it since the get-go — all the voodoo research you did and chasing down the girl from New Jersey — I thought you'd like to know what's happening."

"From the sounds of it, what's happening is Buddy Drown is about to walk into an ambush."

"That's right."

"I hate to miss it. It's the vicariousness of it that rankles."

"The *what*?"

"The vicariousness of it."

"What the fuck you been smoking?"

"No, it's off a talk show I was watching. They were saying how you have to be sensitive about what you say in front of disabled people."

"I'm sensitive, aren't I? I don't talk about sex in front of you anymore."

"Some of those shows aren't bad, you know. *Oprah*, *The View*. Better than those crime shows you watch all the time."

"Those crime shows, for your information, are educational. They're research. *Cold Case Files*, for example, is pretty much all about DNA."

"Do you take notes?"

"Fuck no, why would I take notes? I remember whatever I need to remember."

"I do. I take notes."

"While you're watching *Oprah* you take notes?"

"Yes, I do."

"Okay, that's it, end of conversation. You're making me agitated, and I don't want to be agitated today."

They were both quiet until Trick said, "You working tomorrow?"

"Tomorrow's Friday, so yeah, I'm working."

"Instead of working, how about we go to the track?"

"We go to the track on Sundays."

"So? Let's go tomorrow. We're retired, right? We can do anything we want. Besides, you'll have earned it."

Young thought it over. "I'll pick you up at eleven."

***

At lunchtime, Young went out and bought a meatball sub for himself and a veggie sub for Stella. They sat at their desks, unwrapping the wax paper and talking through the open doorway between their offices.

"Something's up," she said. "What is it?"

"No idea what you're talking about."

"I heard you talking to Trick. Something's up."

"Oh, a case we're working on. We're putting it to bed tonight."

"You've only got one case, so it must be Buddy Drown."

Young looked through the doorway at her. "That's right."

There was a pause, then Stella said, "Maybe you should take tomorrow off."

Young chewed thoughtfully for a moment, then said, "Funny, that's what Trick said. You two conspiring?"

"No."

"Then why do you want me to take tomorrow off?"

"I don't *want* you to take it off, I just think you should *give* yourself a day off."

"Which is it, you worried about my well-being or *you* want tomorrow off?"

After another pause, Stella said, "Both, I guess."

"No, you better come in. For the morning, anyway."

Stella thought about arguing, then changed her mind.

Shortly before four o'clock, Young phoned Wheeler at Homicide.

"You ready for tonight?"

"I'm ready."

"But are you psyched?"

"I'm psyched."

"How about Barkas? Is he psyched?"

"He's psyched, too. How about Mr. Harvey?"

"Oh, he's plenty psyched. Now listen, have you got the money?"

"Twenty-five hundred. Urmson authorized it."

"He doesn't know I'm going to be there, right?"

"It hasn't come up, but I think he *assumes* you won't be there."

"Good."

"But he wants to come along."

"I told you: no way. He'll just fuck things up."

"I don't know, he seems pretty determined —"

"Talk him out of it, Wheeler."

"I'll do my best."

"Now listen, I want you to sign out an unmarked, then you and Barkas swing by my place at nine o'clock sharp. We'll collect Mr. Harvey, and off we go."

"We have to pick up the snitch, too, right?"

"Yup, he's expecting us at nine-thirty."

"How do I look?" Priam Harvey asked as he walked from the entrance of his apartment building towards an unmarked Chrysler Intrepid idling at the curb. He was wearing his white plantation suit, freshly pressed, his Panama hat, white socks and loafers, black shirt and tie, and geriatric sunglasses.

"Very Cuban," Wheeler said, standing by the open back door of the Chrysler. She turned to Young, who was crammed in the front seat beside Barkas, who sat behind the steering wheel cleaning his teeth with a toothpick. "Sarge, tell me again why Mr. Harvey has to be involved."

Young sighed. "Because we want Drown to recognize him. Mr. Harvey always wears that suit when he goes to jazz joints, and Drown will recognize him."

Wheeler ducked her head back into the car and slid across to the far side of the back seat. "Why is that a good thing?"

"Because we don't want Drown to be nervous. He's seen Mr. Harvey so often ..." He turned to Harvey, who was easing in beside Wheeler. "How many times you been to Buddy Drown's gigs?"

Harvey took his time before answering. "Over the years, I'd say a dozen."

"And you've talked to him?"

"Several times."

"Always wearing that outfit?"

"Always."

Young looked at Wheeler. "We don't want Drown to think he's a narc."

"But I still don't see why we need Mr. Harvey at all. Why couldn't it be just you and me and Barkas?"

"Did you look after Urmson?"

"Yes, I did. He agreed to be standby. And no, he doesn't know you're involved. Now back to my question: why couldn't it be just you and me and Barkas?"

Young shook his head in exasperation. "I just told you: because we want Drown to recognize Mr. Harvey and let him into the meeting, so he can open the door for us later. It can't be you or Barkas seeing as how Drown's never met you, and it can't be me because I was there that night at the Sapphire when Drown was playing and he might remember me and get suspicious. We want him dealing with someone who's been around the clubs a long time, someone who won't waggle his antennas."

Wheeler sighed. "Okay, fine, I give up. Is he wired? Are you wired, Mr. Harvey?"

"No, he's not wired." Young snorted. "If Drown suspects something and finds a wire, it'd be game over."

"That's right," Wheeler said. "It would be very bad. And there's a strong possibility it will be very bad even without the wire."

"It's okay, Lynn," Harvey said. "I appreciate what you're saying, but I volunteered for this mission."

"I know you volunteered, but not without encouragement." She nodded at the back of Young's head.

"Campbell asked me to do it, and I said yes. He didn't force me."

"What I don't understand is *why* you want to do it. You could get killed."

Harvey's voice changed, and his expression became solemn. "Because Buddy Drown killed my son. That's why I want to do it."

Shortly after 9:00 p.m. Buddy Drown opened the sliding glass door off his kitchen and stepped outside. It was a moonless night; the sky was pitch-black. Behind him, the light from the kitchen cast a yellow rectangle onto the deck, wider at the far end, narrower at his feet. His shadow was cast onto the rectangle: skinny legs, widening torso, enormous shoulders and head. The only movement was that of his right arm as he lifted and lowered his cigarette.

He could hear the ticking of the wall clock in the kitchen. At first he didn't think about anything. He inhaled, then sighed as he exhaled. For a moment he was happy, but then, without any provocation he could identify, the old grievance kicked in: at six years of age he had been proficient on the recorder, star of the high school marching band at sixteen, *enfant terrible* of the Toronto club scene by the time he was twenty; then he started drinking and doing drugs and sleeping with every jazz Annie who winked at him; the next ten years were a blur, and by the time he came out of it, no one was interested in him anymore. He had made bad decisions, no question, but he just hadn't gotten any breaks, either. He had been so talented and imaginative, so ambitious.

Early in his thirties he began to reconstruct himself: for ten years he toured with a mediocre swing band in Europe — an invisible member of the five-man reed section. Now, in hindsight — as he blew smoke rings into the night air — he wished he had moved to New York and worked his way up the way Mulligan had, and Jackie McLean. Instead he had taken the safe route, the structured route. He had chosen the weekly paycheque over starving in an upstairs garret on Bleecker Street and playing every night in the black dives, earning his stripes, slowly becoming the legend he knew he could have become and should have become.

After he returned to Toronto at age forty-two, he resumed playing the local clubs and gradually developed a reputation. He became "famous among his friends," as he liked to put it, a big fish in a small pond, the éminence grise of Canadian tenor sax players, always welcome to sit in with any of the homegrown trios or quartets or quintets — especially if he had some blow to dispense, or pills, or weed. Like the Kingston Red he had picked up earlier in the day from his supplier, who, at Drown's request, had divided the brick into sixty-four quarter-ounce baggies. *At forty a pop to my dealers*, Drown calculated, *that's a grand in my pocket. Not enough to retire to Florida, but nothing to sneeze at either.* His dealers would sell it for whatever they could get, fifty-five or sixty. Plus the supplier had given him — on consignment, no less — one hundred ten-milligram amitriptyline, one hundred twenty-five-milligram amitriptyline, and one hundred one-milligram lorazepam tablets.

Drown snapped what was left of his cigarette into the darkness of the garden. His shadow went still as a statue. A drug dealer. No matter how you cut it, that's what he was, what he'd become. Not a sax legend, a drug dealer. And not even a legend among drug dealers. The fact that he didn't do much of the actual selling was small consolation. It raised him one rung above the hustlers he supplied, who, in turn, were one rung above the misfits, addicts, street people, bored yuppies, general fuck-ups, and downwardly spiralling university students who consumed his product.

He contemplated smoking another cigarette. It was nice out here on the deck, in the spotlight provided by the kitchen. Not too cold. He turned and peered inside at the wall clock. Ten after nine. He'd better get going. He had to drive all the way downtown, and he prided himself on never being late.

As he re-entered the kitchen and closed the glass door behind him, Ursula came down the hallway from the bedroom. She was wearing her dressing gown and fuzzy slippers and carrying an empty wine glass and a small plate with the remains of a sandwich on it.

"Going out for a while," he said, lifting his blue sports coat from the back of a kitchen chair. "Little gig at the Rex. Tom Maloney asked if I'd sit in." As he stepped past her, he looked away from the bruising on her cheek.

Poor Paul was standing beside the Ninja when Barkas steered the Intrepid out of the laneway and into the opening in front of the garage. Poor Paul had removed his motorcycle outfit and was zipping up a green nylon jacket.

Young said, "Wheeler, frisk him, then put him between you and Mr. Harvey."

Barkas stopped the car, Wheeler emerged from the backseat, told Poor Paul to raise his hands and spread his feet. She patted him down, called over her shoulder, "He's clean," ushered him into the back next to Harvey, then slid in on his other side.

Young half-turned from the front seat and said, "Good to see you, Paulie."

"I don't know about this," Poor Paul said.

"It's all good. Meet Mr. H. He's the 'customer' you'll be introducing to Mr. D."

Harvey smiled at Poor Paul and said, "My pleasure."

Poor Paul said, "I don't see why you can't do this thing without me."

"Oh, you're in," Young said. "Make no mistake about that. You're all the way in."

Poor Paul squirmed his shoulders. "I feel like a fucking sardine in here."

"Show him the money, Mr. Harvey."

Harvey slid his hand inside the jacket of his plantation suit and removed an envelope. He opened it and riffled the bills in front of Poor Paul's nose. "Twenty-five C-notes," he said.

Young said, "Do your job, Paulie, and you keep five. Deal?"

Poor Paul didn't answer.

Wheeler nudged him with her elbow. "Answer the man."

Poor Paul mumbled something.

"Speak up," Wheeler said.

"I said I'll do it for seven."

Young smiled. "You'll do it for whatever the fuck I say you'll do it for." He turned back around so that he was facing front. "Okay, Tony, let's go."

* * *

"Where the fuck is he?" Drown muttered. "He knows the rules."

A thin black-skinned man wearing a brown fedora and gold-coloured John Lennon glasses sitting opposite Drown at the card table said, "No junk till we drunk."

"It's not like I changed the venue on him."

A white woman in an Eddie Bauer ski jacket sitting beside the black man said, "It's not the first time he's been late." The blood red of her jacket matched her fingernails, lipstick, and pixie-cut hair. "I can't wait around forever, Mr. D. It's an early Christmas this year, you might say, and my clients are already sitting under the tree."

A tall, freckled man standing to Drown's right laughed at this. "And that makes you Santa Claus?" he said.

"That's right," the woman said playfully, "and I'm in a hurry. I want to slide down the chimney and give them their gifts."

The freckled man sat down and leaned towards her. "How 'bout I slide *up* your chimney?"

"In your dreams," the woman said. Then they heard what they were waiting for: a knock at the door, a pause, then two more knocks in quick succession.

"Let him in," Drown said to a small Hispanic man seated to his left.

The man stood up, walked to the door, and opened it. Poor Paul stepped in.

"It's eight minutes past ten," Drown said, looking up from his Rolex.

"I know," Poor Paul said anxiously, "but there's this guy outside. He wants to talk to you."

"What guy?"

"He wants to be a new customer."

Drown's eyes narrowed. "Who is he? How'd he get here?"

"I brought him."

"*What!*" Drown roared. "You *brought* him? How many times have I told you? Never never never bring people here! If anybody brings people here, it's me, not you, you fucking moron!"

Poor Paul raised one hand to the side of his face as if to ward off a blow. "But he's got money. Twenty-five hundred — he showed me — and he knows you. He said you wouldn't mind. I thought —"

"He knows me? What's his name?"

Behind Poor Paul, Priam Harvey leaned into the doorway, Panama hat in hand, and looked directly at Buddy Drown. "Forgive the intrusion, Mr. Drown," he said. "Just want you to know off the top what a big fan I am. Saw you at the Sapphire a few weeks ago."

Drown scrutinized Harvey as Harvey surveyed the room and its occupants. The small basement was illuminated by a single bulb above the card table that was front and centre. The gloomy far end of the room was jammed with racks of clothing. Around the table sat four people: Drown in his familiar blue sports coat; a skinny black man in a brown hat and gold glasses; a punk woman in a puffy jacket; and a freckled man with red hair and a nose ring. A fifth person, a short, white-haired Latino who reminded Harvey of the bandleader Tito Puentes, stood beside him at the door.

Drown placed his hands palms-down on the card table in front of him, took a breath, looked up at Poor Paul, and said, "The first rule of our club is we arrive on time for our meetings," then turned to Harvey and said, "and the second rule is nobody calls me by my real name. Refer to me as Mr. D."

Harvey inched further into the room until he was standing next to Poor Paul. "Sorry, it won't happen again."

Drown said, "Gabby, shut the door."

Harvey heard the door swing to behind him. "Please don't blame him" — he jerked his thumb in Poor Paul's direction — "for bringing me here," he said. "It's all my doing. I latched onto him. I told him I had a business opportunity for you."

"And where exactly did you latch onto him?"

"At his garage down on Eastern Avenue. He was repairing my car. Did a fine job, too, I might add. And then our conversation turned to other topics."

In front of him, Poor Paul shifted uneasily.

Drown said, "What kind of other topics?"

"Drugs, basically."

"I see. So tell me about this business opportunity."

"May I speak freely?"

Drown spread his arms expansively. "Be my guest."

Harvey cleared his throat. "I've been deputized, you might say, by a group of people who are looking for a steady supply of high-quality product."

Drown sat up in his chair. "How did you hear about me?"

"A member of this group I represent made it known to me that, uh ... well, that your talents extend beyond the saxophone. And then, coincidentally, last week when I was getting my car serviced, this gentleman here mentioned your name."

Poor Paul said, "That's not what happened, Mr. D."

Drown held up a hand to silence him. "What's the guy's name that told you about me, the member of the group you represent?"

"Do you absolutely have to know?"

"If you want any high-quality product, then yes, I absolutely have to know."

"All right." Harvey paused. "Scotty Turpin."

"Well, it's a small world, isn't it. Being a big fan, you probably know that Scotty plays bass for me from time to time." Drown's tone, which had been liquid at first, was hardening with each word. "But I already look after him, if you know what I mean."

Harvey hesitated. "He wants more. A regular amount each month."

"More what?"

"Kingston Red, among other things."

Drown leaned back, and the metal chair he was sitting on screeched. "That just a lucky guess, or you really know the man?"

"I really know him. And I speak for his piano player and his drummer as well."

"What do they want?"

Harvey slid his hand inside the jacket of his plantation suit. "I've got —"

A gun in the hand of the freckled man was pointed at Harvey's head.

"— a list," Harvey finished weakly.

"That's all right, Liam," Drown said, and the freckled man lowered the gun and laid it on its side on the card table. Drown looked back at Harvey, who had removed his hand from his jacket. "I've seen you around the clubs, I'll give you that much. But tell me this, why do Scotty and the other people you claim to represent need you at all? Scotty could have come directly to me. He knows that, and so do the others."

"Mr. D," Poor Paul said, "I —"

"Shut up," Drown said, without shifting his gaze. "Shut the fuck up. Now what about it?"

Harvey shrugged. "I don't know. Maybe they figure if anything goes wrong, they don't want to be involved."

"They tell you this?"

"No, but —"

"Who else do you represent?"

Harvey licked his lips. "Uh, a few more musicians, about a dozen jockeys, and a couple of —"

"*Jock*eys?"

Harvey nodded. "I work in the industry. And a couple of trainers, too."

"Let's see that list."

Harvey looked at Liam, then slowly slid his hand inside his jacket. His eyes widened. "I must have left it in the glove compartment." He turned towards the door. "I'll be right back. I won't be a minute."

"Hold everything," Drown said. "Gabby, go with him."

The Hispanic man opened the door.

Poor Paul said, "I'm going, too."

"Stay where you are," Drown said, "Gabby can manage ..." Then he cocked his head, looked hard at Poor Paul, and said, "Gabby, shut the door!" but Harvey was already halfway out. Gabby grabbed hold of Harvey's arm and was pulling him back in when his grip was broken by Poor Paul, who chopped his way between them like a race walker, saying "I'm going, too, I have to go, too!" In the light from the basement, Harvey hurried up the steps behind Poor Paul, heard a *pop-pop* behind him, and, at the same time as he felt a punch in the back of his right arm, saw the hair at the back of Poor Paul's head feather as if someone had blown on it. Poor Paul pitched forward on the steps, and Harvey scrambled over him to the top and rolled into the darkness. He heard Young's voice above him say, "Stay down, Mr. Harvey," then, "Tony, out front!"

He heard running footsteps, then Young say, "Wheeler!"

He looked up to see Liam emerging from the stairwell with Gabby close behind him. Liam stopped, and Gabby stopped, and the two of them peered into the darkness.

Wheeler shouted, "Police! Lay down your weapons!"

Gabby and Liam turned in the direction of Wheeler's voice, and Liam raised his gun. Harvey looked above him, and Young was standing astride him, both arms extended as he aimed his Glock. He fired, and Gabby fell backwards into the stairwell. Liam turned towards Young, and Young fired again. Wheeler fired, too, and Liam staggered forward and collapsed on his face. In the ringing silence that followed, the light from the basement vanished, and everything was plunged into darkness.

"Tony!" Young bellowed.

From a distance: "You all right, Sarge?"

"Stay there! They're coming out the front!" Young unclipped a flashlight from his belt and aimed its beam down on Harvey, who lay on his side in a fetal position between Young's feet. "You okay, Mr. Harvey?"

Harvey was gritting his teeth and clutching his shoulder. "I'm all right," he said.

"Wheeler?" Young said.

"Right here, Sarge."

"Secure the area. Call in backup and an ambulance for Mr. Harvey. And a chopper, we can't see anything back here. I'm going out front."

He stepped over Harvey and walked to the stairwell. He shone his flashlight down on Gabby and Poor Paul, then turned his attention to Liam, kicked the gun out of his hand, studied him for a brief moment, then turned and lumbered up the alleyway towards the streetlights.

Harvey watched him go, his ears filled with the frantic sound of his own breathing. Then he passed out.

Trick turned off the television. Once again, he had been sucked into watching *Survivor*, and once again he was angry.

What's happened to our society? he asked himself. *Why are we are so afraid of having our own adventures that we end up watching these fools pretend — pretend — to be marooned on a desert island, and then we convince ourselves, just as the fools have convinced themselves, that the whole thing is real, that they really are members of a tribe, that they really are warriors, and that it's not pretending at all?*

Furious, he propelled himself into the kitchen, opened the door to a low cupboard, and removed a box of Wheat Thins. *What's happened to us? Why are we chained to our televisions?* From the fridge he took a package of salami slices and a carton of milk and set them on the counter.

He lifted a jar of pickles from the fridge, wedged it between his right wrist and the arm of his wheelchair, and managed to remove the lid with his left hand, but the jar squeezed free, fell to the floor, and spilled vinegar brine and slices of garlic dill across the linoleum.

"Fuck!" Trick said. "Fuck, fuck, fuck!"

When the front door of Kuka's Fashions opened and the black man in the brown fedora and the white woman in the red ski jacket emerged with their hands in the air, Young and Barkas were waiting, crouched behind a parked car, guns drawn and aimed. As Young stepped from behind the car to approach them, sirens sounded, and moments later, as he watched Barkas handcuff first the man and then the woman, several squad cars screeched to a stop behind them. The last wails of the sirens died down, and Big Urmson was at Young's shoulder. "What are you doing here?" he said.

"Just passing by."

"Come on, Sarge, what've we got?"

"There's four down out back."

"*Four?*"

Two uniformed officers led the prisoners towards the cruisers. Young watched as the man was navigated into the back of one cruiser and the woman into the back of another.

Barkas said, "Where's Drown?"

Young turned and looked at him. "Oh shit," he said, and charged back down the darkened alleyway like a linebacker after a fumble. Barkas sprinted after him. As they came to the rear of the building, the beam of Young's flashlight picked up the electric blue of Drown's sports coat. He had Wheeler in a headlock, her face buried in his flank, a gun pointed at her temple.

"Stop right there!" he barked. "Stop right there, or I'll blow her brains out!"

Young panned the flashlight down to Wheeler's blonde head, then back up at Drown's face.

"Shine that on the ground, motherfucker, I'll blow her brains out! Throw your gun down! Throw it over here!"

Young hesitated, then slid the Glock across the gravel towards Drown's feet.

"Now shine that light in your face!"

Young did as he was told. With the toe of one shoe, Drown felt around for the gun in the darkness, his eyes never leaving Young for a second. When he found the gun, Drown half-knelt, picked it up, and dropped it into a side pocket of his sports coat. He looked back at Young. "You're Campbell Young, aren't you?"

Young nodded in the flashlight beam. "That's my name."

"Big as a house, just like the Greek said. Why'd you have to stick your nose in, big man?"

Young said, "We know you killed Peter Georgiadis, Buddy, and we know why, but why'd you kill Tal Cooper?"

Drown laughed. "Young man with a horn thought he could seize *my* turf? I don't think so. Tried to be nice to him, talk a little music with him, and what's he do? Acts like he's never heard of me! Ungrateful motherfucker. But I knew about his habit — hell, *ev*eryone knew about his habit — so I told him I could get him some smack. Well, then I had his attention, then he knew who I was. So I said, 'And you know what else, Mr. Cooper, it would be an honour if you'd let me prepare you a meal. I'm an excellent chef,' I told him. 'I'll make you a seafood feast you'll never forget. Just like home. I'll even bring it to your hotel room, and we'll do a little business while you're eating, how's that sound?' Well, he *loved* that idea, so I set it all up, and everything went like clockwork. Mr. Cooper's last supper was a great success, even *he* said so, but then he began to feel a little off, and then he began to feel a *lot* off, and then he had to lie down, and then he did some writhing around and a lot of moaning, and then, while I was packing up the leftovers and the dishes and the wine glasses ... well, he died." He adjusted his hold on Wheeler's neck.

Young took a step forward.

"Stay where you are, big man. The lady and I are going downstairs, and we're going to wait there till you arrange safe passage."

"Okay," Young said. "Whatever you say. Just don't hurt her."

"How many cavalry you got there with you?"

"I'm alone. The rest are out front."

"Shine that light over here now, along the ground. Very slow, very easy, so I can see where I'm going."

As Young cast the flashlight beam across the ground, he reached his other hand into the darkness behind him, found Barkas's arm, and pushed him to circle around behind Drown and Wheeler.

Drown said, "Safe passage to the airport and first-class tickets." He turned his attention to the top of Wheeler's head. "Ever been to Havana, sweetheart? We'll join the Social Club, what do you think of that?" He tightened his hold on her neck, and she cried out.

"You're hurting her," Young said. "Don't hurt her."

"Get over here and shine that light on the stairs."

As Young drew nearer, he heard the distant *whup-whup* of a helicopter.

"Wheeler," he said, as Drown led her around Liam's prostrate body and two steps down the basement stairs, "are you all right?"

"Shut the fuck up!" Drown said, raising the barrel of his gun towards Young, who stopped at the top of the stairs.

"Wheeler," Young repeated.

"I warned you," Drown said, and turned the gun towards Wheeler. "I told you to shut up."

"Now's the time," Young said, and directed the beam of his flashlight into Drown's eyes. In the shadows on the opposite side of the stairwell, Barkas dropped to one knee and, from a distance of three feet and using a trajectory level with Drown's ear, shot him through the temple. Drown's gun discharged, and he and Wheeler tumbled over the bodies of Gabby and Poor Paul to the bottom of the stairs. Young leaped down after them, snatched Wheeler from Drown's embrace, bolted back up to the top of the stairs, and fell to the gravel. "Wheeler," he said to the body limp in his arms. "Wheeler!"

The sound of the helicopter intensified as it drew overhead and the powerful beam of its searchlight poured down on the scene. Young laid Wheeler on her back on the ground. "Wheeler, are you okay!" he shouted over the noise.

Her eyes were shut. Her hair, white in the brilliant light, was littered with bits of twig and dead leaf. Her mouth was closed.

"Wheeler," Young pleaded. "Wheeler, for fucksake!" He shook her by the shoulders. "*Wheeler!*"

Her lips parted, and he saw the perfect white teeth and the pink meat of her tongue.

Her eyelids fluttered open. Young looked at the brown eye first, then the blue one. They squinted in the light from the helicopter, and he leaned forward until they were in his shadow. For a few seconds they gazed without focus — at his chest, at the strangely illuminated night sky above him — before they settled on his face. "Am I ever glad to see you," she said.

"Are you hit?"

She took a deep breath and exhaled slowly. "No. I'm okay. Did we get him?"

Young plucked a small sliver of bark from her hair. "Oh yes," he said, "we got him."

Friday, November 30

Young knocked at the door of his aunt's room and let himself in. The two old women were sitting together on the loveseat. Gladys was bent over a small white box on the coffee table in front of her. Petergay was knitting. The television was tuned to a game show.

"Well," Young said, pulling three cans of Blue out of the pockets of his windbreaker, "if it ain't Jack Benny and Rochester." He snapped open the cans and set them on the coffee table. "What are you two up to?"

"She goin' through her pictures," Petergay said, "decidin' which ones to keep and which ones to th'ow away."

"Why does she want to throw them away?" Young asked, fetching two plastic cups from his aunt's bedside table drawer.

Petergay shrugged. "You best ask her."

The box his aunt was bent over contained a pile of loose photographs. As she spread them on the table, Young saw that some of the photos were in colour, some were black and white, some were large, some small. Without looking up, Gladys said, "They're of people I used to know. School friends. People I went on holiday with. Children I looked after when I was a nanny."

"Right, but why throw them away?"

"They're all dead now."

"The children, too?"

"Well, no, but I'll never see them again, will I, so why keep them?"

"What's that one there?"

"Oh, that's when my friend Joyce and I went on a cruise. The *Cristoforo Colombo*. Ten days in the Caribbean. That's us at the captain's table. Oh, my goodness!"

"What?" Young asked.

Gladys pointed with a shaking finger. "See the man with the cigar? He was the first mate. An awful womanizer. One night he asked me to go for a moonlight stroll on the deck with him."

"Did you?"

"Certainly not. And when I declined, he turned right around and asked Joyce!"

"Let me guess. She said yes."

"That's right, she did, and she told me later he put his hand under her skirt and touched her knee. She had to slap him."

Petergay said, "I woulda slapped him *oh*vuhboard."

"But she did meet another man, an American. In textiles, as I recall. She ended up marrying him and moving to Philadelphia. We wrote each other for years, but eventually we lost touch. She had twin daughters, I remember that much."

Young said, "You know, Aunty, if you'd thrown that photo away, you'd never have told me that story."

She smiled at him. "You keep it then, dear."

He took the photo and put it in the pocket of his windbreaker, stood up, picked up one of the cans of Blue, took a long gulping draught of it, set it back down, belched softly, and said, "Don't let your beers go flat. See you next week."

"But you just got here," Gladys said, looking up from her photographs.

"I've got an appointment this afternoon."

"What kind of appointment? With a doctor?"

"No, at the racetrack."

"Oh, you!"

Petergay said, "The news say they catched that man what kill the musician."

"That's right," Young said.

"He dead, right?"

"That's right."

"I guess you have nothin' to do with it?"

Young shook his head. "Not much."

"You never told me did you visit my grandson."

"Yes, I did. He was a big help."

"Well, that somethin', I guess. What his name again?"

"Claude Johnson."

The old woman nodded. "That right," she said. "Claude Johnson." She turned her attention back to the television.

"You two behave," Young said, and stepped towards the door.

"When you come next time, Nephew," Gladys said, "I'll have a list of chores for you."

* * *

Young stopped at a strip mall and found a phone booth outside a florist's shop. He dropped a quarter into the slot, punched in the number, and waited.

"A-1 Investigative Consultants, Stella speaking. How may I help you?"

"It's me. Any calls?"

"Nope, not a one."

"Just as well. I was going to come in but I guess I don't really need to. Besides, me and Trick are going to the track."

"Well, good for you. After last night, you deserve an afternoon off." She paused. "I guess that means I can go home."

"That's right. You have a good weekend, and I'll see you Monday."

"Wait a minute while I look at my planner.... No, there's nothing happening Monday. I could use the time to take Nicky to the barber. He looks like a sheepdog."

"Can't you do that today? You've got the rest of the day off."

"No, today I'll take him to the mall and buy him a winter coat."

"Can't you do both? It's not like —"

"They're not even remotely in the same part of the city, Boss. The mall's up at Don Mills and Sheppard, and the barber he goes to is down on Kingston Road."

"Take him to a different barber."

"He prefers this one."

"He pre*fers*? What is he, four years old, and he's got opinions about barbers?"

"We tried other ones, but they scared him. This one doesn't scare him."

Young scratched his head. "Fine. I'll see you Tuesday."

"Oh wait! I've been meaning to ask you, did the Sears guy ever deliver the barbeque?"

"What barbeque?"

"Your new barbeque."

"I didn't buy a barbeque."

"But they phoned last week — last Friday —"

"Must be a mistake. What would I do with a barbeque? I don't even use my hibachi anymore."

"Well, that's very strange."

"Forget about it, Stella. See you Tuesday."

On his way to pick up Trick, Young lifted his Mets cap off the passenger seat searching for his cigarettes. They weren't there, but the CD Priam Harvey had given him was. He popped open the lid of his portable CD player, removed Bob Seger's *Greatest Hits*, and inserted *Goombay Bop*. He skipped forward to number six. Following a smattering of applause, a strong young male voice said, "Thank you, ladies and gentlemen, that was 'Freetown High Times.' And now for your musical delectation, I would like to perform an original composition of mine called 'Last Man Best Bone,' which is an old Bahamian expression my grandmummy used to say back in Lewis Yard, where I grew up. Last man best bone. What it means is — drum roll, please, Wycliffe — what it means is whoever laughs last laughs best. Hope you enjoy it. Okay, boys? Uh, one. Two. Uh, one, two, three, four."

Trick said, "How's Jamal?"

"Better now," said Debi. "He was pretty traumatized by the whole thing."

Young, returning from the buffet, said, "What do you say I get him a puppy?"

Debi shook her head. "I don't think it would be a good idea. Not yet."

"I was thinking it could be *his* dog, as opposed to mine."

"That's sweet of you, Daddy, but I think you should wait awhile. His life's kind of upside down at the moment."

Young said, "Where's Ant'wawn in all of this, or did he really go back to Jamaica?"

"Yes, he's gone."

Trick said, "How are you holding up?"

Debi offered a thin smile. "I'm all right. You'd think I'd have learned my lesson by now. You'd think I'd be cured of men."

Young said, "We're not *all* bastards and pricks."

"I know, Daddy, but I've been thinking about it a lot." She patted the *Racing Form* on the table in front of her. "There's a big difference between picking the right horse and picking the right boyfriend, and with the horses I'm usually up a few bucks at the end of the day, so I think I'll just stick with them awhile. Speaking of which, you remember Mr. Berry? The guy who wanted me to train for him?"

"The guy with the Carson City colt."

"That's right. Well, he phoned me yesterday, and — ta-daa! — I'm officially his trainer, and he wants me to go down to Kentucky next month and spend some of his money at the two-year-olds-in-training sale."

Trick said, "Your star is rising."

Young nodded. "You may not have found the right boyfriend yet, but you picked the right profession."

Debi had a filly to saddle for the seventh race. "I guess I won't see you guys afterwards," she said as she stood up. "I'll be busy back at the barn, so I'll say goodbye now."

Young said, "Tomorrow's Saturday. Maybe I'll drop by your place around noon, take Jamal out for a Whopper and a movie."

Debi tilted her head. "That would be nice. Can I tell him you're coming?"

"Nah, let it be a surprise."

After she left, Trick said, "She doesn't know about last night?"

Young shook his head. "I don't like to worry her."

Trick studied him. "Everything go according to plan?"

"It was a bit messy, but we came out of it all right."

"I've been meaning to ask you. Did you ever figure out if the seventy-four cents was actually a clue Buddy Drown left on purpose, or was it just a handful of foreign currency that somehow found its way into Tal Cooper's saxophone case?"

"Oh, it was a clue, all right," Young replied, spearing a meatball with his fork. "Drown thought he was a lot smarter than the rest of us. He thought he'd done such a good job of making Tal's death look like a voodoo murder that he decided to slide in a private joke. He never thought anybody would connect the seventy-four cents to Cannonball Adderley. Hell, he never thought anybody would even add the coins up." Young examined the meatball. "That was his downfall — he got cocky. Once we knew the murder was jazz-related rather than voodoo-related — which we figured out when we realized the evidence at the scene was mostly just harmless obeah stuff, as opposed to serious voodoo stuff — and once you counted up the coins and told Mr. Harvey about it and he made the jazz connection, we were in business."

"How *is* Mr. Harvey?"

"He's fine," Young said. "In fact, he's happy as a pig. Did him good, all in all. Big badge of honour."

"He was hit in the arm?"

"Upper arm, but just a flesh wound. Treated and released. But that white suit of his may not make it. All covered in mud and blood, and a bullet hole in it, too. He might better get himself a new one."

Ursula Drown sat at the kitchen table in her pyjamas and housecoat. She was smoking a cigarette and drinking white wine. She had found an open bottle of Riesling in the back of the fridge. She couldn't remember how long it had been there, but it tasted all right.

It was late afternoon; the police had come and gone. They had told her Buddy was dead.

The book of paintings was open in front of her, and she positioned three transparent plastic film canisters on the heads of the soldiers in Winslow Homer's *Prisoners from the Front*.

"A motley crew," she said aloud.

The canisters had pills in them, pills she had discovered yesterday afternoon in Buddy's saxophone case. He kept an odd assortment of things in the case — reeds, mints, matches, cigarettes, a tuning fork, a pitch pipe, a clean shirt, a change of underwear and socks. She had been looking for evidence of other women — condoms, hotel receipts — but instead had found a multitude of baggies containing marijuana, along with three bottles of pills. For her it was like winning the lottery, because she knew what the pills were for. Lorazepam for anxiety. Amitriptyline for depression. A potent mix with alcohol. She had removed a few dozen pills from each of the three bottles and placed them in the canisters.

She had not anticipated using them so soon. It had been her intention to hoard them against the day when she couldn't take it anymore. But in the twenty-four hours since she had stolen them, not only had Buddy been shot dead, but she, too, was on her way out. It was ironic that Buddy's death should be the catalyst for her own. She had expected it to be his unfaithfulness or cruelty — a beating, perhaps, or one last act of sexual humiliation — that put her over the edge. But now that he had been excised from her life like a bad heart, she felt only loneliness and fear. Her captivity had been her security, her jailer her protector.

She crushed out her cigarette and lit another. She refilled her wine glass.

"There is no one to comfort / no one to comfort me," she wrote on a piece of paper. "My countertop gleams / My living room's a picture / in a picture magazine."

She uncapped the first canister and poured the pills, which were tiny and round and sky blue, into a clean white cereal bowl.

She looked at the window, the late sunshine slanting through, the plants in their pots on the sill.

"And like my green alfalfa," she wrote, "I lean toward / whatever light there is."

The pills from the second canister were canary yellow. She poured them into the bowl.

The pills in the last canister were small, oblong, and off-white. She swirled the pills in the bowl. They mixed together like paints on a palette.

When she had swallowed all of the pills and finished the wine, she walked through the living room and opened the front door. She watched several cars pass by, a woman pulling a suitcase on wheels along the sidewalk, two boys — raucous as crows — skateboarding. She had half a mind to put her coat on and go for one last walk, one last look around. Maybe she would see someone she recognized from the neighbourhood and have one last conversation. About how cold it was getting, how the first snow couldn't be too far off.

Instead she closed the door, walked back into the living room, and put Buddy's *Ballads* CD into the stereo and pushed "play." The first cut was "Guess I'll Hang My Tears Out to Dry." As the big sound of the saxophone filled the room, Ursula felt a rush of emotion, then hard on its heels a wave of fatigue and dizziness. She made her way along the hall to the bedroom, kicked off her slippers, let her housecoat slide down her arms to the floor, pulled back the bedspread and the sheets, and crawled in. As she burrowed her face into the pillow, she wished there was someone with her, someone she could explain her decision to. Someone to tell her goodbye.

Not only did he take command of the operation, Wheeler was thinking as she settled into bed with a cup of peppermint tea, *just seize command of it, like he'd never even retired, but he shot the smaller man first, which was so smart because in the confusion immediately afterwards we both had easy shots at the taller man.*

The tea helped calm her down, drain some of the hyper-alertness out of her.

And he saved my life, she thought. *I mustn't overlook that tidbit of information. He distracted Drown when I was at his mercy, he set up Tony's kill, and he carried me up the stairs like a fireman carrying a child out of a burning building.*

A little while later, her cup empty and Misty nestled in the crook of her legs, she closed her eyes. On the little portable TV on her dresser, Katharine Hepburn was saying, "Nature, Mr. Allnut, is what we are put into this world to rise above."

Like Wheeler, Trick went to bed early, but unlike her, he fell asleep immediately.

He dreamed he was point guard for the Pistons.

He could slam-dunk like a man on the moon.

Miss Leventhorpe, dressed in red and blue, was a cheerleader. She hailed him from courtside.

He waved to her from the top of the key.

Young rapped on the door. "Come on, let me in."

From the other side of the door Jessy said, "Go home! It's after midnight, for God's sake."

"Jessy, please!"

"I've told you before, you can't just come over whenever you feel like it, whenever you're drunk and horny. How do you think it makes me feel?"

"I'm sorry, Jessy. You're right. I'm a bastard and a prick."

"You got that right."

"Now let me in."

"No!"

"I promise I'll be better —"

"I can't let you in even if I wanted to."

"Why not? Is there somebody with you?"

"Yes, as a matter of fact —"

"There *is*?"

"Yes, and why shouldn't there be? I could spend my whole life waiting for you to show any interest."

"Who's in there with you?"

"Never mind, just go away."

"You're lying, there's no one in there."

"There is too."

"You're lying."

A gruff male voice said, "Lady's got company. Take a hike."

Young was silent for a moment, then said, "I know that voice."

Jessy said, "Please leave. Before you wake up the Ukrainians, please leave."

"I know that voice. Identify yourself!"

"Please, Sarge," the male voice said, less gruffly. "The Ukrainians'll call the cops, and then Jessy'll get evicted, and it'll be all our fault."

"*Dexter*? Is that you in there?"

The lock turned, the door opened, and Dexter leaned his head out.

Young laughed and said, "You two lovebirds got anything to drink in there?"

Dexter shook his head and said, "Trouble follows you wherever you go, Sarge, and I always end up in the middle of it."

The smile fell from Young's face. "That's okay," he said. "Sorry to bother you."

Priam Harvey walked from the bathroom of his apartment, where he had re-dressed his wound and swallowed more painkillers, to the kitchenette, where he rinsed a dirty tumbler under the hot water tap and poured three fingers of Bushmills into it.

He made his way to the living room, slid his son's CD into the slit-mouth of the boom box, pushed "play," then curled up with a blanket on the ratty sofa. He tried to ignore the pain in his arm and focus on "Caribbana Man," but he was too uncomfortable. He sat up, swallowed half the whiskey, found a smokable butt in the ashtray on the coffee table in front of him, lit it, got two drags off it, finished the whiskey, lay back down again, and tried to concentrate on the music.

***

Young walked south on Linsmore Avenue to the
Danforth, then turned west towards Broadview. He
took his cigarettes out of his jacket pocket and counted
them. Seven. Would seven be enough? *Better safe than
sorry*, he told himself, then went into a brightly lit convenience store and bought an extra pack.

On the street again, he smoked as he walked.

There were several bars at his disposal — Terri O's,
the Willow, Allen's, the Black Swan.

When he came to Terri O's, he opened the door,
pushed past a group of people on their way out,
approached the bar, and positioned himself on a stool.
The place was pretty much empty.

"What can I get you?" the barmaid said. She was
rough-looking and agitated.

"JD, straight up."

Several stools to his right, a man with a red scarf
around his neck said, "Darlene, you know I didn't
mean anything."

The barmaid turned to the man and said, "You
know better than to talk to me like that. You know I
have a husband."

"I didn't mean nothing by it."

"Shut up, Steve, I'm serious."

"Are you upset with me? I think you're upset
with me."

"Just finish your drink and go home."

The barmaid poured Young's shot and placed it in
front of him. "You want to run a tab?" she asked.

Young nodded, and she moved down the bar
towards the cash register.

The man turned to Young. "I think I upset her."

"So it seems."

"I'll apologize when she comes back."

Young knocked back the sour mash and waited for

the burn. "Maybe you should just let it go," he said.

"I'm going to have to find myself a new bar," the man said. "I hate it when I have to find a new bar."

"Me too," said Young.

The man got off his stool, knotted his scarf, pulled on his overcoat, and buttoned it. He laid a twenty on the bar. "Maybe I'll try the Swan," he said. "Well, good night."

"Good night," Young said.

When the man was gone, the barmaid came back along the bar and picked up the twenty.

Young held up his empty glass. "Hit me again, Darlene."

Acknowledgements

Luis Angel Almodovar, Frederick Armbrister, Harry Baillie, Dr. Philip Berger, Andy Brakas, Rodney Carpenter, Eardley Culmer, Robert Danielis, Brian L. Flack, Vernette Flynn, Portia Haley, John Heath, Sam Hill, M.T. Kelly, Harold Laing, Patrick Larkin, Carol McCutcheon, John McKinney, Stephen Murphy, Dave Paul, Joan Pratt, Karen Ralley, Doug Seeley, Rick Short, Steve Snider, Fred Williams, Chris Wright.